DESIRE MADE FLESH

The kidnapper turned to face her. He still carried that same tenseness in his bearing, as though he held something within him barely in check.

His irises turned a deep gray, almost black, swallowing his pupils until they disappeared like pebbles dropped into a lake. A shot of silver shone through them, almost opaline. She stared into his eyes, heart raging in her chest.

"Who are you?" she whispered past the lump in her throat, both hopeful and fearful he would answer the question this time.

"Axiom," he said. "My name is Axiom. And I am a god made flesh."

Laurell swallowed hard. The man had clearly lost his mind.

ELISSA WILDS

BETWEEN LIGHT AND DARK

LOVE SPELL

NEW YORK CITY

For Michael. The reality of you rivals any hero I could dream up.

*For Mom. You always said I could do anything I set my mind to.
You were, as usual, right.*

LOVE SPELL®

November 2008

Published by

Dorchester Publishing Co., Inc.
200 Madison Avenue
New York, NY 10016

ISBN 10: 0-505-52791-X
ISBN 13: 978-0-505-52791-2

The name "Love Spell" and its logo are trademarks of Dorchester
Publishing Co., Inc.

Printed in the United States of America.

10 9 8 7 6 5 4 3 2 1

Visit us on the web at www.dorchesterpub.com.

ACKNOWLEDGMENTS

I'd like to thank my editor, Alicia Condon, for sharing my vision, and being such a pleasure to work with. I'd also like to thank my agent, Michelle Grajkowski, for being so enthusiastic about my work and so darn patient with me. Thanks to my wonderful critique partners in crime, June Bowen, Cheryl Mansfield, and especially Jean Mason, who jumped in at the eleventh hour and made sure my i's were dotted and my t's were crossed. Special thanks to Cheryl Wilson for your encouragement and friendship. And to Julie Leto and Diana Peterfreund for your willingness to lend an ear or advice when I really needed it most.

Certain people have been my cheering section during my journey to publication and deserve recognition for their love and support: Jeffrey Gordon, Diane Stein, Nanci Clifford, Trudy Leone, Nickole Grams-Deleon, Amanda Wright, Adrienne Russo, Jami Lin, Debra Glass, The Witchcrafters, As Always, and the women and men of Tampa Area Romance Authors. May your good karma increase tenfold! And thanks to Tristyn and Selena who are endlessly excited about my writing and always willing to give me quiet time when I tell them I need to work on my books. Last, but not least, I'd like to express my gratitude to Donna Jeanne Guerra for opening my eyes to the magic in life nearly fourteen years ago and ensuring that I'd never look at the world the same again.

BETWEEN
LIGHT AND
DARK

axiom: (1) A self-evident truth that requires no proof. (2) A universally accepted principle or rule. (3) A proposition in logic or mathematics that is assumed without proof for the sake of studying the consequences that follow from it.

Webster's American Dictionary, College edition

Rage, rage against the dying of the light.

Dylan Thomas

PROLOGUE

You would expect beings as powerful and wise as gods to see the foolishness of discrimination, but even gods can be blind to such evil when it suits them. Mobius sat at the head of the oblong table surrounded by gods of varying levels of wisdom and foolishness, and shook his head at this thought. His jaw set as he scanned the room to rest briefly on each of the white-robed deities surrounding the table. He knew many would disagree with his recommendation. It could not be avoided.

The rest of the thirteen members of the Divine Council eyed him with interest, clearly eager to get on with the vote.

Mobius's deep baritone broke the silence. "This will be a difficult decision for all of us to make, but I believe we have at our disposal an appropriate candidate. I have every faith he would serve us well."

The goddess Willow nodded. Her golden hair shimmered under the soft light and brightened the otherwise stark white meeting room of the Divine Council, kept purposely barren to prevent distraction from the serious work done there. She stepped closer to Mobius, white robe swishing over the sparkling quartz-crystal floor, and her signature scent of verdant soil and spring rain followed.

"Make your recommendation, Mobius," Willow urged. "I, for one, will be glad to have the matter decided. We've much work to do."

Mobius smiled at Willow, the newest member of the Council, a weather goddess with the ability to control the elements. Her smooth, youthful face belied her ancient wisdom. She was ever the peace-keeper of the group, and he was thankful for her presence.

"I'd like to propose we utilize Axiom for this mission." Mobius's announcement met with general rumblings among the group. Helios, a war god whose ebony skin shone with blue highlights, frowned and pounded one large fist against the tabletop, getting everyone's attention quickly.

"A Gray God? You wish to send a Balancer to head up such an important mission?" Helios's words rang with concern.

Mobius noted that same unease reflected in the expressions of several others of the Council. "Yes," he confirmed. "A Gray."

"Highly unusual, don't you think?" Helios pressed.

Before Mobius could respond, Willow interjected, "The Grays have been integral in keeping the etheric and astral energies equalized. They are a large part of the reason the Umbrae have been relegated to the Astral Plane and are unable to move into higher realms—ours included."

Rahkma, a towheaded protection deity, lifted his hand and waved Willow's words away like pesky insects. He tilted his head, startling turquoise eyes narrowed.

"Mobius, you make no secret you are a proponent of furthering the Grays' involvement in the Divine Council. We all know of Axiom's desire to attain a seat here, and this mission, if successful, could go a long way toward helping him achieve his goal. I am not fully convinced integrating the Grays so deeply is a good idea. How can we be certain the Umbrae will not eventually find a way to tap into the Grays' dark halves and turn them against us? For that matter, how can we be sure they won't do the same should we send a Gray on this mission? We all know they're easier to turn when on the Earth plane."

Rahkma's words elicited more rumblings of discord amongst the group. The discussions grew heated, and the voices of the gods and goddesses hit a noisy pitch.

Mobius shook his head. He rubbed his hands over his face, suddenly tired. "Enough!" His voice reverberated, commanding respect. The group quieted. All eyes turned to him.

"We have discussed this matter before at length. There are no guarantees in this, no way to be certain the Umbrae won't interfere with our plan. But sending another Light God will only result in the Umbrae making an equally aggressive effort to infiltrate the humans. Neutralization is the best approach. We need a Balancer god to bring in the Balancer in the flesh. We must utilize the strengths of both the Light and the Dark. I am convinced it is the only way."

"But Axiom, Mobius? Are we not asking a lot of a rather young god?" Helios asked.

"We ask only that which we would ask of ourselves," Mobius responded. "Axiom is young, yes. But he is driven. And he is one of the strongest of the Balancers. We need someone like him, someone focused, someone who—"

"Won't be distracted by the pull of the Umbrae or of Earth life." Willow finished Mobius's sentence for him.

Mobius flinched, well aware the entire Council knew of his own similar but failed mission. At first, it had seemed successful, but like most of their battles against the Umbrae, his success had been short-lived. The night had a way of finding new and ingenious ways to further its goal of overshadowing the day.

Willow spoke in her usual diplomatic manner. "We've argued this point until its edge has dulled. Let us make our vote. The potential candidates are listed on your ballots. You know Mobius's recommendation."

The Council set about plugging their votes into the clear, crystal tablets that lay before each member. The sound of their fingers tapping on the keys echoed through the otherwise silent room. Long moments later, they had placed the tablets into slots carved into the stone tabletop, and the automatic tabulation system spit out a palm-sized amethyst stone. Mobius glanced at the stone, careful to keep his expression blank before passing it to Willow.

Willow smoothed her hair from her face and raised one perfectly arched eyebrow. "Axiom of the Grays is the chosen one."

Rahkma seemed particularly annoyed by the news. He opened his mouth to speak, but Helios touched his arm and shot him a warning look. The Council would only bear so much impertinence toward the Divine Director—or any other member of the Council, for that matter. If they could not remain united in their vision, how could they defeat the Umbrae?

Mobius mentally probed the Light Realm, searching for Axiom's presence. *Come. The Council would speak with you,* he commanded the Gray God.

A moment later Axiom appeared in a sea of sparkling gray, the air shimmering with the telltale signature of a Balancer in motion. Axiom stood, arms folded across his broad chest, granite eyes glittering.

When he spoke, his words held all the arrogance and determination of one who is accustomed to success. "I am ready to serve the Council in any way I am able. I am most grateful for your confidence, and this is my promise to you: I will not fail."

CHAPTER ONE

Earth
Lake Geneva, Wisconsin
October 1

"Won't you reconsider accepting your inheritance, Miss Pittman?" Mr. Robert Abrams, whom Laurell always referred to simply as Abrams, spoke in his usual clipped, formal manner. Normally, Laurell found his British accent pleasing. Today, it grated on her nerves. Much as did the fact that Abrams had insisted on meeting with her again before she left town.

The thin, bookish man who served as the family's long-time attorney and executor of Hollywood legend Elaine Pittman's will cocked his head to one side and watched Laurell with what appeared to be real concern. As long as she'd known Abrams, he'd never expressed any detectable emotion. The idea of someone refusing such a large sum of money clearly had the poor man out of sorts.

"I wouldn't take Mother's money when she was alive. I won't take it now. You know which charities to donate to," Laurell reminded him. She would keep only what she'd need to keep Graves Manor going. That was different. *That's for Grandma Helen.* Her father had died before she was born, and Laurell and her mother had never gotten along. Her grandmother had been the only real family she'd known.

They stood in the middle of the large, circular driveway of Graves Manor, the only remaining asset in the Graves family legacy. The mansion had been built as a summer home shortly before the Chicago fire of 1871 forced Laurell's great-grandfather to retire from his brewing business. Laurell's mother, Elaine, had agreed to keep the mansion going. She'd set up a house account and provided for her mother's needs. It was the one selfless deed Laurell could remember her mother performing.

"Your grandmother was always adamant about keeping Graves Manor from falling into strangers' hands, but if you do decide to sell, I will assist however you wish." Abrams's words intruded upon her thoughts. His tone indicated his assistance in selling the house would not include his approval. *But of course, Grandma considered him a friend. He wants to honor her wishes.*

"I've no immediate plans to sell," Laurell reassured him, adjusting the backpack she wore, as one strap threatened to slide free of its clasp.

She'd once thought to raise children of her own here someday. A pang of grief swept through her. Eventually she'd be forced to let the place go; there would be no child to inherit it. She pushed these thoughts from her mind. Abrams was watching her expectantly. "You've had your hands full, getting Grandma's affairs in order, and now my mother's."

"I am happy to help in any manner I am able," he said.

"Yeah, well, I appreciate all you're doing. I know I haven't been around much." *That's an understatement.* She hadn't spoken to her mother in years. And she hadn't visited her grandmother in six months, hadn't even known her grandmother had cancer. *Some granddaughter I turned out to be.*

Abrams cleared his throat. "Such a tragedy. To lose your grandmother and mother within weeks of each other."

Laurell opened her mouth to respond when a frisson of electricity shot through her, stealing her words. She gasped in surprise. Something foreign stirred in her belly, and her limbs tingled.

"Are you quite alright?" Mr. Abrams asked. "You've gone pale."

Laurell gave a forced half smile. "I'm fine," she said. Whatever it was, the sensation had quickly disappeared.

Mr. Abrams twisted his hands and shifted from one foot to the other. *Nervous energy,* she thought. *He's trying to find something soothing to say. Or maybe he's afraid I'm about to croak, too.*

"There's some other reason for our meeting besides giving me a second chance to change my mind about Mother's money, right? You told me on the phone you needed to deliver something to me."

"Oh yes, yes. How could I forget?" Abrams hurried to his car and returned with a large black book. He handed it to Laurell. Her eyes swept over the worn leather binding. The words scrawled across the front read *Book of Shadows* and rang with an odd familiarity she couldn't place.

"What is this?" she asked.

Abrams shrugged. "I thought you might know."

She shook her head. "No idea. Where did it come from?"

"It was your grandmother's. Along with Graves Manor, it was passed to you at her death," he explained. "I should have given it to you sooner. My apologies. It slipped my mind during the rush to get Helen's affairs in order. Then with your mother's passing . . ."

Laurell ran her fingers over the cover and absently stroked the smooth leather. It smelled old, like a library book no one had checked out for years.

"Grandmother didn't give you any info about it?"

Abrams didn't respond at first. His gaze held a distant focus, as though he were deep in thought. He blinked. "Pardon? Uh—no. No information at all, I'm afraid."

Poor thing. No doubt this was too much emotion for the man for one day. She decided she should put him out of his misery.

"Well, if there's nothing else—" Laurell offered him her hand and he took it, his fingers icy cold against hers. For a moment, he gripped her hand so tightly, it hurt. She started to pull away, and then he abruptly released her hand. It happened so fast, she wondered if she'd imagined his death grip.

"It has been my pleasure to work with you and your family, Miss Pittman. If I can be of further service, please don't hesitate to contact me," Abrams said.

"Thanks."

He paused for a moment, as though struggling to produce some words of comfort, but gave a weak smile instead. He climbed into his beige sedan and drove away in a swirl of dead leaves.

Laurell held the book against her chest. In her other hand she clasped the roses Abrams had given in condolence. What to do with them?

She sighed and followed the winding cobblestone path leading to the family gravesite. She stopped in front of her grandmother's grave and knelt to place the flowers on the ground. Her chest felt empty, cavernous. She was alone in the world now. In that moment, she hated her mother almost as much as she'd once loved her. How could it be that her mother preferred death to the shame of her husband's betrayal? Riley had been a total fake; any fool could see he'd married Elaine for the status it afforded him. She bit her lip. *How could Mother's reputation have meant more to her than I did?*

Laurell glanced at the grave closest to her grandmother's. Despite her resolution not to visit her mother's plot, she moved in front of it and dropped her backpack to the ground. Something compelled her to reach out and touch the words etched into marble. ELAINE PITTMAN—1961–2007—MAY HER STAR SHINE ON.

Riley had picked out the headstone. He'd presided over the funeral with his usual bad acting, milking his role as grief-stricken husband. The press seemed to have forgotten he and Elaine had already filed for divorce.

If Laurell heard him tell his story about how Elaine had threatened to kill herself when he told her the marriage wasn't working, and "then—(gasp, horror, shock)—she did it" one more time, Laurell swore she'd shove one of the man's overpriced designer shoes in his mouth. *Maybe it would break one of his overly bleached teeth.*

A harsh October wind whipped through the solitary graveyard. She shivered and pulled her peacoat higher and tighter around her neck. It did nothing for her ears, which had begun to ache with the cold.

She momentarily regretted chopping her hair into its pixieish cut. Her mother wouldn't have approved of the haircut. Of course, that had been part of the pleasure in getting it chopped. Laurell rubbed her hands over her arms to ward off the cold, thinking her mother would have hated her size-twelve figure as well. She certainly didn't look the part of a Hollywood actress's daughter.

A swift gust rustled the leaves around her feet and made the tall oaks and fragrant pine trees sway in a macabre dance. It would rain soon; the air had a metallic scent she could almost taste.

"Laurell."

She thought she heard a man's voice call to her, distant, urgent. She glanced around the empty graveyard. No one there but the ghosts of her dead ancestors. Her mind had to be playing tricks on her. Graveyards were spooky places to hang out alone.

This would be the last time she'd visit Graves Manor for a while. Tomorrow she'd go home and start hunting for a new job. She could only live off her meager savings for so long. And school would start up again in a couple of weeks. She was only her thesis away from obtaining her master's degree in religion. Once she finished . . . who knew? At least she'd be the one to decide.

A drop of moisture skimmed her forehead. Then another. *Time to go.* She stood, brushing leaves and dirt from her jeans.

"Laurell." This time, the call came more clearly. Who had found her here? Abrams? Had he come back to make yet another plea for her to take her mother's money? God, she hoped not. It was getting to be annoying.

She opened her backpack and stuffed her grandmother's book inside, then slung it over one shoulder. A shiver whispered over her skin. The look of the graveyard was beginning to get to her, all shadows and half-light.

She started along the winding brick path back toward Graves Manor, where her little Honda waited, gassed and ready for the long journey back to Florida.

The house loomed in the distance, peeking between an opening in the oaks. Laurell was about to call out to Abrams when a man appeared in the clearing. She stopped in her tracks. *Not Abrams.*

This man was tall and dark haired and wore a midnight blue double-breasted suit. Who was he?

There it was again. The same strange tingling she'd experienced before had returned in full force. Next came a massive outbreak of goose bumps. She shook her arms hoping to erase the bizarre sensation, but the feeling only strengthened.

The man strode toward her and halted ten feet away. He stared, but said nothing. The sensations increased, pulsing through Laurell like an electric current. Her heart fluttered, and her stomach clamped down with such force, she regretted her hastily devoured lunch. Every nerve ending in her body sang with a need unlike anything she'd ever experienced.

Her muscles twitched with the effort to move, but she couldn't budge an inch. An irrational longing washed over her. She ached to be naked and skin to skin with the man. She struggled to push the urge away, but it persisted.

What's happening? Why can't I move? Panic surged, but before it could reach its peak, a rabid desire ate through her anxiety.

The man's body tensed, his hands clenched into fists. Was he experiencing the same sensations as she?

A moment later, Laurell's paralysis broke. Her legs moved of their own accord. She ran toward the man, eager to touch him. *Stop!* Her brain protested. *Go!* Her body ignored the plea.

She came to an abrupt halt in front of him, her hands on his chest and her face turned upward. He grasped her arms. His eyes, deep and gray as the autumn sky, glittered into her own. She drank in the sight of him. Thick black hair curled over his brow. The chiseled planes of his face and the soft curve of his lips, almost too pretty for a man, left her transfixed. One of her fantasies had come to full, glorious life. He stood at least six foot three, towering over her five-foot-seven frame. *I should be afraid*, she thought. Instead of fear, it was his rugged beauty that consumed her.

"Laurell," he whispered.

His voice touched her in places it shouldn't have been able to. She sucked in a breath in response to a jolt of pleasure between her thighs. *Who are you? What are you doing to me?*

A pained expression took over the man's face, and his body shook. Then he moaned something unintelligible and pulled her sharply against him.

Laurell inhaled musk and sandalwood. His scent. Some part of her mind acknowledged she should pull away and run. Some part of her tried. She grimaced, splayed fingers across his chest, and pushed hard, desperate to disengage.

Just as it seemed she might break the spell he'd cast over her, another blast of raw, frenzied need rocked her to the core. Her hands momentarily fell limp, and a second later, she observed her fingers as though they belonged to someone else, caressing the stranger's taut stomach. She moaned in frustration. To her consternation, the sound came out breathy, inviting.

The man's head bent. The heat in his gaze made clear his intent and she gasped out a feeble, "Wait—"

His mouth crashed into hers, and he kissed her hard and deep, eliciting impossible sensations throughout her body. Invisible hands tugged her nipples and brushed the folds of her sex, setting her flesh on fire. If he'd asked her at that moment to let him take her, despite all logic and reason, she'd have let him. Right there in the mud and the leaves and in front of the specters of her ancestors.

Laurell managed to work up the strength to pull her lips from his. She tilted her head back just enough to focus on his face again. His silver eyes flashed with desire. More energy raged through her, hot and earthy. *Too much. It's too much.* Then the world spun and went black.

CHAPTER TWO

"She's coming to. Hand me some water."

Laurell's eyes fluttered open. She blinked, and a black ceiling swam into view. Her hands brushed the smooth leather of the seat she lay sprawled across. *Seat?* She started to sit up, and her vision zigzagged.

"Careful, abrupt movements could cause additional vertigo. Your body is adjusting."

She choked down nausea and jolted upright anyway, glancing quickly around. She sat in a parked limousine. A silent driver occupied the front seat, his face obscured by the cowboy hat he wore. The man in the suit perched next to her, his brow furrowed in obvious concern. He held a glass of water out to her, and she jerked back instinctively.

"Don't touch me," she spat out.

He sighed and set the glass in a side holder. He glanced toward the front of the car at the man behind the wheel. The driver adjusted his rearview mirror as though to assure eye contact with her captor before shaking his head and saying, "We shouldn't stay here much longer. You're too easy to track from the car."

Laurell's back stiffened. *Great. A wanted man.* She slid toward the door and grabbed the handle. It didn't move. She ran her fingers over the door panel and found no way to unlock it.

"Do not be afraid. I will not harm you."

At his words, Laurell spun back around to face her kidnapper, ready to demand he unlock the door, but the words died in her throat. She realized something very strange. She wasn't afraid. Angry, yes. Confused, absolutely. But the raw terror she'd have expected to experience in this kind of situation didn't exist. She could sense her fear—buried back somewhere in her brain—struggling to be set free, but failing miserably.

Instead, her thoughts continued to focus on the beauty of the man in front of her and the way his thick arms made the suit coat bunch up. *These aren't my thoughts*, she realized. *Why can't I control them?*

There could be only one explanation. "You drugged me."

"I have utilized no drugs." He lifted the glass of water again and took a sip as though to prove his point. Laurell observed his movements with a sort of hypersensitivity. The tilt of his head, the bend of his arm, even the way his fingers circled the glass appeared magnified and vivid. Along with the bizarre visual phenomenon, she experienced that same current of energy shimmering over her skin.

"What did you do to me?" she demanded, absolutely certain he'd done *something*. A girl didn't just get kidnapped by some strange man and feel no fear. Nor would said girl be so focused on sexual attraction during so dire a predicament. Unless she'd been drugged.

"What did you do to me?" she demanded again. He kept staring at her like some kind of interesting science experiment.

"It is because we are in such close proximity. I had to use the yearning to locate you, but I overestimated my ability to ward during our first meeting. I apologize."

He seemed almost embarrassed by this admission, though Laurell had no clue what he'd just confessed.

She frowned. "So you *are* doing this to me?"

He glanced at the driver without answering.

"We should go," the driver warned. Even from where Laurell sat, she could read the tension in the driver's shoulders and neck.

"Drive," the kidnapper told him. The car lurched forward, throwing Laurell back against the seat.

"Where are you taking me?" Anger coiled in her belly. So, fear had taken a vacation, but anger remained and was gaining strength.

"Somewhere safe."

"Safe? This is kidnapping!"

"If I had asked you to come with me while the yearning was in force, you would have agreed. I have avoided the use of force. It would not bode well for our future relations."

"This isn't forcing? You've locked me in your car against my will." She paused, and her eyes narrowed. What did he mean by "relations"?

The man sighed. "Soon we will be somewhere protected. Once there, I can explain everything, including who you are."

Laurell bristled. "I know who I am. Who the hell are you?"

Before the man could respond, the driver accelerated and made a sharp swerve. The quick movement sent Laurell sliding across the seat, straight into the man's lap. She grabbed his arms to keep from falling on her back. As soon as she touched him, a sharp jolt of desire kicked the air from her lungs. Her sex quivered, and her nipples sprang to life. An unbearable ache settled into her groin. Her rear tingled where it pressed against the length of him. It took every bit of willpower she had not to bear down and grind herself against that bulge.

"What the—" she gasped. She didn't *want* to have sex with the man.

"They're tracing us. You've gotta ward." The driver's voice carried a frantic note.

"It is not I they are picking up. It is she. She has no knowledge yet of warding," her captor exclaimed.

"You'd better do something fast or they'll be on our ass and following us to the safe house."

"I am trying, but my own ward is tenuous."

Laurell's hand moved of its own accord up the man's broad chest. She ran one finger over his neck, touching the dark stubble on his chin. Everywhere she caressed him, she sensed an invisible finger brushing her in the same spot. What would happen if she dared press her bottom against his groin? She did just that, and experienced another wave of pleasure. Her thighs were immediately moist with her arousal.

"Enough!" The man lifted Laurell off him and forcibly pushed her to the other side of the car. Unable to help herself, she reached for him, and he raised his hands.

"Stay back!" he cried.

He clamped his eyes shut and sat with his hands folded under his chin as though in deep concentration. A cool blast of air washed over Laurell, and the lustful energy dissipated. The driver slowed the car.

"They've lost the signal," the driver announced.

Her kidnapper opened his eyes and nodded. He looked different, tired and strained.

"I am uncertain how long I can ward for us both. How much farther must we travel?"

"We're an hour or so from Madison," the driver responded. "Can you hold until then?"

"I will have to."

Laurell hugged her knees to her chest and straightened her coat around her jean-clad legs. She wondered if she was in shock; a queer calmness had taken hold of her. She had no way to escape until the car stopped and the men unlocked the doors. No use panicking, even if she could. If he'd meant to kill her, he could have done so while she was unconscious. Which meant he had some use for her, didn't it? Perhaps he knew she was Elaine Pittman's daughter. No doubt he hoped to gain her fortune. Laurell stifled a hysterical laugh. Too bad for him, she had no fortune.

Laurell gritted her teeth. She'd find a way to escape. She had to. No one else would come to her rescue. No one would even look for her. The only friend she'd had, a perky brunette who shared her major and love of late-night pizza, had recently moved to Pennsylvania to be with her fiancé. That was it in the friend department. Laurell didn't make friends easily. Not since she'd realized people's perverse need to befriend those related to the famous.

No one spoke for the remainder of the drive. It seemed eons before the car stopped. Glancing out the window, she realized they were in an area that was only slightly familiar to her. She hadn't come to Graves Manor much since moving to Florida—or Madison, for that matter—but she vaguely recognized the warehouse district just outside the city. Was her captor going to tie her up in some storage facility?

The kidnapper turned to face her. He still carried that same tenseness in his bearing, as though he held something within him barely in check.

His irises turned a deep gray, almost black, swallowing his pupils until they disappeared like pebbles dropped into a lake. A shot of silver shone through them, almost opaline. She stared into his eyes, heart raging in her chest.

"Who are you?" she whispered past the lump in her throat, both hopeful and fearful he would answer the question this time.

"Axiom," he said. "My name is Axiom. And I am a god made flesh."

Laurell swallowed hard. The man had clearly lost his mind.

CHAPTER THREE

His driver saw them inside, provided a tour of the steel, one-story building that had been converted to a large studio apartment, and left.

The girl had remained silent after his departure. Axiom slanted a sideways glance at her. *She is beautiful in the flesh.* When he had observed her from the Light Realm in preparation for the mission, he had noted her attractiveness, but now he saw her true beauty.

Not that appearance really mattered. The yearning would see to it he desired her regardless of what she looked like. Still, he acknowledged Laurell's particular brand of beauty.

Her wide, dark eyes, high cheekbones, and full lips rivaled any goddess's fine features. He was not terribly fond of the short hair, but when he had touched it briefly while carrying her inert form to the car, the strands had been soft against his fingers. He also found the slight red sheen pleasing. And when she had pressed her body against him, it had been more than just a pleasant experience. Her breasts were large and round, her hips full and voluptuous. Axiom's pants tightened around his crotch. *Careful,* he thought. *You'll unleash the yearning again.*

He noticed that Laurell had moved as far from him as possible. She sat on the far side of the opulently decorated room, on a four-poster bed that dominated the space.

She was sipping from a glass of water that Wayne, the driver, had handed her as soon as they'd entered the safe house. Or rather, she pretended to sip it. *She still thinks I drugged her. She will learn to trust me.* At least he hoped she would. He did not wish to attempt a mating without having developed at least a cursory friendship with the woman.

Laurell shivered, and Axiom focused on the stone hearth, where firewood had been laid out in preparation for their arrival. Within moments a flame burst to life and heat engulfed him, accompanied by the pleasant aroma of burning logs. He stood and removed his coat. He glanced at Laurell, who shrugged out of her own coat and set it atop the backpack she had retrieved from the limousine.

"Laurell?"

Intent on arranging and rearranging her coat next to her on the bed, she jumped when he spoke.

Laurell cleared her throat and raised her chin defiantly, but he could read anxiety in her every movement. Her vulnerability made Axiom want to touch her, to stroke her cheek soothingly. He frowned and brushed the urge aside.

Clearly, he had overestimated the ability of his human form to control human emotion.

"Would you like some food?" he asked. She did not answer, just gave him a wary glance.

He crossed the room to the kitchen. He removed his suit jacket and unbuttoned the top of his white dress shirt, rolling up his sleeves before reaching into the refrigerator. Having been on Earth for several days now, he found he rather enjoyed the little things about being human. Like eating. And preparing food. It was easier than he had expected. He ducked inside the refrigerator and emerged with a handful of food supplies. Two slices of bread, some ham and cheese. In moments the meal was ready. Tomorrow he would prepare eggs the way Wayne had shown him. He brought Laurell the sandwich and some potato chips and held them out to her.

"Eat this. You will feel better."

"I don't want food. I want to know how you did that trick," she said, the word *trick* edged with disdain.

Axiom lifted an eyebrow. "Trick?"

"You know, the thing with your eyes. Making them change like you did in the car."

Axiom shrugged. "There was no trick. It occurs when I utilize certain powers."

Laurell frowned. A moment later, her face lost its color and she hugged her arms around her middle, clearly in pain.

"Eat," Axiom urged.

"How am I supposed to eat at a time like this?" she snapped.

"If you do not eat now, you will experience more pain. Your body is depleted from the yearning. Eat." She stared at the plate of food he still held in front of her, no doubt willing herself to ignore the hunger pains, which now were almost unbearable. Her face contorted, and she moaned.

"Eat," he said again. Her face had gone white and her body shook. Still, she refused to pick up the sandwich he had brought her. *Stubborn human.* "What must I do to convince you it is folly to refuse this food? You must eat immediately, or your body will fail to function. At the very least, you will find yourself unconscious."

Axiom feared he would have to force-feed her, but clearly the idea of being unconscious again in his presence seemed to her a worse fate than being drugged with food.

"Fine." She yanked the plate from his hands and took a ravenous bite of the sandwich.

"In addition to your hunger, are you tired?" he asked.

She nodded between bites.

"Until you learn to ward the yearning, its energy will deplete yours."

"What exactly is the yearning?" Laurell's words came out garbled between mouthfuls of food.

"The sensations you have been experiencing since we met."

Laurell arched one eyebrow. "'Met' is an interesting way to put it." She swallowed another bite of sandwich. "So you're saying this yearning thing makes me want to jump you against my will."

"In essence, yes."

Her look was dubious. He pulled a chair to the end of the bed and sat, studying her as she chewed and swallowed. His own stomach rumbled.

"The yearning is what attracts us," Axiom continued. "Its energy is potent. Its presence also masks other emotions. It is keeping your fear in check right now."

"Bullshit. You drugged me. You're probably still drugging me with this food, and if the side effects weren't so damn painful, I wouldn't touch it." Laurell swallowed another bite of sandwich and glanced down with a look of disappointment. Only a few potato chips remained on the plate.

He noticed her color starting to improve, and her body no longer shook. *A good sign.* He sighed and took the plate from her hands.

"Hey," she protested. "I wasn't finished with that."

"I will return it to you in a moment. First, you must reach acceptance of certain things. We have no time for disbelief."

Her eyes shot daggers at him. Her lips pursed into a thin line.

Before she could object, Axiom took her hands in his. A second later a rush of heat engulfed him, and he sensed it moving through her as well. His limbs were on fire. He was filled with the pain of desperate, frustrated sexual need. His groin hardened.

If the agony of the yearning was unbearable for Laurell, it proved doubly so for Axiom. His immortal side allowed him to experience Laurell's sensations as well as his own. He could literally feel the throbbing in her sex and the immediate dampness between her legs.

Laurell slid from the bed and onto Axiom's lap, straddling him. His arms encircled her, pulling her against his chest. Their lips met in a kiss that was anything but tentative. His tongue pushed into her mouth, and hers pressed back eagerly. His senses reeled with the sweet fragrance of her skin and the softness of her hair. He suckled at the crook of her neck, delighting in the goose bumps his touch elicited.

Axiom knew the moment when her inhibitions broke completely under the power of the yearning. He knew when her thoughts filled with him, with the texture of his thick hair as she wound her fingers into it at the nape of his neck, with his earthy scent, and with the taste of his mouth—salty and hot. The pleasure he brought her magnified his own.

He saw himself through her eyes, experienced her pleasure along with his own. *Unbearable. Exquisite.* He had imagined this many times. Before he had been sent to Earth, Mobius had encouraged him to observe Laurell, so befriending her would be easier. Axiom had studied her often, wanting to be certain his mission would be successful. He had wondered about what it would be like to touch her, hold her, kiss her, mate with her.

Laurell pressed her pelvis to his and rubbed herself up and down the length of him. Her nipples hardened as they brushed against him through the thin layers of her bra and T-shirt.

He had been trained to deal with the yearning, to control it as much as possible. When Laurell ovulated, however, not even his immortal powers would be able to withstand its pull.

For now, however, control it he would. Axiom thrust one hand into Laurell's hair, tangled it there, and tugged her mouth from his. His arms trembled with the effort to hold her away from him.

He focused all of his will to slam shut the door of desire just as consciously as he had previously opened it. The sensations stopped. She gasped and scrambled from his lap, chest heaving. Long moments passed while he waited for her to recover. When she could speak, she stared at him, incredulous. Her eyes narrowed, mouth twisted. He would not have been surprised had she thrown something at him.

"How. Is. This. Possible." Each word emerged between Laurell's teeth as though she spat out something putrid.

"It is not of this world."

"Why is it happening?" she demanded.

"Because it is necessary for us to come together and fulfill our duty. The yearning makes it impossible for us to fail."

Laurell bit her lip and pressed shaking hands to her face. When she removed her hands, she was a bit calmer, though Axiom sensed that her composure would be short-lived.

"Our duty?"

"Is it not obvious? We must mate."

CHAPTER FOUR

"I won't be forced to have sex with anyone." The words burst from Laurell's mouth on a growl, and she darted to the far side of the room. The fire heated her backside, but it wasn't half as hot as the heat that scorched her face from the anger raging inside her.

Axiom was at her side in a heartbeat. *He moves too fast to be human.* As soon as the thought rushed into her mind, she pushed it aside. She couldn't start believing his madness now.

Axiom touched her arm, and she jerked away. She stood stiffly before the fire, anger as hot as the orange and yellow flames ripping through her. The man was crazy. And he had drugged her somehow. That was the only possible explanation for the dulling of her fear, the strange ravenous need for food at such an odd time, the unrestrained and all-consuming desire to have sex with him.

How else could he control her body this way? How else could he make her own flesh turn traitor to her will? How could he make the appropriate emotion of fear turn to lust?

At the moment, his hold on her senses seemed to have dissipated a little. She could actually feel her heart fluttering from something other than sexual need. Laurell clenched her fists and willed herself to calm. She despised being afraid. Fear meant having no control. *I control my own life and my own destiny, dammit.*

A god. Yeah. And I'm a goddess. She'd seen enough horror movies to know the best tack to take when dealing with a nut. She had to hide her rage and stamp out any signs of fear. And not by replacing the fear with lust, either. Somehow, she had to fight the drug he'd given her.

Axiom sighed audibly and interrupted her thoughts. "Our duty is not just about the mating, though I hope that will be an enjoyable activity for us both." He paused.

Laurell whirled to face him, glaring. Enjoyable? Right. Rape was not enjoyable.

Axiom touched her arm again, and the now-familiar frisson of the yearning rushed through her body. "Let me explain how this came to be."

"Fine. Talk," she said.

If he was talking, time was ticking, and the drug would be wearing off. But how had he drugged her in the first place? She bit her lip.

"When you were between lives, you volunteered for this mission," Axiom said.

"I volunteered?"

"Yes, to assist in bringing the Earth Balancer." Laurell's confusion must have been stamped across her face, because he added, "The Earth Balancer is the one mortal who can keep Earth from being overrun by dark, destructive forces."

"Riiiggght," she drawled. "So, this person has the ability to ward off evil?" He nodded. "You mean a person who has superpowers or something?"

"In a manner, yes. His very existence, his—" He frowned, as though searching for the right word. "His DNA has a special quality that counteracts the Dark. It works in a similar manner to my own ability to battle the Umbrae in the higher realms."

"You make it sound like we're in the middle of a war," she said.

"Yes, a war." Axiom nodded briskly. "One that has been waged since time began. Between the forces of Dark and Light."

She frowned. "Why do you need this Earth Balancer? Why not just send more gods down to protect Earth?"

"The Light Gods have attempted this previously. Unfortunately, when you shine light into darkness, the darkness disappears only temporarily. Once the Light returns to its source, as it must in order to revive itself, darkness returns. And as for the Grays, our ability to neutralize the Umbrae is not as effective when we are in the flesh. We're able to fend the Umbrae off temporarily, but doing so greatly depletes our energy."

"How is the Earth Balancer different?"

"He will be a being of flesh and will carry both the light and dark energies of an immortal Gray. The Earth Balancer will possess the ability to neutralize the Umbrae on the Earth plane."

"I see," she said, studying Axiom more closely. His chiseled features, dark hair, piercing gray eyes, and muscular build were like something out of one of her hottest dreams. *Focus. Kidnappers are not sexy.*

"You called yourself a Gray. What is that exactly?"

"I belong neither to the Light nor Dark, but contain elements of both, thus the term Gray." His eyes clouded. "I am a Balancer on the higher planes."

"Mm-hmm," Laurell agreed, though she had no idea what the man had just said.

"Are my words unclear?" he asked with raised eyebrows. "I detect confusion in your features."

She sat up straighter and cleared her throat. *Be nice*, she reminded herself. *You're supposed to seem interested; placate the man.* "No, I get it. Really. You're here to bring the Earth Balancer."

"That is correct. It is important that you fully understand. Please ask for clarification when needed."

It suddenly occurred to Laurell she had been in Axiom's presence for what had to be almost two hours, and he hadn't made any move to harm her. He clearly believed the things he told her. She sighed, allowing herself some relief. So maybe her worst fate was rape. A horrible enough thing to be sure, but better than death. Perhaps he'd convinced himself of this whole elaborate story to keep from admitting that he would be taking her against her will.

"I still don't understand my role in all of this. Or yours for that matter."

Axiom leaned forward. "I am certain I explained this to you already. I am to father the Balancer. You are to be his mother."

The words rang in Laurell's ears. Tears pricked her eyes. There was no way he could know. No way. But his oh-so-casual statement twisted like a knife through her gut just the same.

"Fuck you," she ground out.

His brow furrowed. "I do not understand your anger."

"Of course you don't. You can't possibly understand the irony of you and me having sex to give birth to some supernatural baby who's going to save the world."

Laurell forgot about her plan to stay calm. In the space of a few weeks she'd lost her grandmother and her mother, had been kidnapped and then drugged into almost screwing a stranger. *Now this?* She wanted to cry. Instead, she laughed, a raw hysterical sound that burst out unbidden.

Axiom's spine went rigid, and he crossed to the couch and lay down.

Laurell's eyes widened. "What are you doing?"

"Going to sleep."

"In the middle of a conversation?"

"Yes. I find I am not as amused by our situation as you."

"You think I'm amused?" she retorted.

"Your behavior would indicate it, yes. Apparently mating with me is a laughable matter to you, but it is, in truth, gravely important." Axiom closed his eyes, dismissing her.

Laurell's jaw dropped. He seriously intended to ignore her and go to sleep. Fine. She didn't care. She'd had enough of his crazy stories anyway. And the exhaustion she'd experienced ever since they'd met was catching up with her.

Her limbs responded slowly as she yanked the covers back from the bed and crawled atop the mattress. She didn't bother to remove her shoes or socks, just in case she got an opportunity to make a run for it during the night. Maybe while Axiom slept she could look for a way out or at the very least search for a weapon in the kitchen. She was dubious about her ability to fend him off should he decide the time was ripe for—what had he called it? Oh yeah, a mating—but she'd put up a fight he'd not soon forget.

She pulled the comforter up to her chin. Axiom turned off the lamp near the couch. The couch springs screeched in protest as he settled into his makeshift bed.

"Go to sleep." His words sliced through the darkness as though he knew her plan to stay awake and attempt escape. "You are weak from the yearning, as am I. I can only ward for both of us for so long. Especially when we are this close. Tomorrow, I will teach you to ward for yourself."

What was this warding thing he kept mentioning? She opened her mouth to ask him, but couldn't get the words out. Her mind was foggy. What was it she was supposed to do? *Something important.* She struggled to keep her eyes open, but for the second time that day, she fell into darkness.

Today, I'll escape. The words reverberated in her brain as she woke. Laurell opened her eyes and surveyed the unfamiliar room thinking she'd slept very well for someone who'd been kidnapped. *Bet Axiom would say it was from the yearning.* More likely it was from the drugs he'd given her.

Her heart fluttered in her chest, and she bolted upright in bed. The details of the day and night before flooded into her mind. She crept from the bed to the couch, half expecting Axiom to still be asleep on it. It was empty. Realizing she alone occupied the room, her heart slowed.

She exhaled and the air clouded. Without the warmth from the fire, the room had grown frigid.

Laurell shivered and slipped into her coat. She crossed the room. As she'd suspected, the only door to the apartment was locked. And after tearing the place apart, she located no phone. She did manage to find a sharp kitchen knife, and she wrapped it in a kitchen towel that had a ridiculous picture of a dancing block of cheese on it. She carefully tucked the weapon in her jeans, but seriously doubted her ability to use a knife on the man.

She was not a violent person, and he was more than twice her size, but having it gave her some small measure of comfort. Realizing Axiom could return at any moment, she began a mad scramble about the place.

There were only a couple windows, set up high. A dresser along the far wall caught her attention. Ten minutes and a lot of muffled groaning and strained muscles later, she was able to push the dresser under the window. She climbed atop it and found herself at eye level with one of the windows.

Hiking her body up to the window ledge with nothing to lever herself could present a problem. Laurell scanned the room again and spotted a small step stool in the kitchen.

She placed the stool on the dresser and climbed up on it. It teetered precariously, and she sucked in a breath and stilled her movements. The window had no latch; it clearly wasn't meant to be opened. She'd have to break it. Gritting her teeth, she performed a mental checklist of the items in the room that could be used to smash the glass.

"Do not even think of it." Axiom's voice broke through her thoughts, and she jumped in surprise, losing her balance. Her frantic swipe at the window ledge proved ineffective. She careened backward and straight into Axiom's arms.

CHAPTER FIVE

Axiom held her as though she weighed nothing. His jaw clenched, and a pulse beat erratically at his throat. Anger seeped from his skin until the air grew pungent with it. Laurell tensed and forced herself not to flinch under the harshness of his piercing eyes.

"Stop it," he muttered.

"Stop what?"

"Fearing me."

Laurell frowned. "In case you haven't noticed, you're sort of scary," she retorted.

"Were you afraid when I kissed you last night? Or when you were grinding yourself against me?"

Heat flooded Laurell's cheeks, and she pushed at his unyielding chest. "Put me down. Now."

Axiom's eyes narrowed, and he looked for a moment as though he would refuse, but he released her. Once she stood on her own, Laurell backed away from him. She took a seat in one of the chairs before the fireplace and pressed her hands between her knees to hide their trembling. The drug finally must have worn off. She was afraid.

Axiom sat across from her, and though she stared at the fireplace, she could sense his steady gaze.

"I understand your fear. I know this situation is nothing you could ever have imagined or prepared yourself for." Genuine concern tinged Axiom's words and made Laurell lift her head. What did he know? An insane man who insisted he was a god and went around kidnapping women, promising them babies and making them sex crazed couldn't possibly understand her heart.

"You don't know squat," she finally said.

"I know you better than you think," Axiom told her.

"What is that supposed to mean?" Laurell spat out. Who did he think he was anyway? *I am a god made flesh.* His words from the evening before flooded back to Laurell, sending a shiver through her limbs.

Axiom sighed. "Laurell, this resistance is accomplishing nothing. We waste valuable time. I must be able to trust that you will not attempt to flee every time I turn my back. You need to understand the seriousness of your actions."

Before she could respond, Axiom stood and crossed the distance between them. He knelt in front of her chair and yanked her hands from between her knees, clasping them between his.

"I am sorry for this."

"For what?"

A moment later, she knew exactly what. The room went black. A wave of energy hit her. It was nothing like the pleasure of the yearning. It held a desperate, dark note. Grief and hopelessness enveloped her.

She saw creatures, ugly and twisted, their blackened, scaly bodies bloated and vile. She smelled sulfur, thick and putrid, and it filled her nostrils and twisted through her lungs. One of the creatures reached out thin, withered fingers toward Laurell, beckoning her. Its other hand burrowed into the tangled mass of bodies that lay next to it. As it did so, heads lifted, and those poor souls tangled in the mass cried out.

She sensed the fear and despair of millions of souls, trapped in the Dark, kept forever from reaching their rightful home in the Light.

Their screams pierced Laurell's eardrums, plunged into her own soul, and filled her with terror.

She shrieked, and their cries mingled with her own. She could no longer tell where their pain ended and hers began.

The vision ended just as abruptly as it had begun. Laurell blinked, realizing she was back in the safe house.

Her breath was labored, shallow. Axiom hovered over her, granite eyes fixed intently on her face. Her heart fell back into her chest. She jerked away from him and scrambled backward until her spine hit a chair. How had she ended up on the floor?

Shivering, she wrapped her arms around her legs and rocked herself. Her eyes stayed open wide. If she closed them again, would she see those creatures? She shuddered at the thought.

Axiom rose and returned to her side moments later with a glass of water. He forced it into her hands. Minutes passed while she sipped the water and regained her composure.

"Explain what just happened. What were those things and how the hell did you do that?" Laurell's voice came out edged with the horror of the vision she'd experienced.

"They are the Umbrae. They are those who would wipe out the Light and rule the Earth. I shared a re-visioning with you, a memory of mine."

Laurell barely registered Axiom's words. The screams of tormented souls still reverberated in her head. "I don't want to see them again."

"Hopefully, you will not have to." Axiom sighed and lifted her chin, forcing her eyes to meet his. For the first time, she didn't shrink back. She hadn't the energy.

"Please know I regret having to show you in such a harsh manner. I did not know how else to make you believe me."

Laurell shrugged out of his grip. She had to get control of herself. "Fine. I get it. I have to help you save the world.

Somehow, you and I will make a baby who will rescue the planet." The words sounded hollow to her ears, but Laurell knew in her gut what she'd just experienced was real.

"You never drugged me, did you?" Her words were less a question than a statement. "This is all real, isn't it?" She watched Axiom carefully, still hoping for a rational explanation.

He grimaced and nodded. "Again, I am sorry, but yes. It is real."

Laurell's head fell into her hands and she let out a hysterical laugh. *What a joke. What a cruel joke.*

"You are in shock. I should get you warm. I will light the fire." He stood and helped her to her feet. She wobbled toward the fireplace on unsteady legs, but refused the chair he offered, afraid she'd be unable to stand again if she sat. She watched Axiom toss a log into the fireplace.

"God knows I *should* be in shock after all I've been through over the past twenty-four hours, but no, I don't think I am," Laurell told him.

Axiom's hands stilled. "Then why did you laugh again? What amused you this time?"

"You."

He jerked around to face her. "Me?"

"Yup. Because, you don't even realize how ridiculous it is to think I can give birth to the savior of the planet."

Axiom's jaw hardened. "Ridiculous how?"

Laurell's heart twisted as though it would rip in two. "You ever hear of a thing called endometriosis?"

He raised his eyebrows in question.

"Well," she continued, "I've suffered from it my whole life. One of its side effects is infertility."

He didn't respond to that bit of news, but sorrow tinged his features. *Why is he sad? I'm the infertile one.* Laurell straightened her spine and stubbornly blinked away the tears that threatened to spill.

"I can't have kids, Axiom. You've got the wrong girl." Head held high, she stalked past him toward the door. She refused to let him see just how deep the admission cut. Having a child of her own had been her one shot at having a family. A real family.

The scent of sandalwood alerted her to Axiom's presence behind her. His arms wound around her and held her. His unexpected tenderness almost did her in. She let herself linger there for a moment, just enjoying being touched. It had been a long time since she'd been held by anyone.

She remembered the knife then. Could he feel it in her jeans? The thing had become damn uncomfortable there, scraping against her back. Thank god for the dish towel covering it. And her baggy sweatshirt.

Laurell tensed and pulled herself from his arms. He started to touch her, but she raised her palms to him. "Just give me a minute, okay?"

Axiom nodded and settled her into a chair with a blanket. This time she sat gratefully. She was so damn tired. Suddenly she didn't care if she never got out of that chair again. The fire crackled and spit. She heard pots banging, cupboards slamming shut.

The air filled with the scent of fried eggs and bacon. Her stomach growled. Moments later, Axiom handed her a plate of food and a glass of orange juice. He sat in a recliner next to her, and silence reigned as they consumed their food. Out of the corner of her eye, she observed him. He ate with vigor, sighing with unrestrained pleasure when he chewed the bacon. Her own belly pulsed with want of food and she forced herself to chew her eggs slowly, though she was ravenous with hunger.

"I guess you like bacon," she mused aloud.

He nodded. "I find the flavor pleasing." Axiom chewed some jam-slathered toast, then licked his fingers, getting each last crumb. A frisson of heat jolted between her legs at the sight. She frowned and pushed the desire away.

"Why do you eat like that?"

Axiom paused and tore his eyes from his food to give her a blank stare. "How is it that I am eating?"

"Like a pig." She was being nasty. It felt good. She hated how vulnerable he made her feel.

Axiom swallowed and blinked. For the first time his expression was one of uncertainty. "I apologize. I am still becoming accustomed to food consumption."

She sighed. "Gods don't eat, I take it."

Axiom shook his head. He glanced at her still half-full dish and said, "You had better eat more than that. You still need to regain your strength." He turned back to his meal. When his plate was spotlessly clean, he took his dish to the sink. Laurell cleaned her plate quickly when his back was turned. She was so damn hungry.

She drained her juice and walked the glass over to him. One lock of hair curled over his forehead as he scrubbed a skillet with focused vigor, then took a dish towel to it.

"Thank you," she murmured.

Axiom paused in his task and glanced at her, searching her face for sarcasm. He looked back at the pan.

"I do not mind cleansing our dishes. I have observed humans doing these small tasks. It is in some fashion enjoyable to me," he said.

Laurell didn't respond. She nodded and turned to walk away, but Axiom stopped her. "Laurell."

She turned back to him. His gaze was serious. He reached out one hand as though to touch her. She instinctively tensed, and his arm dropped to his side.

"The illness you have dealt with, the one you believe left you barren . . . it is a terrible thing. I do regret you had to endure such a trial."

He must have sensed her pulling back into herself at his words, because his voice took on a soothing note.

"Illness or no, you will bear my child."

She bit her lip. "How can I have a kid with you? I told you—"

"Laurell, I am not truly human. I inhabit this body, yes, but I am still a god. You will bear my child."

Laurell froze. His words washed over her, thick with possibility. Elation and fear bubbled through her, one vying with the other for dominance. *Impossible,* she thought. *How can I believe him?* It hurt how much she wanted to believe. What if he spoke the truth? What then?

Later that day, while Axiom showered, Laurell retrieved her backpack from its place beside the bed. She pulled the smuggled knife from her jeans and slipped it inside. She wasn't even sure why she still felt the need to keep the thing. Axiom had made no move to harm her, and she was even starting to think there was some truth to his stories.

She frowned. Better to have some weapon than none. For all she knew, Axiom wasn't the only threat. Her hand brushed the cover of her grandmother's *Book of Shadows.* She wanted to read it, but not with Axiom hovering over her shoulder. She'd wait a bit longer.

Surely she'd get some privacy soon.

CHAPTER SIX

Anne, High Priestess of Hidden Circle Coven, shoved several bags of groceries into her Chevy S-10 pickup truck and climbed into the driver's seat. She glanced in the rearview mirror and pushed her chin-length, strawberry blonde hair from her eyes, thinking she needed a haircut.

She pulled the truck out of the grocery store parking lot and headed north toward home. The winding, hilly roads of Black Earth, Wisconsin, were dappled with sunlight. Thick with trees and brush, the forest she loved soon became the only scenery, a collage of colors: green, brown, orange, and amber.

Goddess, she adored the fall in Wisconsin. In fact, she loved everything about living way out here in the woods, surrounded by foliage and birds and all the other little scampering creatures of nature. She rolled down the window, frowning at the effort this required. The truck was old; the turning mechanism for the driver side window was rusty. Fresh, pine-scented air filled the vehicle, and the breeze whipped her hair around her face.

Anne yawned. She was tired, hungry, and had to pee. *Should have gone at the grocery store.* She drove a few miles more and remembered a small dirt road that left the highway and merged with the woods. She and Reese had picnicked there in the past. Once, they'd spent an afternoon of passion in the bed of her pickup truck atop a blanket she'd bought on a trip to Mexico. The place was secluded and far enough away from the road that no one would notice if she made a pit stop there.

She spied the dirt road, slowed, and turned the truck down the narrow path. It really was more path than road. Anne stopped the vehicle and climbed out, grateful for the sneakers she wore. The ground was muddy from a recent rain. She stifled another yawn, yanked her jeans down, and did her business. Exhaustion was kicking in. She needed to rest. The late nights working with Helen and getting the safe house ready had worn her thin.

As she zipped her pants and turned toward the truck, a rotten, sulfurous odor permeated the air.

A stabbing sensation knifed her gut, knocking the air from her lungs. Her gaze flew to her abdomen, expecting to see some instrument cutting her. Nothing. Out of the corner of her eye, she detected movement. She turned, but saw no one. Searing pain sliced through her head, and she stumbled backward into the side of the truck.

She grabbed onto the vehicle with one hand and lifted the other to her face. She touched something wet and warm.

"What the—" Her heart raced. Blood, bright as a cardinal's feathers, stained her palm. Where was it coming from? She felt warmth on her belly and glanced down to see her pale blue T-shirt quickly turning that same shade of crimson. She lifted her shirt with trembling fingers. A large wound there was emitting copious amounts of blood. Instinctively, she put her hands to her middle and pressed in, trying to stop the flow.

A bizarre buzzing sound filled her ears, and she blinked twice, uncertain whether she imagined what she was seeing or if it was real. The air a few feet in front of her shimmered and twisted. One clawlike black hand appeared, then two. They pulled the air apart as though it were a solid structure. To the hands was added a misshapen head with hollowed-out eyes and a thin, willowy torso. The buzzing noise became a low keening that came from the thing in front of her. The creature had two glowing pinpoints for eyes, and it stared at her.

Run. Move. But she couldn't. Another burst of razor-sharp pain, this time in her chest. The creature, slightly transparent, moved close to her, so close she was shrouded by the thing. Its form clung to her face like cobwebs. She could feel it shifting against her, and it moaned and undulated in orgiastic pleasure. *Help me. Help.* She tried in vain to make her limbs wake up, but it was no use.

The creature spoke into her mind. *You will not mother the Earth Balancer. You will die now, witch.*

Her heart plummeted, and she knew. She knew it was the truth. *Goddess keep me*, was the last thought to flutter through her mind before the pain became so unbearable that she sank gratefully into unconsciousness.

The woman was driving him to insanity. Axiom gritted his teeth and forcibly pulled Laurell back into the circle of his arms as she moved to scurry away. *Damn stubborn human.*

"Cease fighting me, Laurell," he told her for the third time that day. She seemed to think hiding on the other side of the room would somehow make it easier to avoid the yearning, although distance mattered little once its energy was unleashed.

"I don't see why we have to practice practically on top of each other like this," she protested.

"I already explained this to you. We must be prepared for all possibilities. That includes warding the yearning even when we are close to consummation."

As expected, she remained stiff against him. Equally expected, the yearning surged and pulsed through his body, tendrils of desire reaching out from her skin to his.

The roundness of her jean-clad bottom against his groin and the swell of her full breasts resting on his arms caused his pants to tighten around a fierce erection. His mind merged with hers, and he could sense the shivers that ran through her as she recognized his hardness.

A small sigh of pleasure escaped her lips. For a moment, he almost lost his own warding. Axiom's head bent seemingly of its own accord, and his face burrowed against her neck. He breathed deeply of amber, recognizing it as the fragrant oil Laurell had dotted on her neck and wrists that morning after bathing. Had she applied the scent to please him? He knew it unlikely, but smiled at the possibility. His lips curved against the softness of her neck.

Laurell shivered and let her head fall slack against his chest, lips parted. Axiom narrowed his eyes at the sudden urge to taste her mouth. He lifted his head and shook it to clear away the tenuous hold the yearning had tried to place upon him. His ward was in place. Hers was not.

"Laurell, draw your energy back," he urged. "Envision your aura disengaging from mine."

"I'm trying," she gasped, her words tight, as though speaking was an effort.

"Breathe and then block. See your aura harden like a shell around you. Do just as I demonstrated."

Laurell took a deep, shuddering breath and a moment later, the yearning disappeared. Having regained control, she immediately stepped out of his embrace. He frowned. Why did he already miss the sensation of her body against his? *It must be remnants of the yearning.*

Laurell brushed a stray lock of hair from her eyes and slumped into the nearest chair.

"We must practice more," Axiom told her sternly.

"Just taking a break, slave driver," she quipped. "Here, sit. I want to pick your brain some more." She motioned to the wingback chair next to her.

Reluctantly, he sat. "Fine, but we must continue practicing in a moment."

She nodded. "Explain how the Umbrae find us."

He ran one hand through his hair and forced back his frustration. Why did mortals enjoy talking so much? *Especially this mortal.*

"The yearning is potent energy," he said. "Just as it pulls us toward one another, it leaves behind a trail which the Umbrae can identify," he explained. "However, you need not be concerned or let this distract you from our practice. We are safe inside this dwelling."

Why was she asking these questions again? For what did she search? Besides trying to keep a physical distance from him, she had been uncommonly cooperative since they had risen that morning.

"I'm getting better at warding, aren't I?" Laurell asked.

Axiom tilted his head to one side. "Better, yes. As good as you need to be? No."

She grimaced, but then shrugged his words off and grinned. "I have to admit, I like knowing I have the ability to prevent the yearning from taking over," she said. "You've no idea how good it feels not to have the urge to tear your clothes off right now."

Axiom didn't find that news as comforting as he should.

"I'm just so tired," she told him with a yawn.

"Warding can drain your energy. Especially if one of us is doing all the work. That is why we both need to become as adept as possible," he advised. Standing, he held his hand out to her. "Break is over."

Laurell frowned. "Fine, but you're fixing dinner. I don't think I'll have the strength."

"I would expect nothing less."

Laurell's dreams that night were vivid and disturbing. Several times she woke, heart pounding, eyes wide, only to find herself staring into the peaceful darkness of the apartment. She couldn't remember what had pulled her from slumber or what she'd been dreaming about. Morning light had just started to peek through the windows when she finally tumbled into a deep sleep.

A stark, barren landscape stretched out before her; the earth under her feet was red and claylike. No air moved in this place, no wind stirred her hair or brushed across her skin, and there was a faintly sulfurous odor.

Scanning the area, she realized she stood alone, the only living thing in sight. Not even a blade of green grass peeked from beneath the dirt. The sun overhead shone unrelentingly; her face and neck burned from its heat.

Dimly, Laurell realized she wore a long, white robe, its cloth dirty and tattered. Her feet were bare. Twenty or so feet ahead, a light suddenly appeared from out of nowhere and spun clockwise, growing larger with every turn. Her pulse sounded in her ears, and she held her breath. Then, a woman stepped out of the light.

Laurell sucked in a breath. *Mother.*

The other woman studied her for a moment, familiar brown eyes wide with concern, long, chestnut hair curling over her shoulders. Her heart-shaped face and full lips were twisted with worry. She wore a robe similar to Laurell's.

"Am I dead then?" Laurell asked.

"No, but I am," Elaine told her. "This is the Astral Plane. You're asleep."

"I've read about this place. People believe we travel here when we sleep."

Her mother smiled and nodded. "Yes. It's true."

"Not how I pictured it." She'd thought the Astral Plane would be a star-filled night, brimming with possibility.

"Think it differently," Elaine instructed.

"What?" Laurell blinked, confused.

"Think it differently, and it changes. Your mind is all that counts here."

Laurell frowned, but did as Elaine suggested. Immediately, a million diamonds surrounded them, scattering across the violet sky, and the earth under their feet glowed like an opalescent gem. A jasmine-scented breeze wafted by.

Elaine smiled. "You always did have a wonderful imagination."

Laurell scowled. "How would you know?"

Elaine's lips curved. "I knew."

Her mother's expression quickly turned serious. She moved closer, her thin fingers reaching out to grasp Laurell's hands. Laurell backed up.

Laurell's gaze narrowed. "Why are we here?"

"I came to bring you a message."

"From the grave?" The words held a sardonic ring Laurell couldn't control.

"Yes. From the grave. It's possible when you are traveling here, on this plane. I've been watching you as you learn your powers. There will be much more training to come. It's vital you learn quickly and well. You have an important duty to fulfill."

"You're talking about Axiom. And the child."

"Yes. And you."

Laurell tilted her chin, waiting.

"Perhaps I am a poor choice of messenger," Elaine continued, "since I was never there for you before. But I'm your family, Laurell. Like it or not. I love you, and I want to help."

Tears blurred Laurell's vision. In her entire life, she could recall only two occasions when her mother had said those three words to her. *Talk about lousy timing.* She blinked the moisture away.

"How can you help me now? You're dead," Laurell pointed out, not bothering to hide the anger in her voice.

"I can help. You just have to trust me."

Laurell's eyebrows flew up. "Trust you? I don't even know you."

"I want to make things right." Elaine's words rang with sincerity, and her eyes pleaded. Laurell refused to be taken in. The woman had been one of Hollywood's highest-paid actresses, she reminded herself.

"What do you want, Mother? I mean, what do you *really* want?"

"I have a message for you. You must pass it to Axiom. Alright?"

Dubious, Laurell nodded.

"The witch who cast the protection spell . . ." Her mother's expression turned pained. "She's dead. The Divine Council is trying to figure out how this happened, but—" Elaine's head shot upward.

An eerie screech filled the air. Elaine clenched Laurell's hand so hard it hurt.

"What's going on?" Laurell demanded. A slow hum had begun to vibrate through the atmosphere, and the crystal ground beneath them shifted.

Elaine's face turned white and she spun left to right with jerky movements while scanning the area. "The Umbrae. I must go."

"Wait! I didn't get to—" Before Laurell could finish her sentence, the circle of light that had brought Elaine to the Astral Plane reappeared and scooped her up within it.

Laurell hadn't time to reflect further upon her mother's cryptic message. Above her, a shimmer of black swooped through the sky. It arched and dove toward her. Laurell's flesh prickled with fear.

She jolted up in the bed and into Axiom's arms. He clasped her tightly against his chest and rubbed soothing circles against her back until she calmed.

The dream faded, and she was able to collect herself enough to pull back from him. He lay sprawled across the sheets like some dark, sexy dream. His body was tense, brow furrowed.

"Why are you in my bed?" Laurell demanded, suddenly aware the gown she'd worn to bed had come open and her breasts were nearly exposed to his gaze. She yanked it closed and pulled the covers to her chin. If he'd noticed her quick movements, he didn't let on.

His gaze focused on her face. "You were having a nightmare. You called out in your sleep."

"Oh. Sorry if I woke you."

Axiom shifted closer. He wore only a pair of black boxers, the broad expanse of his chest bare, his long legs stretched out before him as he reclined on one muscular arm. Even without the yearning, which she held in check, the look of him was enough to make her want to throw herself on top of him and press her naked flesh to his. She had to stop thinking sexy thoughts—she'd only encourage the yearning.

"Of what were you dreaming?" Axiom asked.

She sighed as the remnants of the dream tumbled over her. "Mother."

"This was not a pleasant dream, I gather."

Laurell shook her head. "They never are."

"Do you dream of her often?"

"More so since she died." She glanced away from him, trying to hide her expression.

"Talking about her is upsetting to you. I am sorry."

She burrowed back down beneath the covers. "I'm just tired. I didn't sleep well last night."

She turned her back to him, hoping he'd take the hint, but he didn't leave the bed. Instead, cool air hit her legs as he lifted the blanket and crawled beneath. The next thing she felt was his arm around her waist and his body pressed against hers, warm and comforting. She tensed.

"I will lie with you for a while," he said. "You are shivering and in need of comfort. I can warm you."

He was right: her whole body trembled. Laurell didn't point out that he could simply light the fire. She sort of liked having him there, next to her. It had been years since she and her ex-boyfriend had broken up. Years since she'd let anyone hold her like this. How had Axiom managed to break past that barrier twice since they'd met?

"Besides," Axiom continued, "this is good practice for warding the yearning. And if we are to mate, we must become more accustomed to one another."

She bit her lip. She didn't want to start talking about sex or she might lose her hold on the yearning. A change of subject was in order. She sat up, disentangling herself from his arms.

"Axiom," she said, "tell me what it's like on the other side."

CHAPTER SEVEN

"What is it you wish to know?"

Laurell shrugged. "For starters, how is my grandmother? My father?"

"Did you not just speak with your mother? Did she not report of their well-being?"

She frowned. "How could she have? It was just a dream." A dream that had already lost its urgency, its details drifting away like feathers in the wind.

"It was much more than a simple dream. It was her first contact with you as your Liaison."

"My what?" Laurell chewed a nail.

"Your mother has requested to be your intermediary between the Earth Realm and the Light Realm. She is to consult with you and guide you. As long as she contacts you in the astral, she can do so without the Umbrae picking up the scent here on the Earth plane."

"Why do I need an intermediary? Isn't there someone who can contact you directly? I mean, you being a god and all?" Laurell asked.

"The gods and goddesses cannot contact me—or any of us for that matter—without leaving a metaphysical trail that would be all too easy to track. Their energy is very thick." As he sat fully upright, the sheets pooled at Axiom's waist, baring the magnificence of his massive chest to her gaze.

Laurell's eyes were drawn there, but she forced herself to

look at his face instead. He licked his lips. Had he done that on purpose? The yearning started to roll through her belly and snake its way toward her thighs. Quickly, she shielded. Hmmm. She liked being able to do that.

She blinked and focused on his face. "I'm sorry, what did you say?"

"I was explaining that the gods and goddesses cannot contact us here without being detected by the Umbrae." Axiom tilted his head to one side. "If they could assist us here, I know they would. It is an honor to be part of this mission."

Something about the way he said those words made her think.

"What exactly do you get out of this? I mean, besides the esteemed privilege of having sex with me?"

Her sarcasm elicited a small smile from him. "Is saving mankind not reason enough?"

Laurell narrowed her eyes. Something in her gut told her there was more. "There's something else you want, but what I can't figure out is what a god could possibly need."

He shrugged and brushed a piece of lint from the bedsheets. "I wish to be the first Gray to serve on the Divine Council. When this mission is successful, I'll have proven myself worthy."

"I see." The straightness of his spine and the way he refused to meet her gaze told her she'd hit upon a touchy subject. "This Divine Council . . . they're the decision makers up there in god world, right?"

"Yes," he confirmed.

"Why aren't Grays allowed to be part of the Council?"

Axiom cleared his throat. "It is how it has always been." As if that were answer enough.

"So they need you, but they resent needing you."

His jaw clenched. "They tolerate us because they must.

Without our ability to neutralize the Umbrae, the darkness would infiltrate the Light Realm."

Laurell shook her head. There was racism in godland? Maybe gods and humans were more alike than she'd thought. "What does the Council get out of sending you to Earth? Why do they care what happens to us here if they've got a bunch of Gray Gods to keep the Umbrae at bay?"

"Humans and gods were formed from the same source. We are all connected. Therefore, what happens to humans affects the gods and goddesses. When only a marginal number of humans are infected by the Umbrae, it will have little impact in the Light Realm. But if the Umbrae are able to turn enough humans, it could mean the end of us all."

She frowned. That didn't sound good. "And you? Were you formed from the same source too?"

Axiom nodded. "Yes, but the Grays are more recent creations, considered to be anomalies."

"You mean you're an accident? I don't get it. This source you spoke of, I guess it's like what we think of as God, right? I thought God didn't make mistakes."

"I do not wish to discuss this further. Your incessant questions are bothersome."

She clenched her teeth. "Oh, excuse me for wanting to understand why I've been kidnapped to save the world."

"You sound angry. This is—"

"Yeah, I know," she cut him off. "An honor." She sighed loudly. "Well what if I don't want this honor? What if I don't care that I agreed to do it? I clearly didn't realize what I was getting into. Can't the Council pick someone else? Isn't there a backup plan?"

He sighed loudly. "If you refuse to cooperate, there will be a meeting of the Council and a contingency plan will be instigated, but I am not privy to what that plan may be. And you are missing a very important point."

"What's that?"

"Even if by some chance the Council decides to relieve you of your duty, it is unlikely the Umbrae will grant you the same reprieve. They will kill you anyway, just in case you might change your mind."

Laurell's jaw tightened. Perhaps that was a chance she was willing to take. At least *she'd* be making the decision to walk away. At least she'd have some control again over her body and her mind.

"Ugh!" she groaned. "This sucks. I can't tell reality from make-believe anymore. Gods and goddesses and babies that can save the world . . ."

Axiom leaned toward her. The sheet slid farther off his torso, the lean muscles of his stomach completely bared to her view. A jolt of desire throbbed between her legs. A vision flashed in her mind's eye of Axiom atop her, their limbs entwined, his hips pumping against her own. Heat flooded her face. *Damn the yearning anyway.*

His hand grazed her leg. "I am quite real. I thought we had established that by now." The place where his skin brushed hers, such a soft, slight touch, sent a jolt of need that spiraled through her body and made her gasp aloud.

She pulled her energy back and slammed the door on the yearning, then tossed the covers aside. She jumped from the bed.

"You just used the yearning on me," she accused, eyes narrowed.

"I had to. You said you thought I was not real. We cannot backtrack. There is no time for that."

"Dammit, it was a figure of speech. Do you take everything literally?"

Axiom shrugged. "I am sorry if I have upset you."

She turned her back to him and yanked a pair of black jeans and a purple sweater from the dresser. It had disturbed her the first time she'd delved into the clothes someone had left for her at the safe house. She didn't want to know how the heck someone out there, likely Axiom, seemed to know all her sizes, right down to her panties.

Her ears perked at the sound of his footsteps as he retreated to the bathroom. Good. She didn't want to see any more of his naked flesh. Naked Axiom was more than she could handle right now.

She had dressed, brushed her teeth and hair, and sat perched with a cup of coffee at the kitchen table before she brought up the dream again. Axiom slid into the seat across from her and gulped down a glass of orange juice. He filled the glass again and finished it in a flash. His sigh of delight irked her for some reason. Why should he be in such a good mood?

Laurell picked up their conversation. "Mother said she was trying to make things right with me, but I have to ask whose bright idea it was to allow her to be my Liaison. I couldn't stand her when she was alive. Now I have to deal with her when she's dead too?"

"If the Council saw fit to grant her wish, there must be a sound reason behind the decision," Axiom said.

"Why didn't my grandmother volunteer? At least that would have made sense." Laurell thought for a moment and then shook her head. "Never mind. I think I know the answer to that." *Grandmother is still trying to repair the rift between Mother and me. Even in death she is meddling.*

Laurell took a sip of her coffee, enjoying its bitterness. She cleared her throat and tried to sound nonchalant as she asked, "You never answered my question. How is my grandmother? My grandfather? What about my father? Do you even know?"

Axiom glanced up from the container of yogurt he had opened. "The last I knew of her, your grandmother was in the Light Realm. Your grandfather is reincarnated. Your father as well. He is presently a school teacher in Chicago."

Laurell blinked. "Reincarnation, huh?"

"Yes," Axiom said. "You find this difficult to believe?"

"I find a lot of things hard to believe, but I'm trying to keep an open mind." More details of her dream reappeared. "There was something else Mother said."

"Good. It is important to remember as much as you can about her visits."

"She said the witch is dead. I'm not sure what witch. She seemed to think you'd know. Oh, and the Council is trying to figure out what happened to her."

A flash of silver light and a gust of wind literally knocked the coffee cup from Laurell's hands. Folgers dark roast spattered across the table. It took her a moment to realize Axiom had moved from the table to the far side of the room and held a cell phone to his ear. If she'd thought he traveled fast before, she realized then she hadn't seen a damn thing.

She focused on the cell phone. How had she overlooked it during her attempt to escape? Probably he'd had it on him. At least now she knew there was a phone nearby. Not that she had much confidence in her ability to wrestle it away from him.

"Wayne," Axiom spoke into the cell phone, his words laced with concern. "We must leave the safe house."

CHAPTER EIGHT

Wayne, whom Laurell was getting a good look at for the first time since her abduction, wore a stone-faced expression across his broad features as he stared at Axiom. He appeared to be in his early fifties. A good old boy type, wearing a leather jacket, a cowboy hat, and boots. Not like a witch at all.

"So let me get this straight. You're a witch and you belong to a whole coven of witches," Laurell said.

"That's right," Wayne said. "What's wrong? I'm not what you expected a witch to look like?"

Laurell frowned. "Frankly, no."

Wayne glanced away from her and back to Axiom. "So we're off to Fiona's then?"

The three sat at the kitchen table, dressed to hit the road. Laurell cradled a plump duffel bag to her chest like a shield, waiting for one of the two men to speak. She had shoved all the toiletries and clothes she could find into the satchel Axiom had produced. Her backpack hadn't been large enough, though she'd refused to leave it behind. The *Book of Shadows* remained tucked inside, pulling at her to be read.

It seemed they had to leave the safe house. The High Priestess of Wayne's coven, Fiona, owned some fifty acres of land in Black Earth, Wisconsin. In other words, in the middle of nowhere. Laurell knew enough about the northern Wisconsin landscape to know Black Earth consisted of nothing more than woods, gravel roads, and more woods. Her chances for escape were quickly dwindling.

"Wayne," Axiom said. "I do regret having to go to Fiona's. I know it is not what she or her sister Anne would have wished."

"Well, Anne had hoped ta keep you and Laurell at arm's length. The safe house was a good way of assisting without putting the entire coven in danger."

"I understand, but if the Umbrae are responsible for Anne's death, it means they may already know about the safe house. We cannot risk staying here. Particularly with the full moon so close," Axiom said.

"If they found Anne, how can we be sure they don't already know about the coven too?" Wayne asked.

Axiom sighed. "There is no way to be certain. Perhaps Laurell will receive another visit from her Liaison soon and she will have an answer."

Both men looked at Laurell then. *What's that? Have a chat with dear old Mom again? Sounds lovely.* "Who is Anne?"

"The former High Priestess of Hidden Circle Coven," Axiom said.

The witch who died. Laurell cringed, her desire to extricate herself from the mission increasing with every moment.

When she said nothing, the men returned to their conversation.

"In the meantime, at least we have you to warn us if you sense them near," Axiom said.

Wayne sighed and tugged at his chin. "I only wish I were able to detect them sooner. A five-minute warning doesn't seem like nearly enough time."

"It will have to suffice," Axiom said.

"Maybe we shouldn't go to Black Earth," Laurell piped up before she could stop herself. "I mean, it's in the middle of nowhere. What if we need backup?" Both men turned to look at her with raised eyebrows as though they'd forgotten she was there.

"The coven is the safest place for us. The members have been carefully selected for this mission. Like you, they volunteered before incarnating," Axiom said.

Laurell cringed. She didn't like being reminded she'd chosen to become involved. She was willing to believe Axiom was not of this world. She'd seen enough of the Umbrae in the brief glimpses she'd had of them to know they were dangerous and terrifying, but she refused to accept she was the only person who could mother the Earth Balancer.

Why should she be forced into such a circumstance now? Everything she'd worked so hard to build was crumbling. Her independence, her anonymity, and the quiet life she'd created had been torn from her grasp the moment Axiom burst into her life. She was going to be forced to have sex with a stranger.

It didn't matter that he was the sexiest man she'd ever seen. It wasn't her choice to be with him. And as if things weren't bad enough, she had to feign friendly chats with her mother on a regular basis. At the moment, death seemed preferable.

Axiom had said the Umbrae would find her and kill her even if she refused to take part in the mission. He'd also said they could only track her via the yearning. Since she could ward against the yearning, this didn't seem like much of a problem.

Laurell snapped her attention back to Axiom and Wayne. "So, Wayne, you're psychic, huh? So how does your ability work? Do you see a good outcome if we go to Black Earth?" *It's worth a try.*

"I'm an empath, not a fortune teller." Wayne swigged from his soda can.

"Not just any empath," Axiom pointed out. "He can

sense when the Umbrae are near. We will want to keep him close to us when we are not in protected space." Axiom's shoulders stiffened.

Did Axiom fear the Umbrae too? Why? Laurell bit her lip. If a god feared the Umbrae, perhaps the situation was much worse than she knew. Her resolve strengthened. *All the more reason to get the hell away from Axiom.*

The landscape flashed by in a blur of farmland and nearly naked trees. The scenery changed to winding roads and deep woods as they left civilization behind and drove closer to Black Earth.

"The coven is taking Anne's death real hard," Wayne said, his voice heavy with sorrow.

"She was a strong witch and a friend of the Light," Axiom said. His chest ached. No innocents were to be lost. Those were his orders. Even though he had never met Anne, he felt the pain of having failed her.

"She was one headstrong woman. Always pushing boundaries and testing herself."

"Laurell indicated the Council is investigating Anne's death. I am certain she did not bring it on herself." Although he knew Wayne's description of the witch was accurate, he sensed there was more to her death than a lapse in magical judgment.

"I am grateful her sister will step forward to see the mission through," Axiom continued.

"Yeah, well, Fiona's a tough cookie."

Axiom sipped one of the sodas Wayne had packed and savored the sticky sweetness of the liquid as it slid down his throat. He enjoyed the way it tickled his nose and burned. A strange yet exhilarating sensation.

Thinking of strange yet exhilarating things, Axiom glanced at the back seat where Laurell sat, arms crossed, eyes focused on the landscape. What thoughts raced through her mind? He had studied her extensively in the Light Realm, yet in many ways she remained a mystery.

"I have to go to the bathroom." Laurell's voice broke into his thoughts.

Wayne raised his eyebrows in question, and Axiom nodded.

"We should stop. This vehicle will need fuel," Axiom told him. Several miles later, a gas station appeared on the right. Wayne slowed the car and pulled up to the nearest pump. In front of them sat a red pickup truck, jacked up and apparently awaiting a tire change. The driver was nowhere to be seen. A faded brown sedan with NRA stickers on the back pulled up next to them. The couple inside could be heard arguing heatedly, their strained voices carrying through the closed windows. The man adjusted his baseball cap and raised his hand to the woman, who cringed and pressed herself against the passenger door.

"Go get me another six-pack, woman. And stop your whining," the man drawled. The woman exited the car and hurried toward the store. The fluorescent lighting at the gas pumps highlighted the ugly bruise on her cheek. Axiom's jaw clenched.

Wayne's cell phone rang. Wayne picked it up and handed it to Axiom after a moment. "It's Fiona. She wants to talk to you directly. She still sounds hesitant about our visit."

Axiom motioned toward Laurell. "Keep an eye on her." Laurell glared her annoyance, but she followed Wayne dutifully toward the restrooms.

"Yes," Axiom said into the phone.

"We need to talk about the girl before you get here."

"What do you wish to discuss?"

"I need to know what arrangements should be made."

"Arrangements?"

"For sleeping."

"She should reside with me when she ovulates. Until then she can have her own quarters."

"Okay," Fiona agreed.

Axiom went straight to the point. "You could have asked Wayne about the arrangements. Why did you really wish to speak with me?"

"I need some assurance from you that my priests and priestesses will be safe."

Axiom ran one hand through his hair. He empathized with her fear, but the situation was beyond his control.

"You know I cannot guarantee anything. My powers remain limited while I am in the flesh, but I will do all I can to ensure the safety of you and your coven." Fiona was silent. He thought she had hung up the phone, but then he heard her soft sigh.

"I apologize for my weakness. I just didn't expect to lose Anne." Fiona's voice broke as she spoke her sister's name.

"It is not weakness you display; it is caution. However, you must remember your own power, Fiona."

"Yes," she agreed. "The circle is cast about the property. We'll need to cut a door when you arrive. Call me when you're close."

The phone clicked and went silent. Axiom glanced out the window. Baseball Cap Man climbed from his car.

"What's taking so long? Stupid woman," the man mumbled to no one in particular and staggered toward the convenience store.

Axiom watched him disappear inside the store. What was keeping Wayne and Laurell? Axiom's gut twisted. Something was wrong. He bolted from the car just in time to see Wayne racing across the parking lot toward him, eyes wide with panic.

"She's gone."

CHAPTER NINE

Laurell's heart slammed against her ribs like a jackhammer into concrete. She moved quickly through the trees, pushing branches out of her way and glancing behind her every so often, expecting Wayne or Axiom to be there. The moon peeked out through an opening in the trees above, bright enough to illuminate her way across the uneven terrain. She had no idea where she was going.

Wayne had followed her to the bathroom, but fortunately had not insisted on coming inside with her. He hadn't questioned the backpack she carried with her, but she'd had her menstruation story ready in case.

Laurell pulled her jacket tighter. The night air had started to seep through the wool peacoat. When it seemed she'd been on the move for at least a half hour, she paused to rest against a towering oak to catch her breath. She wished she were in better shape.

A ripple of energy started at the base of her spine and crawled to her neck. Goose bumps surfaced on her arms. A moment later, the yearning burst forth, and a wave of need washed over her. Her limbs went weak. A deep, painful ache settled between her legs. Her flesh pulsed, and her womb throbbed.

Laurell moaned. Her legs shook and protested with every step. Her mind filled with Axiom and she could think of nothing else but his touch, his scent, his kiss. She slid to the ground at the base of the huge oak tree.

There is no other way to find her quickly. Axiom knew this, yet the moment he released his hold on the yearning and pushed, forcibly, past Laurell's warding, he regretted it. The sensations were agonizing.

"Shit. You're sending a homing beam to the damn Umbrae!" Wayne shouted. As if on cue, Axiom caught a movement out of the corner of his eye. The air became heavy, weighted.

He turned to see Baseball Cap Man eyeing them from the doorway of the store. The man clutched a six-pack of Bud and watched them with narrowed eyes. Something in his gaze wasn't quite right, a strange mix of vacancy and focus. An impossible combination, yet one that was all too familiar to Axiom. The hair on the back of his neck stood up.

"A Finder," Wayne muttered, and Axiom looked away from the man long enough to glance at his friend and realize he'd made the same connection.

Wayne reached into his jacket and pulled out a .40-caliber Glock, clip already in place. He held the weapon against his side, half-hidden.

Baseball Cap tilted his head and nodded as though communicating with an unseen entity before he shrugged and strode toward them, the six-pack falling from his grasp and making a loud pop as it hit the ground. The gas-pump shelter's fluorescent light glinted off the metal of the gun the Finder pulled from his jacket. He lifted it and aimed at Axiom. Axiom reacted quickly, silently cursing the humanness of his body, which would not be impervious to bullets, while at the same time feeling grateful for the speed with which the god part of him could move his limbs.

He dropped to the ground and rolled toward their car just as the bullet whizzed past his head with a hiss. The air vibrated as Wayne fired a shot at the Finder. The Finder took a hit to the shoulder, but kept moving toward Axiom, seemingly oblivious of Wayne and his gun. The Finder had already taken aim again at Axiom's head.

Axiom reached behind himself, fumbling for a weapon. He would not kill a human if he could avoid it. Maiming was another thing altogether. Wayne took a second shot. This time the bullet connected with the Finder's firing arm, causing the man to drop the gun he held. He grunted, dropped to his knees, and picked up the weapon again, this time with the other hand. He fumbled with the gun while his wounded arm hung limply at his side, oozing blood.

The Finder had almost gotten the hang of using the gun with his left hand when Axiom's fingers closed around a cold metallic object. A tire iron? Almost too good to be true. *A blessing from Source and the stranger who'd been changing his tire.* Axiom pulled himself to a crouching position and lifted the makeshift weapon. He sent the tire iron flying.

The Finder's face registered a brief moment of surprise when the tire iron connected with his head. He crumpled to the pavement, his weapon issuing a clickety-clack as it fell from his fingers to the ground.

Wayne rushed to Axiom's side and helped him to his feet. "I don't think I'll ever get used to how fast you can move. Poor bastard couldn't have seen it coming. I sure didn't."

Axiom crouched at the Finder's head and searched for a pulse. The man would live. Hopefully, he would be out long enough to give them time to get away and to clear the energy trail of the yearning.

Axiom stood, breathed in deeply, and exhaled. Strange how his very human body had registered the fear of possible death even while he knew he—a god—could not really perish. That knowledge had not mattered, though, when he had been staring down the barrel of the Finder's gun. The racing of his heart and the blood rushing through his veins at breakneck speed were very real. He did not much care for that emotion: fear. Fear caused humans to live in mediocrity or despair. *Fear is the most ungodlike quality one can experience.* Axiom frowned.

"Why would the Umbrae send a Finder and not just come themselves?" Axiom wondered aloud. "With the amount of energy I was pouring into finding Laurell . . ."

"They ought to have been able to pick up the trail easily enough," Wayne finished for him, then frowned. "Axiom?"

Axiom tilted his head in response, and Wayne suggested, "Maybe they weren't worried about killing you so much as slowing us down."

Axiom grimaced. *Or distracting us.*

Axiom glanced at the front of the convenience store, where the attendant and one customer—probably the guy whose tire iron had been so helpful a moment earlier—crept out of the door and glanced furtively around. Behind them the other half of the Baseball Cap couple scurried out the door, wailing "Chuckie!" when she saw her husband lying on the ground. The police would not be far behind.

He closed his eyes and silently willed each of the innocents to forget what had occurred. They would not remember Axiom, Wayne, or Laurell. Their memories would start with finding Baseball Cap lying on the ground. Baseball Cap would not recall a thing either, but Axiom needed to play no part in his amnesia. Humans never remembered what occurred during the time the Umbrae controlled them as Finders.

"We must retrieve Laurell," Axiom murmured.

Damn him. Laurell thought as many nasty things about Axiom as she could, once the yearning left her body and she could finally breathe again. She let go of the tree she'd been clutching and brushed bark from her hands.

Axiom had lied to her about the warding. Perhaps her ward was useful against the Umbrae, but it proved defenseless against Axiom. He could, and clearly would, break through it anytime he wished. *What else has he lied about?*

Laurell clenched her teeth and trudged forward, pushing branches out of her way. Up ahead, moonlight shone through the trees and lit a clearing. A bird hopped from limb to limb above her. She could make out its silhouette against the moon. She squinted, and a tiny stream of light flickered off the bird's blue-black wings.

"Hey there," she murmured to the bird. "Can you show me how to get back to a road?" The bird bent its head and moved closer to her as though it would answer, but of course it simply sat. And stared.

It was so dark. She wished she had a flashlight. Her limbs were still shaky, but she forced herself to keep walking. As she moved, the trees rustled. She glanced up and saw the bird flitting from tree branch to tree branch as though it were following her. *Must be lonely.*

Laurell had only moved a few more feet when her skin prickled and the hair on her arms stood up. She froze. The blood in her veins seemed to slow. She sucked in a breath and glanced quickly around. No one there. *But I'm not alone.* The air was heavy with a presence, something . . . *not nice.*

Her stomach clenched. Her skin crawled with the kind of sick dread she'd only experienced during her brief astral meetings with the Umbrae. *Oh my god.* The air in front of her shimmered and shifted. An outline began to form.

Her breath came out in quick little bursts, leaving white trails in the chill air and creating an eerie spotlight for the thing that was emerging out of nowhere. The creature was so black that despite the dark of the woods, she could see it. It appeared solid; there was an impenetrability to the thing that made the night air seem thin and bright in comparison. The creature hung in the air, just in front of her. The smell of sulfur filled her nostrils. Long, crooked fingers reached out toward her, and she backed slowly away.

Shit. I can't outrun the Umbrae. She turned to try anyway, but something bitter and frigid filled her lungs, stopping her. She couldn't breathe. She gasped for air and her vision filled with all-consuming blackness. *I take it back. I'd rather stay with Axiom. Live.* These thoughts, fractured and frantic, raced through her mind. She clawed at the air in front of her but the thing had no form to grab on to. Her awareness narrowed to the burning in her chest and her body's struggle for oxygen. She closed her eyes, willing the pain to stop.

Her eyes popped open again at a movement to her side, and she registered the burst of heat accompanying it. The Umbra released its hold on her and she tumbled to the ground, gasping for air. She could see again.

A flash of silver. A man standing in front of her. *Axiom.*

His hands were raised toward the creature, emitting streams of light. The creature writhed and squirmed, letting out a hideous squeal. Axiom's face contorted, as though the effort pained him. The creature still reached for her. She could finally make out its eyes, crimson specks of light, focused on her.

Someone yanked her to her feet and away from the Umbra and Axiom. *Wayne.* She'd never thought she'd be so grateful to see the burly man. She crumpled against him and held on to him tightly. But she couldn't tear her gaze from the battle being waged in front of her. Axiom grunted and another burst of light blazed from his hands, thicker and more brilliant, edged with sparks of silver.

Finally, the creature retreated. The air opened up and sucked the thing back into the hole it had crawled out of.

"You okay?" Wayne stepped back from their embrace and studied her face, squinting, trying to see her in the darkness. She shivered and nodded.

A moment later, Axiom stood next to them, his hand on her arm, his grip viselike. He was breathing raggedly, his expression haggard, as if the battle had taken a toll.

"How'd you do that?" Laurell muttered, her teeth chattering.

Axiom glared at her, but didn't answer.

Laurell's brow knitted. Axiom was pissed at her? *Bullshit.* She was pissed at him first.

Silently, the three trudged back to the car, which was parked on the side of a dark, country road. Laurell didn't bother to protest. It would have been pointless. She was shivering hard, and her legs were Jell-O. She stumbled once, twice. She couldn't seem to keep her balance on the uneven ground. Eventually, Axiom must have grown tired of her bumbling. With a low growl he scooped her up in his arms to carry her the rest of the way.

Laurell held herself stiffly. "I can walk."

"No, you cannot," he responded. "And we do not have time to waste."

When they reached the vehicle, Axiom tossed her inside unceremoniously, and then climbed into the front passenger seat next to Wayne. Axiom threw a blanket over the seat to her without so much as a word.

Her eyes shot daggers at the back of his head. She

couldn't help herself. Anger was easier to cope with than the fear she'd experienced at the hands of the Umbra.

They drove in silence. It seemed hours passed, though it was probably only one. Finally, she couldn't take the silence anymore.

"Why did you come after me?" she asked. "Why can't you just find someone else to knock up?"

She didn't miss the frustrated shake of Wayne's head, or the way Axiom tensed at the question. Wayne glanced at Axiom as though to say, *Who's going to answer this ridiculous question—you or me?*

Axiom spoke, his words flat and measured. "We have discussed this at length. You are the chosen one."

Laurell shrugged off the blanket, suddenly warm. She rubbed her fingers over her eyes, exhaustion making her limbs heavy. The shock was starting to wear off. She wanted to sleep, but questions bubbled in her brain like a pot of stew on a hot stove. If she didn't get some answers, she might just boil over.

"There's got to be more to it than that," Laurell insisted. "If this was just about me volunteering for the gig, then I wouldn't be worth the trouble to follow. You could just go pick up whatever girl fits the number-two volunteer slot."

Wayne spoke this time. "You'll understand the rest once we reach Fiona's. If you can behave yourself until then, we might just be able to keep you from getting yourself killed." Laurell's gut clenched at Wayne's condescension.

"You act like this is all my fault. You kidnapped me, remember? I'm the one being forced to have sex with a stranger. And you blame me for trying to get away?"

Neither man answered her question. Wayne watched her from the rearview mirror. "Has Axiom filled you in on the Finders?"

"I don't think so," Laurell said.

"They are the human tools the Umbrae use to do their dirty work. The Umbrae can control folks who have let their dark sides get out of balance. They can also tap into people whose minds aren't their own—say, from drugs or alcohol. Unfortunately, we ran into just such a Finder at the gas station after you took off."

Before she could respond, Axiom turned in his seat and glared at her, apparently deciding to join the conversation. "If you did not understand the urgency of our situation before, I hope what happened tonight has made it clear. Not only could you be dead right now, but others, innocents, could have died because of your actions." He ground out his last words with venom.

The air shimmered with Axiom's power, and Laurell's skin crawled.

CHAPTER TEN

Fiona the witch had emerald eyes and cherry red hair that brushed her shoulder blades. Laurell thought the woman resembled all the witches in the fairy tales her grandmother had read to her as a child. Beautiful. Powerful. Young. In her mid-thirties at the latest. At the moment, though, with her jaw set and her eyes hard, Fiona did not seem some fairy-tale character. She was a very annoyed, very human woman.

Fiona had met the new arrivals at the entrance to her property after Wayne called her on his cell phone. The iron gate at the foot of a very long driveway opened, but before they were allowed to pass through, Fiona made quite a show of pulling a long sword from beneath her black cloak and cutting an imaginary door in the air around the gate.

After the three drove through, Laurell turned to see Fiona using the sword in the opposite direction, as though to close that same imaginary door behind them. *What's that red flash at the edge of the sword?* Laurell squinted her eyes shut and opened them again. The crimson glow disappeared.

"What did she just do?" Laurell asked.

"Who, Fiona?" Wayne glanced in the rearview mirror at Laurell.

"I saw her wave a sword in the air and then red light came out of it." Or at least, she thought that was what she'd seen.

"She was cutting a door in the protection circle around the property. It's not as tough to do as you might think."

"You mean a literal door? Using what, magic?" Laurell asked.

Wayne shrugged. "The cutting of the door isn't a big deal. The magical part is the casting of the circle. From inside the circle anyone could cut the door. It's trying to get in from the outside that would cause problems for most folks."

Once they'd driven for another mile, they stopped the car and Wayne and Axiom got out. Laurell watched from inside the vehicle as they waited for Fiona to pull up behind them on her golf cart. They spoke briefly with the witch, though Laurell couldn't make out their words.

Axiom opened the car door then, and stuck his head inside. "You are safe here. Fiona will show you to your cabin. Try to get some rest." Then he and Wayne disappeared inside the main house.

Laurell frowned and stepped from the car. Where the heck were they going?

"Follow me," Fiona instructed, then turned and stalked away as though it were inconceivable that Laurell would do anything else.

As she followed Fiona across the property, Laurell's feet sank into mud and leaves. It was dark, but tiki torches and solar lights lit their way.

Fiona glanced down at Laurell's feet. "Hope those aren't expensive shoes. We've been getting a lot of rain lately." Fiona grimaced at the sky as though angry at the weather's lack of cooperation. "Completely unseasonable, all this damn rain." Fiona's dislike of Laurell was clear.

Moments later, the witch halted so suddenly, Laurell almost walked into her. They stood in front of a cabin, which sat in the middle of a circle of similar buildings. Fiona motioned Laurell inside. "This is where you'll be staying."

Laurell glanced around the cabin. A queen-size bed sat in one corner with a nightstand beside it. A double dresser, comfortable brown chair, and side table completed the furnishings. Laurell noted a small bathroom to the right. The place was small, but had a warm, cozy feel with its earth-toned decor, shag rug, and wood floor.

"Our coven, Hidden Circle, holds spiritual retreats here several times during the year. Usually for the Sabbats, but sometimes we also hold special, focused gatherings for things like learning alternative healing modalities," Fiona told her.

Laurell glanced up from her perusal of the room. "Sabbats . . . that's a pagan thing, right? Some sort of seasonal celebration?"

"You know something about paganism?" Fiona raised an eyebrow as though she doubted such a thing.

"I took a class on paganism in grad school. I'm no expert, but I've learned a few things," Laurell told her.

Fiona shrugged, clearly unimpressed. "Too bad. I was hoping training you would be easier."

Laurell frowned. "Exactly what are you training me in?"

Fiona looked at her as though she were dim-witted. "Witchcraft, of course."

Laurell didn't know how to respond. She set her bags on the floor. "I don't understand."

"This isn't easy for me either. I've never had to train a natural witch before. And obviously, I've never done it under such pressure. I hope you're ready to work hard, because I'm not going to go easy on you."

Laurell stared at her. The antagonism was just too much. "Someone tried to kill me tonight. Strangely enough, it's making it hard for me to follow you right now." If she'd expected this admission to gain sympathy from Fiona, the attempt failed miserably.

Fiona's expression was blank. "We can talk tomorrow. Meals are in the main house. Breakfast is at eight A.M. sharp. Don't be late. I'm not here to be your personal servant, and I'll be cleaning up by eight forty-five, whether you've eaten or not." And with that, Fiona stomped out the door and slammed it shut behind her.

Laurell sat on the bed. Nope, definitely no sympathy to be had here. What the heck had she done to make Fiona dislike her?

Suddenly she felt more alone than she ever had in her life. There was no point trying to escape again, even if it was as easy to cut a hole in the magical force field around the place as Wayne had said. It was one thing to risk her own life, but she wasn't going to be responsible for endangering other people. And according to Axiom and Wayne, that's exactly what she'd be doing.

She sighed. Now that she'd seen the Umbrae up close and experienced their power, she was no longer so certain she was willing to risk her own life.

At least she had a soft bed, and for the first time in days, some privacy.

Axiom took one last sip of coffee and set his cup in the sink, surprised at how much effort that small movement took.

"What are we going to do about Laurell?" Wayne's voice, tinged with concern, echoed through the all-but-empty kitchen of the main house. Fiona had explained earlier that the rest of the coveners were in bed. It was almost three in the morning. She had poured both Wayne and Axiom a cup of coffee before heading to bed herself. It was eerily quiet.

Axiom shuffled back over to the table and sat across

from his friend. "I do not believe she will try to escape again. For all her bravado in the car, she was very frightened tonight."

"Hopefully she gets it now," Wayne murmured.

"I think she does." Axiom stretched, tilting his head to each side. "Not that I expect her to be any less difficult to deal with."

Wayne chuckled. "'Difficult' is a nice way to put it."

Axiom shrugged. "I am hopeful she will soften with time."

Wayne tugged his cowboy hat lower on his head. "It would sure make it easier to make love to her. I wouldn't wanna try to force that woman to do anything."

Axiom frowned. "I will not force her. In fact, I plan to focus on engaging her in friendship. If I can gain her trust, it will make the mission go more smoothly for all of us."

Wayne nodded. "No doubt, but, ahh"—he shook his head—"good luck with that."

Wayne's words rang true, but Axiom brushed them away. *She will come around. She has to,* he thought. "This body is almost depleted. I must rest," he announced, standing.

Wayne eyed him warily. "Are you sure you're okay by yourself? You look pale. I know using the yearning like you did kills your energy. And then fighting off that Umbra. That had to be draining."

Axiom's shoulders tensed. "Your concern is appreciated, but I will be fine after I sleep."

"Well, 'night then," Wayne said.

"Good night." Axiom left the main house and found his way to his cabin. He paused momentarily in front of Laurell's cottage, his closest neighbor. The lights were out, and he sensed she slept. Something he must do, as well.

He entered his cabin and flipped on the light. As soon as he closed the door behind him, a sharp pain sliced through

Axiom's midsection. His breath caught. A wave of electricity rolled over his body, and his vision filled with blackness. He groaned and struggled to get to the bed, one arm wrapped around his stomach while the other stretched forward, feeling his way. His knee struck the bedpost. He fell forward onto the mattress, his head twisted to the side.

His muscles twitched and leaped beneath his skin as though they struggled to break free from his flesh. He could barely manage to breathe. The sound of the blood rushing through his veins filled his ears. He ground his teeth and moaned, then felt his body arch from the bed as the current dived into his gut and pulsed there. He forced his eyes open again, but still couldn't see; a black void had consumed him. That void was digging inside him with sharp claws, like some wild beast on a feeding frenzy. *Be gone, you wicked thing. You cannot take me.* The words reverberated through Axiom's head.

Images flashed through his mind, vivid and appalling. A man beating his wife while she begged for mercy. A woman thrusting a knife deep into a man's gut, her eyes wild with perverted glee while his life dripped away in a pool of red. Bombs dropping on innocent people who screamed in agony. Parents sobbing in despair when the body of their abducted child was located. The horrors of Earth. The despicable evils of this realm. Things he had seen from the Light Realm that made him ache with grief. Illustrations of the Umbrae's tightening grip on the people of Earth.

Axiom tried to push the visions away. Was he under some sort of attack? How could the Umbrae have entered the protected space of the circle?

CHAPTER ELEVEN

The dark energy wanted to control Axiom, to take him over. He would not let it. He forced his arms, suddenly heavy with fatigue, over his stomach, ignoring the way his muscles pulled and twitched with the effort. Sharp pain sliced through his gut, confirming that the energy was trying to enter through his solar plexus chakra. He focused his mind.

Cool air stirred over his skin as he drew in his god force, centered it, and willed it to form a hard shell over his human body. Then he called up the part of himself that was of the Light, the part of him that he so cultivated, and pushed at the thing. At first, it did not budge.

Axiom used more of his god force to battle the entity. He groaned with the effort, his skin taut, his muscles straining. Just when he thought he could not exert an ounce more strength, a sharp snap sounded in his ears. A moment later, all was still. He could breathe again. Praise Source, the pain had disappeared. Whatever had tried to take him over was gone.

Axiom lay dazed for several minutes, blinking at the ceiling and wondering what in the cosmos had just happened to him. He eventually stood on shaking legs and stumbled to the bathroom. He ran his hands over his face, staring at his normally silver eyes, which currently still held the obsidian pools of god force within them. He had utilized much power to fight the thing.

What was it? An elemental, some spirit unleashed by the Umbrae? A new tool they had discovered with which to fight him? A moment later, realization dawned.

No, not the Umbrae. His own darkness. The side of him he held always in check—yet, which simmered beneath the surface—was sensing the blackness, the underbelly of the Earth Realm. The demonic energy of Earth's evils was reaching out to him. It had struggled to touch him and bring his shadow side to life. The darkness had formed into some type of entity. He could see it in his mind's eye, all that evil trying to pummel its way into his midsection. He knew if it ever succeeded, it would turn him—would take up residence inside of him and eat away at his light until all was destroyed, save his darkness. And then what would happen to Laurell, the child, the coven?

He had been warned to guard against the pull of the Earth Realm on his dark side. Darkness wanted only to obliterate light. And the coveners were filled with light energy.

Axiom blinked and observed his eyes returning to silver. His jaw hardened. *It matters not,* he decided. *None within this camp will ever see my shadow side, and it will not be the downfall of this mission.* He had never lost a battle. He would not begin now.

Bright light flashed in front of her closed eyelids and pulled her to the waking world. Sunlight streamed in through the window next to her bed. Laurell sat up and yawned. It seemed as though she'd only just fallen asleep. She burrowed back beneath the covers, hoping to rest a bit longer. Then her stomach grumbled. Breakfast. She jumped from the bed and ran to the bathroom. She splashed some water on her face and took in her red eyes with a grimace.

There was no clock in her room. Breakfast was probably already underway. She dug into her backpack and pulled out the baseball cap she'd shoved inside it on her way to the family mansion so many days before. She slapped it on and glanced in the mirror again. She looked tired and frumpy. *Good enough*, she decided.

Outside, the crisp air carried a gentle breeze, and bright rays winked between the trees. A nice change from the rainy weather of the past weeks.

Laurell entered the main house and was greeted by silence. She stepped through a living room inhabited only by statues of Buddha and goddesslike figures, and came to a dining area.

The six-seater mahogany table was empty. The distinct but faded scent of baking bread clung to the air. On the wall hung a grandfather clock that chimed nine just as Laurell realized she'd missed breakfast. Great.

"You look hungry." A male voice sounded behind her. Laurell spun around. An attractive, broad-shouldered man with thick shoulder-length blond hair leaned against the wall. He eyed her with interest.

"Who are you?" she asked.

The man grinned, pale blue eyes sparkling with amusement. "What? You don't know about me yet? I'm hurt."

Laurell blinked. "I'm sorry, I—"

The man's chuckle cut off her apology. "Just teasing. You are, no doubt, the infamous Laurell. I'm Reese. I'm part of the coven. Anne and I—" He hesitated. "Well, she was special to me."

"I'm sorry," she said, feeling his sorrow. Trying to lighten the moment, she asked, "So you know all about me, huh?"

He shrugged. "Well, not everything of course, but enough to know your importance to the mission. And enough to see that you missed Fiona's breakfast, which never makes our High Priestess too happy." His warm smile made it clear he wasn't too worried about the High Priestess's wrath.

He motioned her to sit. "The pancakes were the first to go, but I could get you some cereal if you want." He skirted the dining table toward the kitchen.

"I don't expect you to wait on me," Laurell responded.

"Oh, don't worry, I won't. I'm getting myself some too." He disappeared around the corner and returned balancing a carton of milk, two bowls, spoons, and a box of cereal. Laurell's stomach growled. Cereal sounded fabulous. She sat at the table, and Reese slid into the chair next to her.

"Didn't you get any pancakes either?" she asked.

"Actually, I did," he said.

"You're eating again already?"

Reese rubbed his taut stomach and winked. "Good genes."

Laurell eyed his trim physique with envy. She never trusted people who could eat like horses and never gain a pound. Of course, she'd always wished she were one of those people. She poured her cereal and took several bites, grateful when her stomach stopped rumbling, then filled a glass with orange juice.

"So how many people are there in the coven?" she asked.

"Including myself, seven."

"An odd number for a coven, isn't it?" She'd always thought covens had thirteen members.

Reese shook his head. "There's no particular number necessary. That's a Hollywood movie thing."

"Well, I only took one course in paganism in school. I'm trying to remember everything I know about Wicca and witchcraft."

Reese nodded. "So you know something about Wicca then? I guess that makes sense, since you're a natural witch."

Laurell glanced up at Reese and shook her head in confusion. "Why does everyone keep calling me a natural witch? What does that mean anyway?"

Reese tiled his head in question. "You don't know?"

Laurell sighed. "It seems I'm the last to know anything."

Reese lifted his eyebrows in question. "A natural witch is a hereditary witch. You know, someone who has magical blood in their veins, whose ancestor was trained in the craft."

"You've got to be kidding me. Someone in my family was a witch?" Laurell's mind reviewed the family members she knew personally or had learned about from her grandmother. In all of her stories of times and relatives gone by, her grandmother had never mentioned anything as interesting as a penchant for the paranormal. As far as Laurell knew, her relatives were a pretty staid, conservative lot.

She shook her head. "No way. It's ridiculous."

Reese winked at her. "Is it?"

CHAPTER TWELVE

The Book of Shadows *is a witch's journal.* The moment Reese had left the dining room, Laurell remembered. She'd read about such journals in her paganism class. She jumped from the table and hurried back to her cabin, heart racing, afraid her grandmother's *Book of Shadows*, which she'd stuffed in her backpack and all but forgotten, might have disappeared.

The book was still there. Laurell let out the breath she hadn't realized she was holding. She trailed her fingers over the worn leather cover, flipped to a random page, and began to read. The entry was from Grandmother Helen. She'd have recognized the handwriting even if the entry hadn't been signed and dated.

I have been having such vivid dreams lately. Visions of darkness and despair. Hardly a night passes when I am not pulled from my sleep trembling with fear of some strange, intangible menace. I've tried scrying for an answer, but my pendulum hangs in stillness and my crystal ball remains cloudy. The tarot spreads I've consulted all point to upheaval and strife, but the particulars elude me. I feel in my bones our family is connected to this situation. I've tried to talk to Elaine about it, but she only listens to my concerns with amused disbelief. She's never embraced her heritage. Now, she thinks the cancer is rotting my brain. I've told her there is a far worse affliction than this disease, and it is coming and she must be prepared. If only Jonathan had lived. He was sensible. He would have listened to me. Everything would be different.

At the mention of the father she'd never known, a familiar emptiness filled Laurell. The entry was dated less than two months prior to her grandmother's death. Laurell's chest tightened thinking of her grandmother, to whom she'd been so close as a child.

So it was true. Her grandmother had been a witch. Based on other entries in the book, her mother's brother, Luke, had been a witch as well. Luke was in a fatal car accident when Laurell was seven, and her remembrance of him was a hazy image of warm brown eyes and a wide smile. The book contained numerous entries by both her grandmother and her uncle; some of the entries dated all the way back to Laurell's great-great-grandfather.

The pages were worn and difficult to read in some parts. It was a wonder the thing hadn't fallen apart, but it was clear each owner had taken exquisite care of the book. Except for Laurell, who'd shoved it unceremoniously in her backpack with her beef jerky, chocolate bars, and wallet. Of course, if she'd had a clue as to how precious it was, she'd have treated the book with more care. She glanced around the room, spied a silky purple cloth covering the dresser, wrapped it around the book, then slid the text under the bed.

That afternoon Laurell met the rest of the coven.

"Everyone, this is Laurell," Fiona announced as she introduced the newcomer to the group of men and women reclining on blankets in the midst of a clearing. Laurell didn't enjoy being in the spotlight. She cringed inwardly, but forced her spine straight and gave the group a weak smile.

Axiom was nowhere to be seen.

Fiona continued her introductions, starting with Reese, whom she seemed to treat with a possessive air. Besides Reese, Fiona, and Wayne, the coven consisted of a heavy-set, middle-aged African-American woman named Hillary, who went by the nickname Hill; a slender forty-something blonde named Lynn; a petite black-haired goth girl named Dawna; and Thumper, clearly right out of college, who had close-cut dark hair and wire-framed glasses that slipped down his nose just a soon as he pushed them up.

Laurell tilted her head to the side and eyed Thumper with interest. "So where did you get a name like Thumper?"

He shrugged and glanced at the ground. "I guess the coven thinks it's cute or something."

"What's cute?" Laurell asked.

"The coven was practicing psychometry, you know, touching something to get information about the past or future? Anyway, he kept thumping the object against his head trying to get an answer," Fiona said, flashing Thumper an affectionate grin.

Thumper nodded and became engrossed in studying his watch. His shyness was almost painful to watch. "I'm more into potions. I'm working on one now."

"A potion for what?"

"I don't exactly know yet. The formula came to me in a dream."

"He was a chemistry major," Fiona said, as though this should explain everything.

"Nice to meet you all," Laurell said. Hillary was the first to stand and embrace her in a warm, patchouli-laced hug.

The others followed suit, with Reese taking advantage of the situation to linger just a tad too long with his hug.

His impish grin and shrug, however, made it impossible to take his actions seriously. Laurell's mouth lifted in a half smile, and she rolled her eyes at him.

Her eyes narrowing at the byplay between Reese and Laurell, Fiona turned to face the group. "Laurell and I are going to start training now. I'll get each of you to assist when the time comes for her to learn your particular area of specialty," Fiona told the group. Everyone dispersed quickly.

"Follow me," Fiona instructed Laurell and set off through the woods. Not knowing what else to do, Laurell followed. She hated being ordered around.

Laurell stepped in between the branches to find herself in the center of a circle of oaks. The towering trees leaned forward, their branches almost completely enveloping the blue sky above the circle, save for a large enough opening to let the sun—and, she guessed, the moon—shine through. In the east, a huge, carved wooden statue of a hawk stood at least five feet tall. Attached to it were real feathers of some sort, which lent the creature a lifelike appearance. A dish sat at the foot of the hawk, half-buried in the dirt. It held the remnants of burned herbs. Laurell breathed deeply. The scent of sage clung to the statue. A soft breeze swept over her, stirring her hair, delicious beneath the heat of the sun.

Laurell sensed Fiona watching her and turned to the other woman.

"Go ahead, walk the circle and connect with the elements. In the east, you've encountered the element of air. In the south, it is fire. The west holds the element of water. The north is where you'll find the earth element. In each direction, at each elemental altar, stop and feel the element outside you and inside you."

Laurell didn't know exactly what Fiona meant by feeling the elements, but she dutifully walked the circle. She was first compelled toward the west, intrigued by a fountain in the shape of a mermaid. She stopped to gaze at the fountain and breathed in the lavender-scented water. She crouched and touched her finger to the water.

Fiona came up behind her. "Think about what water is, what it represents. The blood in your veins. Our bodies are mostly made of water. Water symbolizes your emotions. It's what moves us to get in touch with our inner selves."

Laurell continued to peer into the pool of water, her reflection gazing back at her. A furrowed brow. Round eyes narrowed. Lips pursed. "Breathe in and out a few times and close your eyes. Try to tap into your sources of pain, your raw places. Ask the water element to wash them clean, to soothe."

Laurell obeyed. She closed her eyes tight and let her mind drift to the past. She thought of the father she'd never known, of the times in her life when she'd felt most alone. Her fingers tingled where they still touched the fountain.

"Open your eyes slowly and look."

Laurell's lids fluttered open and she glanced at the fountain. Water flowed upward toward her fingers. Just a little, but enough to make it clear something magical was happening.

"Don't let it go," Fiona instructed. "Think of more things that have hurt you and release them to the water."

She recalled a scolding voice telling her she couldn't wear a particular dress because it made her look heavy. A look of disapproval when she asked if she could cut her hair short so it wasn't so much work to fix each morning. Years of pregnant silence between mother and daughter. The water immediately fell back to the fountain and the tingle in her hand ceased. She glanced at Fiona, who was frowning.

"Try it again," she said.

Laurell concentrated, pulse speeding up, willing the damn water to move. Nothing.

Fiona looked annoyed. "I don't think you're trying as hard as you can. You've got to put your heart into it."

"How can I?" Laurell objected. "I don't even want to be here."

"That's obvious. Maybe you should remember the sacrifices others have made to get you here safely. Like my sister."

Chastened, Laurell turned away and walked to the southern altar, which held a statue of a dragon and a fire pit where embers still released smoke from a recently extinguished blaze. Without being asked, she closed her eyes and strove to sense the fire element. A moment later, heat flared over her feet and legs. She opened her eyes to find Fiona standing beside her with a lighter in hand. She had lit the fire. Laurell stepped back from the flames.

Fiona took Laurell's hand and held it out over the fire, not close enough to touch the blaze, but near enough to be slightly uncomfortable. When she would have pulled back, Fiona gripped her hand tighter.

"You can't run from the flame. Pull it into you and feel your own spark within, your own passion. Fire feeds the soul." Fiona's words washed over her with a hypnotic, dreamlike quality, and Laurell's lids shut once again. Heat flared low in her torso. A current pulsed through her body, settling near her groin, and crimson light filled her eyes.

"Good," Fiona encouraged. "That's it. Now open your eyes and direct your focus to the fire."

Laurell did as told. Her eyes flickered open and she willed the heat inside of her toward the flames. The fire flared and jumped, its flames bursting so much higher, both women leaped backward, away from the blaze.

"Holy shit!" Laurell exclaimed. "Did I really just do that?"

Fiona laughed, eyes wide with amazement. "I guess you won't need much assistance working with fire."

Laurell's breath came out in short little pants and a familiar electricity sprang to life in her veins. *Uh-oh.*

"Oh no," she muttered.

Fiona frowned. "What is it?"

Laurell clasped her hands over her lower abdomen and grimaced. "I think the fire exercise triggered the yearning."

Raw pleasure rippled through her, and she stifled a moan. She grimaced, then willed the walls of protection into place, absorbing the sexual energy deep inside herself. A moment later, she sighed with relief. The warding had worked. Half expecting to see Axiom appear in response to the brief sizzle of yearning, Laurell glanced around the circle. She and Fiona remained alone.

"Have you seen Axiom today?" Laurell asked. She'd looked for him after talking to Reese that morning, planning to demand an explanation as to why he was withholding information. She'd pounded on the door of his cabin, but no one answered.

"He's been sleeping most of the day. I checked on him earlier and he mentioned an energy depletion from your run-in last night with that Umbra," Fiona said.

"Oh." Laurell's gut clenched with guilt. She bit her lip.

Fiona raised an eyebrow. "You okay?"

Laurell nodded. "Yeah. The yearning's gone. I guess I'm getting better at warding." She grimaced. "I hate this, wanting someone I don't even know."

Fiona shrugged. "I can think of a lot worse things than having sex with Axiom. In case you haven't noticed, that is one hot man."

Laurell frowned and ignored the comment. He was hot, yes, but exasperating, too. *And I'm still being forced to have sex with someone I just met.* "Whatever. I just can't wait until this is all over and I don't have to deal with the yearning anymore."

"You know," Fiona began, eyes narrowed with disapproval, "you don't sound thrilled with your role in the mission, but it's—"

"An honor. Yeah, so I've been told." Laurell didn't care if she sounded bitter. She knew the mission was necessary, but she didn't have to like it. "I've been reduced to breeding stock."

Fiona frowned. "You know, there was a time when people saw pregnancy and birth as a magical, honorable, spiritual process. When the Goddess and her life cycles were something to be revered."

"I know about the Goddess movement," Laurell muttered.

"From your scholarly studies?" Fiona raised her eyebrows.

Laurell nodded. "And I'm just a person. I'm no goddess."

Fiona laughed. "You're wrong. All women are reflections of the Goddess."

Laurell shook her head. "Look, all I know is that I want the yearning gone. I'm willing to do my part to save the world, but I'm tired of feeling forced into it."

Fiona sighed. "I agree the yearning is a bit much. Desperate times call for desperate measures, I suppose." Fiona shrugged. "You won't have to deal with it too much longer. I've been told that once you conceive, the yearning goes away."

Laurell perked up at those words. "Really?" Why had the thought never occurred to her? It made sense. The yearning existed to force her to mate with Axiom and conceive the Earth Balancer. Once that objective was completed, the yearning would be unnecessary.

"That's my understanding," Fiona agreed.

"No yearning means Axiom's power over me goes away too, right?" Laurell could barely contain the rush of hope flooding through her.

Fiona's eyes flashed with comprehension. "So you want to get pregnant quickly then, is that it?"

Laurell grinned. "Hell yes, if it means I might actually get my life back."

Fiona sighed and shrugged. "Then I guess you'd better think about some seducing, hadn't you?"

Laurell's stomach clenched. *Damn.* She hadn't really considered that part yet. Her sexual expertise was limited, and the thought of trying to entice Axiom made her heart palpitate.

"You look scared," Fiona observed, eyes narrowed with what Laurell couldn't help reading as barely constrained amusement—at her expense.

Laurell's spine stiffened, and she stood, brushing dirt from her pants. Her stomach grumbled. "I'll be fine. Thanks for your concern."

Without giving Fiona a chance to keep her there with another list of magical tasks to complete, Laurell stalked toward the main house in search of some food to satisfy her sudden and ravenous hunger. *Damn the yearning.*

CHAPTER THIRTEEN

Axiom stepped from the shower, skin dripping with moisture and hot from the heated spray. He slung a towel around his waist, knotting it loosely on one hip, and glanced in the mirror. His eyes still flashed with their usual silver gleam. He'd known they would, but was still reassured. Last night's battle had shaken him more than he wanted to admit. The long rest, however, had restored his energy. He felt strong again, renewed.

A knock sounded at his door, and Laurell entered the cabin without waiting for his response. She stood with hands on hips, eyes narrowed.

"You appear upset," Axiom said.

Laurell made a harrumphing sound in the back of her throat. "Do I?"

Axiom nodded.

"Well, maybe that's because you haven't been telling me the truth. One thing I can't stand is being lied to," Laurell exclaimed.

Axiom frowned. "I have told you no lies."

"Lies by omission are still lies," she insisted. "First, you tell me that once I learn to ward, I can control the yearning. All the while, you have the ability to bust through my ward whenever the mood strikes you."

"I never said I did not have the ability to break your ward," Axiom remarked, confused. Was this what she was upset about? Warding? "I apologize if I did not sufficiently explain the mechanics of the warding. Rest assured that although I can break past your wards, I will only do so when absolutely necessary. It causes an energy depletion best avoided." He reached out one hand to touch her shoulder and offer reassurance. She backed away from him. His jaw clenched. He disliked when she withdrew from him.

"Oh no, you don't. You won't get out of this argument by distracting me with the yearning." Laurell's eyes raked his body, and her face flushed as she noticed his state of undress. Her eyes shot back to his face. For some reason the fact that his near nakedness unnerved her pleased him.

Axiom sighed. "I do not understand the need for an argument. Let us sit and discuss this so we may move forward with the mission unencumbered by mistrust." He sat on the bed and patted the spot next to him.

Laurell did not budge from her place in the center of the room. "Not a chance," she muttered. "Explain about the witch thing."

"Which witch thing?" he asked, one eyebrow raised.

She frowned. "Don't get cute with me. Why didn't you tell me about my bloodline? It might have been helpful for me to know my family is full of witches and that, supposedly, I'm one too."

Axiom knew he must tread lightly. How to tell her the truth without upsetting her further? During the time he had studied Laurell from the Light Realm, he had often witnessed her silent pain over her severed relationship with her mother. He had no wish to increase the rift between them, but he could not evade Laurell's questions and hope to gain her trust. It was necessary, if they were to succeed in their mission.

"Your Liaison had asked for the right to provide that information to you. The Council agreed it would be best that she explain," he ventured.

At the mention of her mother, Laurell's spine stiffened. "My mother was supposed to tell me about this? Why? Because she failed to do so when she was alive? What is this about, anyway? Mother unburdening her guilty conscience or us saving the world? Why are the gods allowing her to run the show?"

Axiom ignored Laurell's words. "How exactly did you learn of your magical background?" he asked. Axiom had not broken his agreement to allow the Liaison to tell Laurell she was a witch. Who had?

"Reese," she admitted. "And my grandmother's *Book of Shadows*."

Axiom raised his eyebrows. Fiona had assured him the coven understood the Council's instructions. As for the *Book of Shadows*, he was not aware one existed for the Graves family, but perhaps it would prove useful to them in the future.

"Tonight would be an opportune time for you to attempt a meeting with your Liaison on the Astral Plane so she can explain further," Axiom suggested.

Laurell scowled. "Yeah. I'll get right on that." She crossed to the far side of the room with jerky movements, then stopped abruptly as though uncertain of her next step. She let out a heavy sigh and rubbed her hands over her face before dropping her arms to her sides.

Axiom frowned. He could not help feeling he had failed her in some manner. He stood up and went to her, reaching out to her again and steeling himself for her inevitable retreat. Surprisingly, when his hand touched hers, she did not move. Her head lifted and her hazel eyes gazed into his, searching. She squared her shoulders, as though coming to some sort of decision, and licked her lips. Axiom's eyes were drawn to the curve of her mouth, to the plump flesh now wet from the sweep of her tongue. A pulse ticked in his neck. He blinked and his gaze met hers again.

Laurell's hands came up and hovered over his bare chest. The hairs there prickled under the heat of her palms, begging them to land. At the same time her fingers curled against his skin, Laurell stood on tiptoe and pressed her lips to his. Axiom sucked in a harsh breath.

That brief press of mouth against mouth was so tempting. He felt the yearning trying to tumble over him, but held it in check. Yet a desire all his own heated his blood.

Laurell's kiss became more heated, her body pressed close against his, and her tongue pushed between his lips. She tasted of sugar, and the scent of smoke from a distant campfire clung to her clothes and tickled his nose. His arousal had to be clear to her. He hardened and strained against the towel still hanging loosely from his hips. He should stop this.

It was not time for their mating, but the sensations were too pleasurable to turn away. The fact that Laurell had initiated the embrace further titillated him.

Axiom's arms closed around her, his hands running slow circles over her back, caressing her through her cotton shirt. He enjoyed the feel of her, the curve of her hips, the way goose bumps broke out on her arms when his fingers brushed them. Heat flared and he choked back a moan. Laurell's fingers left his chest and fluttered across his back, his hips, to rest on his waist. Laurell pulled her mouth from his, ran her tongue over his lips, down his jaw, and then teased his neck.

Her breathing was heavier, her skin hot to the touch. His breath, his skin, soon followed suit.

Break away. This is not the time. But then he told himself the embrace was harmless and he should look at this as a practice exercise. The yearning hovered in the background, teasing with its promise of exquisite pleasure, yet still held in check by their wards.

Distracted by the need throbbing in his groin and the tingling of his skin when Laurell's sweet lips trailed over his chest, he did not think to question her sudden change of heart or why she had gone from avoiding his touch to initiating their intimacy. That was, until her tongue flicked his nipple and the hands around his waist released the towel and sent it pooling to the floor. Her fingers slid over the length of his engorged sex and closed around the tip. He moaned and bucked against her hand.

A moment later, he sensed Laurell's ward break and he knew, without a doubt, she had released the yearning on purpose.

The yearning ripped through Laurell's body, fierce and hot, burning through any remaining nervousness and severing all her inhibitions. Her mind filled with Axiom, with visions of sex acts so carnal she'd have blushed if the yearning allowed her even a moment of clarity. Axiom. The visions were of Axiom. And her. His scent, earthy but tinged with soap from his recent shower, engulfed her. He throbbed in her hand and she rubbed and moved her palm up and down him, imitating a much deeper intimacy. His nipple grew hard beneath her tongue and she flicked and suckled it relentlessly. Her panties grew damp, her thighs trembled, and she pushed Axiom toward the bed. A moment later, they fell onto it, with her on top.

She forgot about the fact she was only seducing him to get pregnant and end the yearning. She forgot this was just a means to an end, a way to gain some control over her life again. Laurell could think only of Axiom. Of his brawny body, so lean, so muscular, so beautiful.

She lifted her head to rake her eyes over him. Thick black hair, chiseled facial features, broad shoulders, defined chest with a spattering of dark hair that trailed down over a taut stomach to his groin, highlighting the long, thick length that she held in her hand. Her hand looked tiny, holding him.

He's gorgeous. Just looking at him could make a girl come.

She increased the pumping motion. His back was arched, his head thrown back, eyes slitted as they peered up at her. He let out a deep groan.

His hands closed over her breasts, and he tugged her nipples between index finger and thumb. She shuddered. She couldn't take it; she needed him to touch her bare flesh. Laurell released Axiom and sat astride him. She pulled her T-shirt over her head and tossed it away. Her bra followed. Axiom's silver eyes darkened to gray as they rested on her naked, ample breasts.

She grabbed his hands and closed them over her chest, her small hands cradling his, encouraging his caress. Axiom sat up abruptly, his hands leaving her chest to circle her waist and cup her bottom. Now she sat in his lap, bare chest to bare chest, his coarse chest hair tickling her nipples. His mouth ground against hers and the yearning flared deeper, more urgent.

Her sex pulsed and ached, almost unbearably. She rubbed herself against his hardness, silently cursing the jeans she wore and wishing no layers separated them.

He only allowed her a couple of presses against him before he pushed forward, and Laurell found herself lying on her back. One hand tangled in her hair and forced her head back so he could lick her ear and suckle the crook of her neck. She sensed movement at her waist and realized dimly his other hand was making quick work of her button and zipper. A moment later, seeking fingers touched the waistband of her panties.

The yearning ripped through her, electric, raw. She cried out. Her eyes fluttered open and met his. His face was flushed, his gaze full of arousal. She grasped his shoulders, dug her nails into them. *Touch me. Touch me*, she thought. *Oh god, touch me before I explode.*

As though he heard her silent plea, his fingers dipped beneath her panties and skimmed the light hair over her mound. She parted her thighs, urging him farther. His hand slid through her slick folds to flicker over her aroused bud. Her hips arched. One circular swirl over that sensitive flesh. Two. Three. And she came. Hard. But unlike a regular orgasm, this one didn't retreat after it had reached its peak; instead, it decreased only slightly, just enough to let her breathe. Then it hovered and pulsed again and again. Laurell gasped and forced her mind to clear just a little.

She grabbed at her jeans and, since Axiom held most of his weight off of her, managed to tug them down to the top of her knees, her panties going along for the ride. She reached between them to stroke Axiom's erection again. He had to enter her. She'd never get pregnant this way. She fought against the waves of orgasm that continued to lap at her, struggled to focus, lifted her hips and her sex toward Axiom's aroused flesh until the tip of his penis nudged against her pubic hair.

"No." Axiom's voice broke the spell. Her orgasm waned. His features twisted into a grimace, and he pulled himself off of her in one smooth motion. The towel regained its previous place around his waist. The yearning immediately stopped.

CHAPTER FOURTEEN

Cool air tickled Laurell's chest and made her instantly aware of her lack of clothing. Axiom had left the bed and stood several feet from her, silently watching. She blinked in confusion. Why had he stopped? She tugged her jeans back to her waist, and sat up.

"What's wrong?" she asked, self-consciously crossing her arms over her chest as her eyes made a frantic sweep of the room. Where was her bra? Where was her shirt? A scrap of blue cloth peeked out from beneath a chair near Axiom. She leaped from the bed and, holding one arm over her breasts, crouched and retrieved it, then turned her back to him and pulled her shirt over her head.

Turning to face him again, she placed her hands on her hips and cocked her head to one side expectantly.

"Well?" she prodded.

"Nothing is wrong," Axiom finally said. He looked shaken, his own breathing still somewhat labored.

"Then what just happened?" Laurell persisted.

"I stopped the yearning. It seemed you were unable to hold your ward."

"I still don't understand *why* you did it." Laurell tried to keep her tone light, flirty. This wasn't going as planned. They were supposed to be having sex.

"It is not time for consummation," Axiom said.

Laurell bit her lip. Not time? They'd both been all but naked and she'd been wet, ready, and raring to go. So had he, for that matter. She crossed the room and touched his arm, running her fingers over his elbow and putting on what she hoped was a seductive smile. She hoped it hid how vulnerable she felt, now that Axiom was one of only three men in her life who'd seen her orgasm face.

"Seems to me like the perfect time," she murmured, stepping closer so her breasts brushed his chest. She slid her hand up his arm and tilted her head, intending to kiss him again and get the party restarted.

Axiom grabbed her shoulders and set her away from him. He shook his head. "It is not time. Please leave my cabin." His words came out firm, almost harsh.

Laurell recoiled as though she'd been slapped. Her face burned. She'd thrown herself at him twice and he was rejecting her. His gaze met hers, and she struggled to camouflage the humiliation she knew must be reflected in her eyes. She averted her eyes. Axiom's hand touched her cheek, the barest brush.

"We can discuss this later. Once I am dressed," he said.

She shook her head. "There's nothing to talk about," she said, and hurried out the door without looking back.

Three nights later, Laurell soaped and scraped her flesh until it tingled. She was trying to scrub the desire out of her body, to satiate the hunger inside without doing what she really wanted to do. *Axiom.* The memory of the yearning and the feelings it evoked was enough to send her mind back down into the lustful gutter again and again. She'd never experienced desire like that, let alone an orgasm of such intensity.

Axiom's rejection only made it even more humiliating that she couldn't stop thinking about their passionate episode.

Clearly, he had some timetable of his own in mind for when they would have sex. *Or "mate," as Axiom put it.* She hadn't even been able to push past his ward long enough to make him have sex with her. And clearly, she was not sexy enough to make him relinquish his control.

It doesn't matter. It's just the yearning making me want him so much. It's not real.

She needed to stop thinking about Axiom. She'd been having a hard time focusing on her witchcraft training because of him. And because of her embarrassment and hurt over being rejected. At least she'd done a pretty good job of avoiding him since the thwarted seduction attempt.

Unfortunately, she still bumped into him at meals and around the contained fire the coven enjoyed in the ritual circle each night. She avoided making eye contact and gave him only a forced hello when he greeted her.

She'd stop thinking about Axiom. Instead, she'd focus on the child to come.

Laurell stepped out of the shower, grabbed a nearby towel, and wrapped it around herself. She picked up a hand towel and rubbed it through her hair. Wiping the steam from the mirror above the sink, she studied her flushed face. *Who are you? Are you even ready to be a mother?* Her reflection didn't respond.

When he'd first mentioned she would deliver the Earth Balancer, Laurell had thought it a cruel joke. An impossible one. Once she began to believe Axiom spoke the truth about the child, her soul had sung. She'd have a child she could raise and love as she herself had never been loved.

She'd be the mother she'd never had. *Focus on the baby.* Laurell sighed and blinked away the tears that threatened to well in her eyes. She was strong. She was used to having only herself to rely on. She'd be fine. *Focus on the baby.* Maybe that thought could keep her fear of the Umbrae and of an uncertain future at bay. At the moment, it was the only bright light she held against the invading dark.

Mobius strode through the sparkling halls of the Divine Council's meeting quarters. His white robe flowed about his ankles like a cloud, and he impatiently kicked it away as he turned the corner and entered the room where Elaine Pittman and Anne, the former High Priestess of Hidden Circle Coven, lay oblivious atop crystal slabs. The goddess Willow watched them intently, lips pursed in concentration as she twisted one shiny blonde lock of hair about her finger.

"Has there been any progress?" he asked.

Willow lifted her head. "Elaine's re-visioning is just about complete. I've scanned all scenes from her memory. She did not see who pushed her from the balcony, but the energy surge she experienced prior to the fall carries the scent of the Umbrae."

Mobius glanced to where Elaine lay, her light gold robe shimmering under the soft lighting of the re-visioning room. Her features were relaxed and peaceful, dark hair curled over her shoulders, arms folded across her midsection. He then looked at Anne, whose face was twisted in a grimace. She wore the same gold robe, as all previously human spirit beings did, but she dug her fingers into the material at her sides, clawing it.

"Her re-visioning is still in process?"

Willow nodded. "It is not going as smoothly."

To say the least, Mobius thought. A large screen hovered in the air several feet above them. Images flashed. Anne's memories.

Though they could be utilized at any time to gain insight into a mortal's history, re-visionings were typically employed when humans first moved from Earth to the Light Realm. Their lives were replayed so they could remember and learn of progress made or not made in that lifetime. It helped determine whether they needed to reincarnate.

In this case, a repeat procedure was necessary for the Liaison Elaine, since Willow felt certain Anne and Elaine's deaths were connected. Anne's re-visioning had been delayed because, since her final moments had been so violent, they'd caused a fracture in her memory of them. She'd needed time to regain her strength and heal before proceeding.

Mobius and Willow observed the screen in silence. The images whizzed by at rapid speed, but Mobius knew they were getting close to Anne's last few days on Earth. "Slow the projection," he said.

Willow placed one slender hand over Anne's head and the moving images assumed a more comprehensible pace. Anne meeting with Laurell's grandmother, Helen. Helen pleading with her to talk sense into Laurell's mother, Elaine. Anne's visit to Elaine, who refused to listen. Anne's attempt to convince her by sharing her visions. Mobius watched this scene with interest. He had viewed it once already, from Elaine's perspective, but hoped seeing it through Anne's eyes would bring additional enlightenment.

During her attempt to convince Elaine to take part in the mission, Anne had shared a vision that racked Elaine's body with energy remarkably similar to the yearning. If he himself had not once experienced the yearning, Mobius would have thought it the real thing.

"Was anyone on the Council aware of Anne's ability to transmit visions in this manner?" Mobius asked.

"Yes," Willow confirmed, "but we did not know she had envisioned the yearning."

Mobius frowned. Well aware of the Umbrae's ability to tap into the yearning and track the parents of the Earth Balancer, the Council had carefully guarded its secret until the mission's launch. "We underestimated Anne's power. It cost us Elaine's life."

With another sweep of her hand over Anne's head, Willow halted the woman's re-visioning and stepped close to Mobius. She glanced at the open doorway and pulled him to the side.

Lowering her voice, she said, "I questioned Anne after she arrived in the Light Realm. She said she'd learned of the yearning from Helen."

Mobius tilted his head to one side. "Helen's psychic abilities were not strong enough to discern the yearning. Especially when we had purposely erased the memory of it from all humans affected during my time on Earth." This new development did not bode well. Not at all. A sinking sensation took root in his solar plexus, and he crossed his arms, not enjoying the feeling one bit.

Willow's lavender eyes flashed with apprehension. "One of the Council members must have implanted the vision of the yearning in Helen's mind. But who would do such a thing?"

Mobius sighed. He could think of a number of those on the Council who did not approve of Axiom's selection, but none who would risk the mission because of prejudice. "Perhaps we've misjudged Helen's intuitive ability, just as we did Anne's powers."

What if we also underestimated the Umbrae's pull on Axiom's dark half while he is on Earth? Willow did not speak the words, but Mobius saw the doubt on her face.

He wanted to groan his frustration. Humans thought the gods were omnipotent. Yet despite their mighty strength and vast abilities, they remained limited. They could not see or know all. Only Source had the ability to tap into all of life at once. Source, however, was not a thinking being, but instead an energy, a force, something that resided in all beings, in varying degrees. The Umbrae hoped to harness Source by stealing the fragments of it that resided within the gods and goddesses. They hoped to weaken the gods via their ties to humanity. So far the mission to prevent that from happening was off to a shaky start.

Mobius shook his head and willed the worrisome thoughts away. He motioned for Willow to resume Anne's re-visioning. He cringed as he witnessed the final, brutal scene of Anne's life. Some weeks after her meeting with Elaine, she'd been overcome by an Umbra.

"Why do you suppose the Umbrae didn't attack Anne earlier? They must have detected the yearning on her after she shared her vision with Elaine," Willow murmured.

"She had a perpetual ward in place; it sometimes occurs in witches who spend a great deal of time working protection spells."

"Which she would have been doing while perfecting the spells for the safe house and the covenstead," Willow murmured.

Mobius nodded. "It's unlikely she even realized it was there. Unfortunately, it would have taken only a small lapse in her ward for the Umbrae to detect her."

"So much death." Willow's voice was low, almost a whisper.

Mobius knew much of death. His own time on Earth, his own mission, had been fraught with it. He cleared his throat, not willing to allow his mind to drift back to that time. *What's done is done.*

"At least it seems clear the Umbrae did not track the coven or Laurell through Anne," Mobius remarked.

Willow said nothing, just stroked Anne's forehead as though to brush away the lines of agitation. Filled with admiration, Mobius's eyes swept over the unconscious witch turned spirit being. Anne had put up such a strong fight during the final moments of her life. She'd resisted the Umbra's attempts to infiltrate her mind, where it might have gained access to her secrets.

"Bring them both back to consciousness. Once they've rested, inform them of what we have learned and instruct Elaine to pass the information to Laurell. At least the coven will be able to rest easy knowing they are safe at the coven-stead."

For now. Eventually, the Umbrae would find a way to ferret them out. They always found a way.

CHAPTER FIFTEEN

Laurell perched on her bed, thankful for a moment of reprieve from her witchcraft training. She flipped through the pages of her grandmother's *Book of Shadows*.

The doctors say I've not long to live, and I sense this is why I'm seeing the visions more often. I woke last night from a particularly vivid dream in which Elaine was giving birth to a child that glowed white and shiny as a pearl. The child was brought to a man, an ugly, twisted man who had the blood of many on his hands. His fear of the child was palpable.

He tried to run away, but others, men and women in long cloaks holding wands of some sort, held the man in place. The child settled small hands on the man's head and suddenly all that was evil within him dissipated. I woke abruptly, thinking I heard someone call my name. Of course, I was alone.

I wanted to make contact with my spirit guides. I felt certain someone wished to get me a message, but I could only grasp fragments of it. In my frustration, I decided to try some automatic writing.

I've never been very skilled at automatic writing, but apparently the messenger wanted to be sure I received this information. So I picked up a pad of paper and a pen and held my hand limply over the page, waiting for the spirit guides to take over. I closed my eyes and silently told the spirits to speak to me through the pen. My hand shook and moved as though directed by an unseen entity. When my hand stilled, I opened my eyes.

Imagine my surprise to see the following words on the paper before me: *Elaine is to mother the Earth Balancer. She must accept her heritage as a witch. You must convince her. She will birth the child that will save Earth from demons threatening to destroy it.*

I called Elaine the next day and read these words to her. She became immediately incensed when I brought up the subject of witchcraft. She reminded me I'd promised not to soil her or Laurell's life with such nonsense. Then she assured me she had no intention of becoming a mother again at age forty-five. She said it had been hard enough becoming a mother at age seventeen. She asked if I was taking my medication and demanded to speak to my nurse.

I was afraid the nurse would take the *Book of Shadows,* so I hid it where I always do. Only my old friend Robert knows where to find it. Along with all my important papers.

Laurell glanced up from the *Book of Shadows* and frowned. *Wait a minute.* Mother *was supposed to be part of the mission?* Mother *was supposed to be the one to mate with Axiom?* Mother *was supposed to get pregnant and give birth to the super-kid and . . . and . . . and . . .* Laurell snapped the book shut and dropped it to the bed with a frustrated groan.

She buried her head in her hands and tried very hard to calm herself. She hadn't wanted this mission. She hadn't wanted anything to do with Axiom or the baby, but he'd convinced her the world rested on her shoulders. This was her destiny, a role she'd been born to fulfill. Even worse, she'd supposedly volunteered for the mission before incarnating. And she'd finally come to terms with all of that, accepted her place, and started to see the bright side of things. Such as it was.

So why had her grandmother written that Elaine was to birth the Earth Balancer? What was Laurell? *The freakin' backup plan?*

Laurell leaped to her feet and paced the room. Rage welled in her chest, sharp as a tack. Just when she thought she understood everything, she discovered more she hadn't been told about this mission. Her first instinct was to confront Axiom again. But his rejection during her attempted seduction still stung. She'd done a pretty good job of avoiding him so far. She intended to keep avoiding him for as long as possible.

An immature and cowardly way to handle the situation, but right now she didn't much care.

She could approach Fiona, but that idea was even less appealing than talking to Axiom. Who then? Reese? He'd been friendly to her so far. He'd spilled the beans about her witchy heritage. He seemed her best bet for a straight answer.

She found him reclining on the couch in the main house, nose buried in a book. His blond hair flowed over his shoulders, freed from its usual rubber band, and he wore blue jeans and a black sweater. An ebony long-haired cat purred in his lap, and he stroked it absently.

"Anything good?" Laurell asked.

Reese peered at her over the edge of his book, and his sky blue eyes crinkled at the corners. "Nothing half as interesting as you." He placed the book on the end table beside him and patted the place next to him on the sofa.

Laurell sat and tilted her head toward the feline. "A witch with a black cat. Sort of a cliché, isn't it?"

He chuckled. "Some clichés are worth perpetuating.

This is Magic. She's been Fiona's kitty for as long as I can remember."

She ran her fingers over Magic's back, enjoying the feel of the sable-soft fur. The cat lifted its head, cracked open one emerald green eye, and let out a satisfied meow before settling back down into its nap. "I have a question for you."

"Uh-oh," he teased.

"It's no big deal, just something I need to know," she said.

"Okay then, shoot."

"How is it that your coven came to learn of me and my family? Or the mission, for that matter?"

"It was through Fiona's sister, Anne, actually. She was the group's psychic."

"So the visions," Laurell pushed, "they sent her to my grandmother?"

"Yeah. I think that's how it happened. Then the next thing we knew, she'd tracked your family down, and she and your grandmother set up the safe house. Not too long after, Axiom showed up here asking for help getting used to his human body."

"That must have been something," Laurell said.

Reese snickered. "Was it ever. He just hovered, observing everything we did and mimicking our movements. Fortunately, he's a quick study. You wouldn't want to see what it looked like the first time he ate."

"I'll bet." Having witnessed his aggressive eating habits before, she could only imagine what his manners must have been like upon first arrival.

"A few days later, he said it was time to go fetch you, and he and Wayne left. That's about the time Anne went to town to get supplies and never returned."

A shadow of grief crossed Reese's face, and Laurell's gut clenched in sympathy. She touched his knee. "I'm so sorry about Anne."

Reese's hand closed over hers. "Thanks. It's been hard on all of us, but especially Fi."

She nodded and allowed him a moment of quiet before asking, "Do you know anything else? Anything about my mother, maybe? Did you know she was originally supposed to mother the Earth Balancer?"

Reese's eyebrows flew up. "Oh no, you don't. Last time I told you something about your family, I was taken out back and flogged."

"What?" Laurell exclaimed.

He laughed. "I'm exaggerating. I was reprimanded though. I'm under strict orders to keep my mouth shut about your family."

Her heart sank. "I wouldn't want to get you into trouble."

"And just what type of trouble are you two brewing up?" Fiona quipped, sweeping into the room. She looked stunning, as usual, in a black velvet skirt and forest green top. The High Priestess's gaze focused pointedly on where Reese's hand still clasped Laurell's.

Laurell's face flushed, and she snatched her fingers from his, feeling as if she'd been caught doing something naughty, but not certain why. She'd been so preoccupied with their discussion, she'd forgotten he still held her hand.

"Hey, Fi, up from your nap?" Reese said.

"Yeah," Fiona said as she flopped into the wingback chair opposite the couch. Her cat green eyes narrowed on Laurell with a suspicious gleam. "Seriously, though, tell me what you two are conspiring about."

"We weren't conspiring." Laurell lifted her chin in defiance. "We were talking about my family."

"No worries, Fi. I already told her I'm not allowed to share any more secrets," Reese interjected before Fiona could respond.

Fiona eyed Laurell carefully. "Glad to hear that, Reese," she said, still looking at Laurell. "Laurell, if you want to know more, talk to your Liaison. My understanding is she asked to be the one to fill you in on all that."

Laurell rose, keeping her expression blank. She refused to let Fiona see how much she dreaded talking to her mother. The woman didn't need anything else with which to torture her. "Maybe I'll do that."

"Get up, lazybones. Time for ritual." Hillary's husky voice boomed through the closed door of Laurell's cabin. She'd been trying to catch a quick nap before supper. Actually, Laurell had attempted an astral travel trip, figuring it would be best to talk to her mother and just get all their business out in the open rather than stewing over it. Instead, she'd simply fallen asleep sans Liaison visit.

"What ritual?" Laurell called out, her words muffled by a yawn.

"Full moon. You've got twenty minutes, so move it, girl! And dress nice! Ritual for us is like church for Christians." Hillary's footsteps faded into the distance.

Laurell sat up and glanced at the clock. She'd slept through supper. Her stomach growled its protest. She'd have to grab a snack later. She slipped on a long, violet skirt Hillary had given to her a few days before, along with several other articles of clothing. "These are my clothes from when I was scrawny like you," she'd said.

When Laurell asked if she wouldn't rather keep them in case she fit into them again, Hillary had laughed. "Oh no, I'm celebrating my goddess curves, not trying to get rid of 'em."

Laurell added a silky black peasant shirt to the outfit and glanced in the mirror. She only wished she had Hillary's attitude about her less-than-perfect body. *Scrawny? As if!*

She ran a brush through her hair, then ruffled the mahogany strands until the choppy layers lay in planned disarray. As she applied some mascara and dotted her lips with gloss, she thought over the day's training.

She'd pretty much gotten the hang of the earth element; after countless tries and lots of focused will and intent, she'd caused a rather impressive crack in a boulder. She'd utilized the air element to whip up a small dust devil, and as for fire, well, it was clear she had a natural ability to tap into that particular element, so she and Fiona had left well enough alone.

Working with water, however, remained problematic. No matter how much power she put into it, she was unable to affect the water. Fiona continued to harp on perceiving the water element within her, imagining it as the blood running through her veins, and tapping into her emotions. No matter what Laurell did, though, she couldn't assimilate this element. Fiona had given her some more practice exercises to work with on her own and told her they'd come back to it later.

It still amazed her, this ability to weave magic. She felt a little like Alice in Wonderland, having stumbled into a strange world where the improbable was possible and nothing was what it seemed. Knowing her grandmother had been a witch and being able to tap into her own previously hidden power, Laurell felt like a Graves for the first time in her life.

Suddenly, being a Graves meant much more than being a Hollywood legend's daughter; it meant having access to unusual abilities and strengths, being part of something bigger than herself. She only wished she'd known her potential when her grandmother was alive.

She dotted some amber oil on her wrists and neck. Dawna, the goth girl of the group who spent most of her time in her cabin writing in a journal, had given Laurell the tiny cobalt blue bottle of essential oil, explaining it had protective qualities.

Protective or not, Laurell adored the scent, sweet with a hint of spice. One by one the members of the coven were stepping forward in their own ways to welcome and befriend Laurell. Each time this happened, a slow and fuzzy warmth spiraled through her. She actually belonged here. Maybe not forever, but for now.

She took one more look in the mirror. Normally, she'd have preferred jeans and a T-shirt, but Hillary had said to dress nice. *That's the only reason I'm primping. It has nothing to do with Axiom being at the ritual.*

She wrapped a black, hooded cloak around her shoulders, enjoying the softness of the velvet against her skin. She had no idea whom to thank for this particular present. She'd found it lying across her bed that morning upon her return from breakfast.

The brisk night air greeted her as she stepped from the cabin, and she was immediately grateful for the cloak. Something drew her eyes upward—perhaps the pull of the moon, which shone bright and vivid against the black sky. She could make out a face with a lopsided smile on its surface.

"Are you coming or what?" Hillary appeared at her side, breathtaking in a black velvet dress with a red wool ruana slung about her shoulders. Her eyes were heavily lined and her lips shone with something glossy in the moonlight.

"Wow," Laurell said.

"Goddess of Willendorf, that's me!" Hillary quipped, grabbing Laurell's arm and pulling her toward the ritual circle.

They followed the beam of Hillary's flashlight and made their way between the trees toward the place where a fire danced and a lone drummer tapped out a primal beat.

CHAPTER SIXTEEN

Axiom observed Laurell from the west side of the ritual circle. She halted at the entrance to the clearing, and Fiona drew a banishing fire pentagram on Laurell's head while the blonde witch named Lynn waved sage around her body. The smoke tendrils from the burning herb curled over Laurell, cleansing her in the manner of the Native Americans.

The scent of the sage drifted to his nostrils, and he tried to concentrate on it, on the rhythm of the drum Reese percussed with such skill, on the coolness seeping from the hard ground through the blanket on which he sat.

He wished to focus on anything but Laurell and the vision she presented, illuminated by moonlight, the image of a powerful goddess in her flowing skirt and the cloak he had gifted her. *Breathtaking.* The fact she so clearly did not know her own beauty only made her all the more attractive.

Fiona pointed Laurell in Axiom's direction, and she strode clockwise around the ritual circle toward him. Laurell folded her legs beneath her, sitting on the blanket as far from him as she could. She kept her gaze averted despite his pointed attempt to make eye contact.

Laurell sat with her back rigid, clasping her hands tightly in her lap. Clearly, she was still angry with him. He had attempted to talk to her several times since their passionate encounter, but she'd always hurried away before he could utter more than a greeting.

"Brothers and sisters of the craft, please stand." Fiona's voice broke through Axiom's thoughts. Reese's drumming ceased, and the coven members, clustered into the four cardinal directions, rose. He stood and offered his hand to Laurell, who teetered as she got up, almost losing her balance. She ignored his attempt to assist.

Fiona walked the perimeter of the circle, sweeping a broom and chanting, "A circle within a circle, protected, and clear of all negativity." Axiom knew Fiona referred to the ritual circle and the larger circle of protection that encompassed the property.

Next, Fiona and Reese consecrated the elements, a task that included saying a blessing over a dish of salt and one of water, and lighting a stick of incense. Dawna collected the incense, Lynn the salt, and Wayne the water. The three then walked the circle once, returned the items to the stone altar that sat in the middle of the circle, then resumed their posts. Next, the coven greeted and called in the elements one at a time.

"Guardians of the watchtowers of the East, element of air, we summon, stir, and call you up to aid and witness our rite," Reese called out from his station in the east. He held up his athame, a short-handled knife used only for magic, and cut a pentagram invoking east. Golden sparks followed the trail of his athame, brilliant against the backdrop of night.

Wayne repeated a similar act in the south, his athame producing red flashes of light as he waved it through the air. Then all eyes turned to Axiom and Laurell.

"Laurell, will you invoke the element of water, please?" Fiona's words were more command than request.

Laurell's brow creased in surprise. "Me?"

"Yes. You and Axiom occupy the west quarter," Fiona explained. Laurell shifted from one foot to the other, then twisted to view the water fountain trickling quietly behind them. She bit her lip and looked perplexed.

Perhaps she did not notice the fountain when she sat down earlier, Axiom thought. Long moments ticked by while Laurell eyed the thing dubiously, as though she expected it to sprout fingers and accost her.

She finally faced forward again. "I'm not sure . . ."

"You need practice with the water element. This is a good place to start," Fiona insisted. Laurell's hands clenched and released the folds of her cloak. She swallowed hard and, for the first time in days, turned her face to Axiom. Her dark eyes were round with dismay and her face was flushed with enough pink for him to perceive her embarrassment even in the dim glow of the tiki torches.

She needed his help. Her eyes begged him for it. That she looked to him for assistance, that she trusted him to come to her aid, produced an unfamiliar surge of tenderness in Axiom.

"I will call the water," he announced. He had never performed a Wiccan ritual before, but had on occasion witnessed them from the Light Realm. The energy produced by a group of witches working in tandem could be quite impressive, and frequently such activity caught the attention of the gods.

Laurell's release of held breath was audible. She mouthed the words *thank you.* He flashed a smile in return. Her lips curved slightly before she looked away. Reluctantly, Axiom returned his attention to Fiona and the ritual at hand.

Fiona stood stiffly, hands on her hips and head tilted to one side, clearly unhappy with his interference. He did not care.

I made Laurell smile, he mused. *Only the briefest glimpse of curved lips, but still a smile.* Which meant she might actually converse with him again. Which meant they might actually forge a friendship before they mated.

He feared he had hurt her by halting their most recent intimate exchange. He could have consummated their sexual union then—Source only knew he desired her fiercely—but since she was not ovulating at the time, it would have served no purpose.

Her aggressive kisses and caresses had nearly pushed him over the edge; she had certainly tested his control of the yearning. He could have given in to the carnal lust of the human body he inhabited, but that was not part of his mission. He was to father the Earth Balancer and do what he could to protect both the child and the mother. Anything else would simply cause him to lose focus. And a warrior who lacked focus was doomed to fail.

He could not afford unnecessary distractions. A Council seat hung in the balance.

Fiona cleared her throat loudly. Axiom blinked. How did Laurell manage to take over his thoughts even when he held the yearning firmly in check?

"Guardians of the watchtowers of the West . . ." he began, holding one hand to the sky.

An hour later, they had almost completed their ritual. The coven had honored both male and female aspects of deity, created a vortex of healing energy and channeled it to the Earth, and then turned their attention to spiraling a protective current to the center of the circle. Fiona then stepped into the midst of that energy, using it to recharge her power. Laurell watched the scene in awe. Sparks of violet light sparked around the redhead and wove through the circle to touch each coven member's outstretched palms.

Laurell's eyes swept over the group. Everyone else hovered in various altered states, eyes either closed or half-open and unfocused. Even Axiom stood still beside her, brows furrowed in concentration, his eyes mere slits. Laurell had started out that way, but when her fingertips began to tingle and her palms itched, she couldn't help opening her eyes. The same violet light shimmered from her own hands and flowed into the circle.

Amazing. She thought working with the elemental energies was incredible. Actually viewing the creation of energy and its transmittal was even more astonishing. *Now I understand why the coven stays together. They strengthen and support each other. Like a family.*

Fiona's voice broke the silence. "At the full moon, occult force and power reach maximum strength. Tonight, we utilized that strength to direct much-needed healing to Mother Earth. At this time, if any of you would like to direct the group's will toward something you wish to create or accomplish, please speak now." Her face glowed in the dim light, effervescent as the moon, which presided above them, pregnant with possibility.

"I have a request." Axiom's deep voice came out husky and strained. He cleared his throat. Fiona nodded, waiting. "I would like to ask that Source remain close to us, that our mission be successful, and that all of those involved in this important work receive their just reward."

After he said the words, Axiom shifted from one foot to the other and glanced furtively at the others, his uncertainty obvious. "It is appropriate for me to request such things, is it not?"

Fiona nodded and gave him a warm smile. "Absolutely." She then instructed the group to clasp hands and send currents from left to right, until it whirled from one person to the next and made Laurell's body vibrate.

"Now!" Fiona's voice boomed. "Raise your hands skyward. Release your intent to the skies. Let the element of air carry it away and sprinkle the ethers with our will."

Laurell's hands shot upward. As the energy exited her

body and spiraled upward, tiny tremors erupted inside her, and she gasped in a mixture of surprise and fascinated delight.

"It's time to recast the protection spell around the property," Reese said. "Remember to let Fiona make the first round. Her abilities are the closest to Anne's. And whatever you do, finish by midnight."

At the mention of her dead sister, Fiona's shoulders sagged. Laurell's chest tightened and she experienced a pang of sympathy. In spite of Fiona's most recent attempt to embarrass her in front of the group by assigning her the one element she knew she hadn't been able to master, she just couldn't be angry. Instinctively, Laurell stepped forward and touched Fiona's shoulder, meaning to lend comfort.

Fiona jerked back. She didn't acknowledge Laurell's attempt to offer comfort. "I'll get started," she said. "Everyone is expected back here to close the ritual."

Then, flashlight and sword in hand, Fiona strolled off into the darkness, purple cloak billowing in her wake.

Reese pointed to the main house. "Last one there has to sit on the back of the golf cart." To their left, leaves crunched and a whirring noise drifted by. Fiona had already claimed a golf cart of her own.

"How may we assist?" Axiom asked Reese.

"By sitting this one out. We'll show you both how to cast a protection circle tomorrow, but unless we absolutely need you, we won't use you to cast. There's that five-second delay to contend with, and you two are both too valuable to the mission to chance if we don't have to," Reese explained before following the others out of the clearing.

Once the group's footsteps had receded and their excited voices dwindled, Laurell wondered what to do next. Axiom watched her intently. Normally, she hated it when he studied her like that, but for some reason, tonight, an air of excitement and anticipation hovered between them. *Is it all me? Or does he sense it, too?*

The wind picked up and swooshed through her cloak, lifting and twisting it about her ankles. The fire blazed from the far side of the clearing in shades of orange, red, and magenta. Thumper had stayed behind and busily tended the flames.

"Perhaps we should sit before the fire," Axiom suggested.

She almost refused. She was still miffed with him. Then again, he had helped her out at the ritual circle. Reluctantly, she agreed and followed him to where Thumper now perched on a log, tapping a languid beat on his djembe drum. Another long log rested opposite Thumper, and they sat there. He nodded his greeting, and Laurell responded in kind.

"The cloak suits you," Axiom said. Her eyes rose to his as she tugged the velvet material around her, burying her hands beneath the excess folds in her lap in order to keep her fingers warm.

"Thanks," she replied. "Someone left it in my cabin."

"I did. Consider it a gift," he told her. His eyes lit with a silver gleam as he studied her features. "You are beautiful tonight. There is goddess energy flowing freely through you."

Laurell blinked. She couldn't be completely sure, but she thought this might be the first time Axiom had complimented her. Although she'd seen his usually reserved demeanor soften into mild amusement once or twice at the safe house, most of the time he just delivered information or instructions regarding the mission.

Laurell offered Axiom a shaky smile and willed thoughts of her botched seduction away. *Please don't let him bring it up. I just want to forget it happened.* She sucked in a deep breath. There. All gone. Now what had they been talking about? Oh yeah.

"Thanks for the compliment. And I appreciate the

cloak," she said. "It's keeping me much warmer than my coat would have. The coat only reaches to midthigh." She spied Axiom's usual suit beneath the long, black jacket he wore. She swore he must own a dozen of them, some navy, some black, one chocolate brown. Didn't he tire of dressing so formally every day?

"Your suit looks nice, but, uh, why don't you try jeans sometime? I mean, not every day calls for formal attire. Especially around here."

Axiom seemed to ponder her words. "I enjoy the look and feel of the suits, but I will consider your recommendation."

"Good," she said, her gaze wandering back to the fire. The heat took the edge off the frigid air.

"We must discuss our mating," Axiom suddenly announced.

CHAPTER SEVENTEEN

Laurell snapped her attention back to Axiom, and her face went hot. Much as she wanted to, she resisted the urge to flee. "Do we have to talk about that now?"

"Yes. You have ill feelings toward me as a result of my refusal to engage in coitus."

An agonized groan erupted from her throat. "This discussion really isn't necessary." *Good Lord.* Could Thumper hear them? Laurell eyed the youthful witch, who thumped a louder, slightly faster tune now on his drum, gaze fixed on the stars above. Satisfied he wasn't eavesdropping, she continued. "Look, you weren't in the mood, right? No biggie."

Axiom ran one hand through his hair, leaving a wavy lock to cascade over his brow. Laurell itched to touch that chunk of hair and smooth it into place.

"I did not reject you for lack of desire, but because you were not ovulating," he said, his expression earnest.

Laurell swallowed hard. Well, that sure as heck explained a lot. She didn't know whether to be relieved or insulted. "I don't get it. I thought you could get me pregnant anytime, anywhere. You being a god and all."

"I never said that. I am sorry you made this assumption."

"Wait a minute. How the heck do you even know when I'm ovulating? My cycle is so screwed up from the endometriosis, I don't even know when I'm ovulating."

Axiom smiled. "I am able to sense your cycles."

"Because you're a god."

"Because I am a god, yes."

Since she'd only tried to coerce Axiom into having sex to stop the yearning, Laurell told herself it shouldn't matter that he experienced no urge to make love with her unless she could conceive the child.

But as he gazed at her with his deep sexy eyes and the firelight danced over the chiseled planes of his gorgeous face, she ached inside. His rejection stung just as much as that of her ex-boyfriend when he had ended their relationship of three years because she could never have children.

It stung just as much as the teasing she'd experienced as a teenager, heavy and awkward, when she'd had a crush on one of the popular boys in school. Somehow he'd caught wind of her secret infatuation. *Stop looking at me, fatty,* he'd said one day when he caught her gazing at him with unabashed adoration in class. *I'd never go out with you,* he'd added, his voice purposely loud so the other kids could hear him.

"Although mating without ovulation is unnecessary," Axiom went on, "I do believe developing a friendship would prove beneficial to us both. It will make the mission go more smoothly if we have built trust in one another. I cannot force you to befriend me, but I strongly urge you to consider it."

Laurell shook her head to clear it. Surely she hadn't heard him right. Had he just asked her to be his buddy? His request was sort of cute, actually. It eased the sting of his earlier words. But only a little.

She hid a giggle behind a fake yawn. "Uh, sure. I'll be your friend."

Axiom grinned. His pearly teeth gleamed and his left cheek dimpled. She'd never noticed that dimple before. Probably because he didn't smile much.

A shout erupted from the trees to their right. Twigs

snapped beneath the weight of hurried footsteps, and someone let out a tortured groan. Another voice—it sounded like Hillary—said, "Take her to the house. I'll get my kit."

Laurell and Axiom jumped to their feet. A moment later, the branches parted and Hillary bounded past them toward the house, cloak billowing behind her, Wayne fast on her heels. Reese appeared, carrying Lynn in his arms. Dawna hovered next to them, eyes wide with worry.

"I told you, you don't need to carry me. I can walk," Lynn insisted. Her chocolate brown cloak was pushed aside, and she pressed a scrap of white cloth to one thigh. It looked like someone's handkerchief. She struggled to be free of Reese's arms, and he sighed loudly and set her on her feet. She immediately cried out in pain. The cloth she held darkened in color. *Blood.*

"Satisfied?" Reese asked. Lynn glared.

"Is she okay?" Laurell asked. "Can I help?"

Reese shook his head. "She'll be alright. I'll take her to Hill. She'll stitch Lynn up, and I'll bet she has a healing salve for the wound."

Axiom stepped forward. He bent and looked closely at the wound. "It is not deep. She will be fine."

Reese gave Lynn a pointed look. "Just because he says it's not bad, that doesn't mean you should walk on it."

"Fine," Lynn muttered. Reese scooped her back into his arms and trudged onward.

Dawna made to follow, but Axiom stopped her. "What happened?"

She twisted her hands, her features scrunched with apprehension. "I was casting the protective circle on the east side of the property. I had my arm held out with my athame pointed, you know, to direct the energy."

Axiom nodded his understanding. "And?"

"Poe was skipping around my feet, and I was telling him to back up so I wouldn't trip over him—"

"Poe?" Laurell interrupted, stepping forward and tilting her head toward the other woman.

"My familiar. Poe."

"Poe's a raven. You know, a bird," Thumper said, joining them. "Dawna can communicate telepathically with animals." Admiration tinged Thumper's words. The look on his face made Laurell certain he had a crush on Dawna.

"Not all animals," Dawna corrected. "At least not yet. So far, it's mostly birds. Anyway, Poe was under my feet, and I told him to move. I bent down for a second to shoo him out of the way, and I thought I saw something swoosh by out of the corner of my eye."

"Swoosh by? How do you mean?" Axiom asked.

"Just that. I thought something moved in the air just outside the circle. I got spooked and spun around. Of course, there was nothing there. Anyway, I guess I still had my arm outstretched. Habit, you know. And that's about the time Lynn walked up beside me. She said she called my name, but I didn't hear her. When I'm communicating telepathically with Poe, I tune out everything else."

"And she walked into your athame?" Laurell prodded.

Dawna nodded. "Yeah. I feel awful. I should have been paying more attention. Especially since there's the five-second delay to worry about." She paused and bit her lip. "I'm gonna go check on Lynn." She pushed past them and headed toward the house. Thumper made to follow Dawna, then halted and turned toward the bonfire. "I've gotta put out the fire," he murmured.

Laurell watched the young man walk away, running his hands through his shaggy hair. "What's this five-second delay thing I keep hearing about?"

"That's how long it takes for the new protection circle to become fortified once the old one has dissipated," Fiona said, entering the ritual clearing, sword sheathed and strapped to her side, crimson hair tousled from a gust of night wind.

Laurell frowned. "Isn't there some way to cast the new circle earlier, then? Before the old one is gone?"

Fiona shook her head. "No. The prior circle dissipates on its own at exactly midnight of the full moon, and must be gone before we can recast."

"Why?" Laurell wondered. "Why not just recast in a different spot or something?"

Fiona sighed. "I guess you need more training than I realized," she muttered, causing Laurell's insides to twist in embarrassment. "The circle isn't just some invisible wall set up to keep out demonic forces. It creates a boundary between the mundane world and the magical one we inhabit. You can't just create one magical world within another. It doesn't work like that."

"So we're in another world here?" Laurell didn't bother to hide her confusion. *To hell with Fiona and her condescending attitude.* She needed to understand this stuff, and if she had to pry the information out of her reluctant teacher, she would.

"Yes, inside the protection circle, we're literally in another place, another dimension, if you will. From the outside, others can't view us. If you were to be standing outside our property right now, you'd see the trees, possibly even my house, but not us. And you wouldn't hear us either."

Laurell's eyes widened. "So the Umbrae can't see us here?"

"Unfortunately, this does not apply to the Umbrae," Axiom broke in. "They do not exist in the world of men, but on a different plane. Their Finders, however, cannot view us here, since they are human."

Fiona seemed to be growing impatient with the conversation. She waved her hands at them as though to wave away any concerns. "As long as you two keep your wards in place during those five seconds, there's no way for the Umbrae to track you here. And once the circle is in place, even if they can see you, they can't get in. Which means they can't get close enough to harm you."

Fiona glanced around the clearing then, eyes narrowed. "Where is everyone? Aren't they back yet from the casting? I sensed the protection spell was secure a while ago."

"You did not hear of Lynn's accident?" Axiom asked.

Fiona's spine stiffened, and she shook her head.

"Apparently Dawna got spooked and Lynn walked up at the wrong time and was injured by Dawna's athame. They're up at the house now," Laurell explained.

"Do not be alarmed," Axiom said. "The wound was not deep."

A dark shadow crossed Fiona's face, and she muttered something unintelligible.

"It's okay. She looked like she'd be fine," Laurell assured.

"I know she'll be okay," Fiona said. "It's just . . ." For the first time, Fiona lost her arrogant self-assuredness.

"Just what?" Laurell pressed.

"An athame should never shed blood. As omens go, this one's pretty bad."

As though to emphasize Fiona's words, a gust of wind barreled through the clearing, kicking up dirt and leaves and sending an ominous chill over Laurell's skin.

The next morning, Laurell found Lynn and Dawna relaxing on the porch outside the main house. Lynn reclined in a lawn chair, her injured leg elevated on some pillows, a blanket strewn across her lap.

"Mornin'," Laurell murmured, sitting down next to the

other two women. Lynn's sky blue eyes met hers with warmth and she nodded.

"How's it goin'?" Lynn asked.

"I'm good. How's the leg?" Laurell motioned to the limb in question and took a sip of coffee from the mug she held in her stiff fingers. It was getting colder by the day.

"My leg's okay. Thank Goddess for Hill. She stitched me up and gave me some painkillers and antibiotics. I'll be good as new before you know it," Lynn said.

"Is Hillary a doctor?" Laurell wondered how she'd missed that bit of information.

"She's a nurse practitioner. And a midwife. We're lucky to have her. You'll be glad she's around when you get ready to deliver."

At the mention of the child she'd yet to conceive, Laurell swallowed more coffee and looked at the sky. No sun today. Clouds puckered over the treetops and a brisk breeze stirred the branches. Brown leaves still clung to some of the tree limbs, but she suspected they'd be bare soon.

"You look frozen," Dawna said to Laurell.

Laurell tucked her head farther into her jacket, trying to keep her ears from the wind. "Yeah, well, it's a tad bit colder here than it is in Florida. How do you guys stand it?"

Dawna flipped her blue-black hair over one sweater-clad shoulder and shrugged. "Used to it, I suppose. It'll be snowing before you know it, so enjoy this weather while you can."

"Snow?" Laurell couldn't remember the last time she'd seen snow.

"We're only a week from Samhain—or Halloween, as the rest of the world refers to it. Weatherman forecasts a white and chilly November," Lynn said.

"Poe, you little rascal, come here!" Dawna jumped to her feet and scampered across the porch to crouch in front of a black bird perched on the edge of the wooden railing. Laurell craned her neck and watched with amazement as the bird hopped across the railing toward his friend.

"Kraw! Kraw!" cried the raven. As it moved, a tiny purple string tied to one of its legs trailed loosely behind it.

"Oh, you goof, your bow is untied." Dawna stroked one finger over the bird's head before retying the bow. The bird watched her, not moving as she finished her task.

"What's the string for?" Laurell wondered.

Dawna glanced over her shoulder. "It's just so I can keep an eye on him and so you guys always know which bird is Poe."

"Hillary came out of the shower once to find Poe sitting on her bed, and she thought he was a wild bird that got in our cabin," Lynn said with a wry smile.

"She was swatting at him with a broom when I came in and found him flying all over the room, squawking," Dawna finished. "I used to share a cabin with Hill."

Dawna turned back to the bird. "You go fly now. Get something good to eat. I think I saw a dead mouse or a squirrel or something on the east side of the property."

The bird tilted its head to one side. "Kraw!" Then the raven took flight and, sure enough, headed toward the east.

"That's amazing," Laurell remarked, shaking her head.

Dawna resumed her seat by Lynn. She stroked the other woman's hand affectionately. "Yeah. Poe's pretty cool. Lynn and I share a cabin now, so he's allowed to come around when he wants."

Lynn grinned. "I'm used to the little guy by now." She lifted one hand and touched Dawna's cheek. "Dawna's familiar is always welcome in our cabin." Their eyes met and Dawna blew Lynn a kiss.

It suddenly dawned on Laurell the two women were a couple. Ah, well. To each her own. The two certainly seemed happy.

Laurell's chest constricted. She'd hoped once to have someone look at her the way Lynn did Dawna. Deep down she still dreamed of loving someone so much she'd do anything for that person. Even put up with a wild bird hanging out in her cabin. What must it be like to love and be loved like that?

CHAPTER EIGHTEEN

Laurell entered the Astral Plane with trepidation. Not only did being there mean communicating with her mother, but the last time she'd visited, the Umbrae had made an appearance. She shuddered. She really could do without seeing those vile creatures again. She glanced at the orange sand beneath her feet and the gray, smoke-filled sky, then remembered what she'd learned from her previous visit. She'd focused her will, and the ground soon sparkled like diamonds, while the sky turned luminescent violet.

The air shimmered, contracted, and a moment later, Elaine appeared, clad in a flowing white dress, her dark hair curling around her shoulders. Elaine smiled. Laurell simply stared.

"I'm so glad to see you," her mother exclaimed.

"We need to talk," Laurell said.

Elaine nodded briskly. "You're right. We've lots to discuss. But first, please know the Council has determined Anne's death was caused by the Umbrae, just as mine was. And they have no reason to believe the Umbrae know of the coven's location. So you should be safe there."

Laurell heard her mother's words, but they passed by ears numb to anything but the words *just as mine was*. She blinked, and her hands twisted at her sides. "Did you just say the Umbrae killed you?"

"Yes, I did. The Council is pretty certain the Umbrae caused me to fall from the balcony," Elaine confirmed.

Laurell shook her head. "No. No, you killed yourself." Was the woman having delusions in her spirit life? "The coroner ruled your death a suicide."

"He was wrong. I was pushed," her mother insisted.

Laurell frowned. "But Riley—"

Elaine groaned. "Yes, I told Riley I'd kill myself if he left, but I said it tongue in cheek. I was being sarcastic, and he knew it. I can't believe he told the newspapers that!"

Laurell bit her lip. She didn't know what to think. She'd just spent weeks angry and hurt that her mother hadn't wanted to go on living—not even for her only daughter.

"Think about it," Elaine continued. "I was at the height of my career. Why would I want to die? Just because Riley wanted to shack up with some whore half his age?"

"But you were always so concerned about appearances," Laurell said. "I thought—"

Elaine sighed heavily and stepped closer. Her slender hands rested on Laurell's shoulders, and her hazel eyes met their likeness in her daughter's gaze. "I know. You had every reason to believe Riley. I was selfish, self-centered, and controlling. Part of me wanted to curl up and hide when I learned of his betrayal. Not because I was hurt so much as because I was mortified that the world would know. But if there's one thing you should know about me, it's that my career came before everything and everyone."

Her mother seemed sincere. Laurell's stance relaxed a bit. The Umbrae had killed her mother. Her chest burned with anger, this time at the evil creatures whose machinations had turned her world upside down. Maybe Elaine *had* left much to be desired as a mother. But she was the only family Laurell had, and the Umbrae had taken that family from her.

"Now that that's out of the way, tell me how you're faring? Are you and Axiom getting on okay?" Elaine asked. She stepped back as though a thought had just occurred to her, and her gaze swept Laurell's middle.

Laurell's jaw tensed, and she shrugged out of her mother's grasp. *Not so fast, Mother.* "You were supposed to mother the Earth Balancer, weren't you?"

Elaine blinked at the sudden turn of topic. "Yes, that's true."

"Tell me what happened to prevent you from fulfilling your mission," Laurell demanded, a familiar ire settling in her gut with a slow, acidic burn.

"Your grandmother tried to tell me about the mission, but I didn't take her seriously. So she sent the High Priestess, Anne, to try to convince me," Elaine admitted.

"But she couldn't convince you either, could she?" Laurell pressed. "You wouldn't listen." *You never listened.* "You cared only about yourself and your career and keeping up appearances. I spent most of my life trying to fit some impossible mold you'd created for the perfect Hollywood daughter. And no matter how much I tried to tell you what I wanted for my life, who I wanted to be, you wouldn't hear me." Moisture pricked her eyes, but she blinked the tears back. She wouldn't cry. She hadn't cried since she was a teenager, and she wouldn't start now. Not in front of her mother, of all people.

"You've every reason to be angry with me, but I want to make things right for you. For us." Elaine reached for her, but Laurell stepped back.

"No. You don't get to ruin my life, then sweep on in for your happy ending. This isn't the movies, Mother." Laurell paced over the smooth crystalline landscape, glancing periodically at Elaine. She enjoyed the whiteness of her mother's face, the way the other woman twisted her hands in concern.

It felt good to tell her mother off. She'd wanted to do it for a long time and probably should have years ago.

"Laurell—"

She ignored her mother's attempt to speak. Elaine's time to talk was over. Laurell had spent too many years listening to Elaine.

"The fact is, you refused to hear Grandmother or Anne and because of that, you're dead. And now, guess what? Once again, thanks to you, my life isn't my own." She paused in midstep and turned to face Elaine, arms folded, limbs shaking with repressed rage.

"I understand your world is topsy-turvy right now, but the mission—"

Laurell cut Elaine off and continued. "I've accepted my place in this mission. I'm committed to seeing it through." She sighed and ran one hand through her hair. "Then again, I don't really have an option, do I? But I do have the choice of whether to talk to you or not. I choose *not*. Tell the Council not to bother sending you here again. You're a piss-poor choice of messenger."

Elaine's eyes widened. "Laurell, don't do this."

"It's done," Laurell said.

A moment later she bolted upright in her bed. Shadows danced across the dimly lit cabin, the night-light casting distorted shapes on the walls and ceiling. Traces of nag champa drifted on the air, remnants of the incense she'd burned earlier that day.

She buried her face in her hands and willed her frantic heartbeat to slow. She should be satisfied, smug, after giving her mother what for. After all, she'd wanted to do that for as long as she could remember. But a hollow cavern echoed where her heart should be, and she wished she could cry. *Just let the tears fall.* She tried, but in the end, she couldn't. If she gave in to the urge now, would she ever stop?

CHAPTER NINETEEN

"Ginger for a stomach upset or peppermint. Soapwort for skin conditions like eczema or acne. Anise is a good anti-septic and also helps nausea—oh, and it's great for a colicky baby." Hillary's words droned on, and Laurell found herself tuning her out without intending to. It had been hours since she'd entered the healer's cabin to discuss the various uses of herbs. For the past several days she'd moved from one coven member to the next, learning each person's magical expertise.

The day before, she'd worked with Dawna, playing "psy-chic games" where she had to guess what shapes or numbers were on the backs of cards Dawna held up. Apparently, since Anne had died, Dawna was the group's next-most-talented intuitive. Despite Dawna's insistence that every-one was psychic, Laurell remained unconvinced. Her own intuition left something to be desired.

Today, she was supposed to be learning about different healing modalities. So far, they'd covered everything from Reiki to oils and herbs.

"Hill, aren't you going to be around once the Earth Bal-ancer is born? I mean, I'll never remember all this stuff. And I'm not sure why I need to," Laurell remarked, halting Hillary's treatise on the benefits and drawbacks of the herb valerian.

"I don't know that any of us have ever discussed what

happens after the baby is born," Hillary said with a look of puzzlement. She scratched her head, close-cropped black curls bouncing beneath her hand. "We were just told to make sure you learned as much as you could from us. You know, 'cause you're going to have to help the child learn."

Laurell frowned. It hadn't occurred to her the coven might disappear once the baby came, leaving her and the child to their own devices.

"I know I'm going to have to be able to help the baby, but what will you guys be doing? Is there some other mission the coven needs to jump on or something?" She tried to keep the sarcasm from her voice, but failed miserably. Sarcasm always laced her words when she was worried or scared.

Hillary's stern brown gaze pinned her. "Hmmph! Don't take that tone with me, young lady. I'm old enough to be your mother, and I won't take any lip from you! We have lives outside this coven, you know. You should be thankful we put them on hold to help you and Axiom."

Laurell sighed, thoroughly shamed. "I'm sorry. I'm just feeling anxious."

"Well, you've lots to be anxious about. Aside from the obvious, why don't you tell me what's on your mind? Maybe I can help." Hillary dropped the sachets of herbs she'd been sorting onto the table in front of her and crossed the room. She folded herself into the chair next to Laurell and patted Laurell's knee reassuringly.

Laurell chewed a nail and glanced over her shoulder toward the door to the cabin. It was closed tight. So was the window next to it. Outside, the wind shook the bushes beneath the window so the branches tapped against the glass. The day was gray and dreary as usual. Inside, though, soft new age music played from a CD player in the corner, and vanilla incense burned.

Hillary's open, friendly face turned to her, smooth cocoa

skin gleaming from the homemade lotion she'd applied earlier during her demonstration of healing creams. Crossing her arms over her purple fuzzy sweater and ample bosom, she tilted her head to the side. "Well? Out with it."

She could trust this woman; Laurell knew it. Still, her face heated with a blush as she thought of how to pose her concerns.

Just get it out. Maybe she can help. "Here's the deal," Laurell began. "I've only had sex with a couple guys in my life. With one of them, it only happened once. With the other, it wasn't any good. And, well, I really lack experience in that department." Now that she'd done her best to seduce Axiom, only to be summarily rejected, she was less certain of her sexual prowess than ever.

Hillary didn't say anything, but her lips thinned, and her brow furrowed in apparent concentration. "So, you're feeling nervous about getting busy with Axiom, is that it?"

Laurell let out a breath she didn't know she'd been holding. Thank god she didn't have to explain further. Hill got it. "Exactly," she said.

"Just what is it that makes you nervous?"

Laurell pointed to her thighs. "My thighs are big, my butt is big, my belly is big, my—"

"Good Goddess, girl! You're not even half my size, and you think you're fat? You got a little meat on your bones, so what? You look like a goddess!" Hillary grinned and motioned to her own ample figure. "Not as much of a goddess as me, of course, but you can't have everything, now can you?"

Laurell groaned in frustration. Maybe Hillary was the wrong person to complain to. No doubt her worries seemed silly and vain to such a self-assured and confident woman.

"Now, now, don't think I'm making fun of you, sweetie. I understand. Really, I do." Hillary stood and grabbed Laurell's hands, yanking her to her feet. "We've been sold a lie in this country. A lie that says women are only attractive if they can wear a size six. Come here."

Hillary dragged her to the full-length mirror occupying a wall near the bathroom. She stood behind her, hands resting on Laurell's shoulders. "Look in the mirror. I see a gorgeous woman with a curvy figure, big hazel eyes, high cheekbones, and a mouth like Julia Roberts. And look at that hair! Silky and shiny enough to make any girl jealous. I see a beautiful goddess. What do you see? Hmmmm?"

Laurell met Hillary's piercing gaze in the mirror.

"Don't look at me. Look at yourself," Hillary urged.

Laurell reluctantly complied. Feeling silly, she stared at the woman in the glass. For a moment, she thought she saw the woman Hillary did, eyes dark and beguiling, cheeks flushed with embarrassment, plump lips tilted in a half smile. She glanced at her breasts. They were admittedly large and perky and probably pleasing to most men. Her gaze traveled over hips she just might be able to imagine as voluptuous and not just wide.

Then her gaze settled on her too-thick thighs, and she heard her mother's voice calling out from a distant dinner table as ten-year-old hands reached for the mashed potatoes: *No seconds, Laure, you know we Graves women have the obesity gene. Don't tempt fate.*

She twisted away from Hillary. "Hill, I appreciate what you're trying to do, but—"

"But you aren't buying it just yet, huh?" Hillary shook her head, one eyebrow arched in disapproval. "Well, I suppose you can always ask Fiona about a glamoury to get you through your night with Axiom."

"A glamoury?"

"A spell to alter your appearance temporarily. Fiona knows how to cast one, but I don't. Maybe she'll show you how to enhance your features so you'll have more confidence." Hillary resumed her seat by the window. "Not that I think you need it, mind you. But whatever it takes to get the deed done, the Earth Balancer needs to be conceived. The sooner the better, I say."

"Yeah," Laurell agreed. "The sooner the better." How in the world would she convince Fiona to teach her a glamour spell? The coven's High Priestess had made it clear she didn't like Laurell, so why would she help her with such a request? *And how will I explain why I want it so badly?* Just the thought made her cringe.

"You want me to do what?" Fiona eyed Laurell with feigned shock. Laurell shifted from one foot to the other, her forced smile drooping a little.

"I know you heard me, Fiona," Laurell said, taking a step farther into the kitchen, where Fiona was stirring a pot of homemade vegetable soup. The scent of beef bouillon and simmering peppers and onions tickled Fiona's nose. She lifted the spoon to her lips and took just a sip of the broth. Tangy, but it needed a bit more spice. She reached around Laurell to the cupboard, found the cumin, and started to tip some into the pot. Laurell's hand on hers stopped the movement.

Green eyes locked with determined hazel ones. "Why do you want to learn glamoury? It's hardly necessary training for the mission," Fiona said.

Laurell pushed a lock of chestnut hair from her eyes. Fiona noticed the other woman's hair had grown a bit since she'd arrived at the covenstead. It curled over her collar and softened Laurell's striking features. Fiona would bet Reese had noticed the subtle but attractive change as well. Reese noticed everything. She turned back to her soup and stirred with a vengeance.

"Does it matter why I want to learn it?" Laurell asked.

"I'm in charge of your training," Fiona insisted. "I don't

want you wasting your time on spells that won't be of any use to you."

"It's not a waste of time," Laurell said, her tone tinged with agitation.

Clearly this spell was important to the girl. Fiona set her spoon on the counter. But why was it so important? She faced Laurell, arms folded across her chest. "Tell me why you want to learn it and I'll consider teaching you," she said.

The brunette's face flushed and Fiona had an inkling she was about to hear something good. Despite Laurell's obvious attempts to appear nonchalant, the glamour spell meant a lot to her.

"I want to use it when I ovulate."

Fiona didn't bother to keep the surprise from her face. "You mean during sex with Axiom?"

Laurell nodded. "It's no big deal. Hillary just thought I could use it for confidence or something."

"She did, huh?" Fiona remembered that day in the ritual circle, the first time Laurell had attempted elemental work. Laurell had clearly been distressed by the thought of having sex with Axiom. Or maybe the girl was just upset she had to couple with Axiom instead of Reese.

Fiona smiled, an idea dawning. "Well, one thing I've learned is you never argue with Hillary."

That evening, Laurell perched on the edge of a chair in her cabin, arms resting on the scratched mahogany table in front of her, eyes narrowed as she focused on the mirror before her. At each side of the glass a lit candle burned. No other light illuminated the room, and shadows stirred and crawled over the walls. In the distance, a bird made a keening sound, the only noise to mar the stillness and quietude of the night.

She peered at the mirror, barely able to see her features, so veiled were they in darkness. She angled forward to form a triangle of candles and mirror, her face the centerpiece. She clutched the charm Fiona had provided, a voluptuous goddess etched in silver and hanging from a black leather cord.

Starlight, star bright, first star I see tonight. The childhood chant burst into her mind unbidden and she almost giggled. She'd never said a spell before. To do so now filled her with the giddy hopefulness she'd experienced as a child wishing upon the evening's first star.

She squeezed her eyes shut and focused her will on the chant Fiona had made her memorize. *Believe in yourself. You have to believe with all you are for this to work.*

"Mighty Venus, goddess of beauty and grace. Enfold me now in your strong embrace. The power is mine to enhance my form as I see fit. An appearance most striking does your magic beget. I take within the ability to transform my outer shell. And all who view me, I enchant with this spell."

Laurell dropped the talisman over her neck. When she'd finished the chant, she opened her eyes and waited expectantly. The air around her shifted, became weighted. A trickle of electricity whispered over her skin and her face tingled. She jumped from her chair and raced to the nearest lamp, flipping it on before resuming her seat.

Hmmmm. The face reflected back to her from the mirror showed no signs of alteration. She crossed the room to get a full-body view in the bathroom mirror. No change. She grimaced. Maybe others would see the changes, but not herself? Laurell didn't remember Fiona saying that was the case. She had said that Laurell and others would sense something was different, would notice Laurell's beauty was enhanced, but the changes would be subtle enough so as not to cause alarm. Like getting a makeover. *I'm supposed to look like me, only at my very best,* Laurell thought.

Maybe Fiona was playing some kind of joke on her. The

redhead had insisted that once Laurell experienced the tingle of magical current, the spell was complete. Well, she'd felt the tingle alright, but so far the spell was a bust.

Fiona sure had some nerve. Laurell wished it weren't so late at night. She'd have to wait until morning to confront the other woman.

She paced the room a few more times, too agitated even to think about sleeping. On her third time past the bathroom mirror, she caught a glimpse of her profile and pivoted for another look. Was it just her, or did her nose suddenly appear larger?

CHAPTER TWENTY

The next morning, Laurell stood in front of her bathroom mirror and craned her neck to view her face from every possible angle. She blinked a few times to clear her eyes. Her features seemed normal again; her nose was its usual size and shape—medium, straight, and nondescript. She must have imagined its change. She really needed to start getting more sleep.

She quickly dressed in her usual jeans and selected a black sweater that hugged her ample breasts a bit more than she'd have liked. She needed to do laundry, so the sweater would have to suffice. She headed to the door, planning to find Fiona and confront her about the spell's efficacy or lack thereof.

Ah! Almost forgot. She halted and scanned the room for the charged talisman. No doubt if she failed to wear it, Fiona would tell her its absence was what had kept the spell from working.

She spied the little silver goddess nestled amidst papers and books on the night table where she'd left it. She slipped the necklace over her head and went to find a certain High Priestess.

"Wow, look at you!" Fiona exclaimed, doing her best to keep her eyes from widening at the sight Laurell presented. The other woman was striding purposefully around the corner of the main house, jaw set, her displeasure so evident Fiona could sense its presence even before she caught sight of her. The brunette bolted up the porch steps and halted in front of her, lips pursed, head cocked to one side.

Fiona tucked the book she'd been reading beneath her arm and rose from her seat. "So," she said. "I see the spell worked."

Laurell's jaw dropped. "Worked? What are you talking about? Nothing has changed. Not even when I wear this damn talisman, which I charged just as you instructed."

Fiona bit back a derisive snort. It had been a simple spell, but a doozy. She studied the other woman, admiring her handiwork. Laurell's features seemed different, but in such a way that one couldn't quite pinpoint what was wrong. Her eyes appeared closer together, her nose longer, lips thinner. Fiona's gaze raked Laurell's body. Just as she'd suspected, the spell made it appear that the natural witch had put on fifteen pounds overnight. Laurell's appearance was striking, alright.

"The spell worked very well, silly. You look gorgeous. Didn't I tell you that you yourself wouldn't be able to see the difference?"

Laurell frowned. "You left that part out."

"I'm so sorry. I should have told you. Only other people can perceive the changes. Goddess, how stupid of me."

Laurell's eyes narrowed as though she suspected she wasn't getting the straight story from Fiona, who flashed her best attempt at an innocent smile.

"Look, if you don't believe me, go try it out on someone else. I think Reese is in the living room." Fiona waved her hand toward the main house with feigned nonchalance.

"Fine, but you'd better be telling me the truth," Laurell ground out, turning on her heel and heading back the way she'd come. Fiona settled back into her chair. Perhaps once Reese got a look at the new Laurell, his infatuation would wane.

"Don't forget to keep the talisman on!" she thought to call out after Laurell. "If you take it off, the spell won't work."

A muffled *uh-huh* confirmed Laurell had heard her. It was almost too easy. A sliver of guilt sliced through Fiona. What she was doing wasn't very nice. It didn't befit a High Priestess. But she couldn't seem to help herself. She'd lost her sister already, and stood to lose Reese, too. She couldn't take another loss in her life at the moment. If one little spell gone awry could keep that from happening, surely the Goddess would forgive her. Wouldn't she?

"You sure you're feeling okay?" Thumper asked with a wrinkled brow and a flicker of concern in his bespectacled brown eyes.

"Fine," Laurell said, agitation creeping into her voice. Why did everyone keep asking if she felt well? First Reese, then Hillary, and now Thumper, too.

He shrugged. "You look tired." Laurell bit her lip. She hadn't had a very restful sleep the previous night, but the way everyone acted, one would think she hadn't slept in days.

"Other than that, how do I look?" she pressed.

Thumper got that expression men get when a woman asks them if her outfit makes her look fat. "Ummm. Good. You . . . well, you always look good."

Laurell sucked in air and willed herself to be patient. Why couldn't she get a straight answer from anyone? Reese had insisted she was beautiful when she'd approached him and asked if he noticed anything different about her. He'd almost convinced her he meant his words, until she noticed how his gaze kept flitting over her face and form as though searching for a lost relic.

Hillary had pushed herbal cold and flu remedies on her and insisted she lie down for a while. She'd sought out

Thumper as a last resort, finding him holed up in his cabin, concocting some strange potion in test tubes and beakers.

"Do you need me for anything?" Thumper's voice pulled Laurell back to the present, his tone laced with nervousness. She sighed and shook her head.

"No. I'll see you at dinner," she said, not missing the relief that spread over his features as she left.

Later, Laurell entered her own cabin and tossed the useless talisman on her desk. Either Fiona had outright lied to her, or she really did look sick. Just to be on the safe side, she decided to take the nap everyone seemed to think she so desperately required.

"What's the deal, Fiona?" Laurell didn't bother to hide her anger when she sought out the High Priestess the next morning after having revisited Reese, Hill, and Thumper, minus the charged talisman. Everyone remarked at the good a full night's rest had done. Apparently, she looked much better. Laurell's lips thinned.

Fiona glanced up from her plateful of scrambled eggs and paused, fork at her mouth. She patted the seat next to her at the dining table. "Hungry? There are more eggs on the stove. Probably not cold yet."

Laurell's eyes shot daggers at her. "Ignoring my question won't cut it. What game are you playing, and more important, why?"

Fiona stuffed more eggs in her mouth. She chewed slowly. "What do you mean?" she finally asked.

Laurell suppressed a groan. "The glamour spell you gave me. There was something wrong with it. Everyone kept saying I looked sick or tired or both." Come to think of it, she *was* sick and tired. *Of Fiona's nastiness.* She should have known better than to ask the other woman for help.

Fiona took a sip of water.

"When I saw you, you looked great. I wonder if something is off with that spell? I haven't used it in a long time."

Laurell folded her arms over her chest and searched the High Priestess's apple green eyes. She wanted to believe Fiona was telling her the truth, but her gut said otherwise. Fiona's gaze remained even, her demeanor calm and collected.

"Doesn't the Wiccan Rede say to harm none?" Maybe she could shame Fiona into honesty.

Fiona blinked. "Have I harmed you?"

Laurell raised her eyebrows. "If I'd put that talisman on and then started to ovulate . . . if Axiom and I had gone off to make a baby, and for some reason my sudden trip into Uglyland caused him to retreat . . . that could have been a bad thing, don't you think? A major missed opportunity? Harmful even?" She didn't mention that the yearning probably would have driven Axiom to have sex with her, even if she were a two-headed, one-eyed, hairy monster.

Fiona stared. *I've got her,* Laurell thought. She waited for the confession.

"I guess you shouldn't use the talisman, just in case." Fiona stood, expression blank, and scooped up her plate and cup. "I'll double-check that spell. Sorry it didn't work for you."

The High Priestess placed her dishes in the kitchen sink. Apparently there'd be no confession this morning.

"Wassup, witchy women?" Reese swooped into the room in a wave of sweet-scented sage that clung to his jean-and-sweater-clad body. He grabbed an empty plate and scooped some eggs and bacon from the stove. "Mornin', Laurell, mornin', Fi," he said.

Laurell mumbled a hello. Fiona flashed him a grin. Reese paused in his breakfast routine and tilted his head, staring at Fiona. "Wow, H.P., you look mighty fine this A.M."

The High Priestess in question viewed Reese through

veiled lashes. Her face flushed. She tossed her loose braid over one shoulder and licked rose-tinted lips, then smoothed her forest green blouse over her matching velvet skirt. Laurell realized Fiona was wearing rather fancy attire for a casual breakfast.

Realization dawned. *Fiona has a crush.* Fiona's lips parted, but before she could respond, Reese pivoted toward the dining room.

"Don't think I forgot about you, au naturel witch," Reese teased. "You always look smashing." Reese winked at Laurell and disappeared into the living room.

Fiona's previously bright expression turned sour. Her jaw hardened. She focused on Laurell. "Eat quickly. We've a lot of work to do."

Now why did that sound like a threat?

Axiom traipsed through the woods, eyes scanning his surroundings with keen focus. Leaves crunched beneath his feet and tiny woodland creatures scurried about—squirrels, birds, snakes, rabbits. He tugged his long, black wool coat around himself, fighting off the unfamiliar chill in his bones. He would not miss this cold when he returned to the Light Realm. He shivered. As a god, he did not experience such things. He was impervious to cold, heat, hunger, fatigue, and desire.

He frowned. Perhaps he would miss the desire. Though he had not yet made love to Laurell, if their passionate encounters thus far were any indication, he would very much enjoy the consummation of their relationship. He had wondered about lovemaking.

Though Mobius spoke little of what had occurred between him and the mortal woman he had joined with during his own Earth mission, Axiom had noticed a wistfulness in his friend's expression whenever she was mentioned. Mobius had warned him not to become too enamored of the Earth woman assigned to mother the Balancer, not to confuse the yearning and the needs of his human body with real emotion. He'd reminded Axiom his time on the Earth plane was limited.

Axiom had no intention of developing tender feelings for Laurell. But when he had watched Laurell from the Light Realm, he had found her attractive in a way he had not found her mother to be. Some part of him had been grateful the mother had not been able to fulfill her part in the mission. He was glad the job of mothering the Earth Balancer had fallen to Laurell instead. Not that he would have wished Elaine dead. Of course not.

But he looked forward to mating with Laurell with an anticipation he had not experienced with her mother. Something about the feisty brunette called to him. He had sensed a kinship with Laurell, though he knew better than to share that information with Mobius. When he watched her one night, huddled in her little apartment all alone, Axiom had understood her emptiness.

He knew what it meant to be an outsider, to never belong.

"I don't pick up anything out of the ordinary," Wayne remarked, ending Axiom's reverie. He pivoted to face his friend. Wayne ran one hand over his lined face and broad nose.

"You do not sense the Umbrae or any Finders?" Axiom asked. Wayne shook his head and pulled his signature Stetson hat down.

The two had been walking the perimeter of the property, inspecting the wooded area for anything suspicious. In particular, they had surveyed the east side, where Dawna had had her strange experience the evening of the full moon. After talking to her about that night, a quiet unease had settled inside of Axiom.

Something seemed amiss, though he could not discern what that might be. Although he did not have the ability to feel the presence of the Umbrae as Wayne did, his keen eyesight allowed him to make a quick and efficient sweep of the property.

Now, his silver gaze investigated the twisted limbs of the mostly barren trees, the collage of brown, amber, and green that made up the forest. Above, a few birds flitted between two towering oaks, beaks open as they emitted occasional screeching sounds.

Perhaps his concerns were unfounded. He had to be wary of the emotions of his human body. He lifted his hands to his face, inspecting his long, thick fingers and clean, short nails as though they were something foreign. He had to be certain his worries were not merely paranoia brought on by this flesh. The Liaison had informed Laurell they were safe in the covenstead, undetected by the Umbrae. He would have to trust that information.

"I don't know what to tell ya, Ax," Wayne said, using the nickname he had recently taken to using when addressing Axiom—and which, for some reason, Axiom enjoyed.

Wayne meandered over with his usual relaxed stride, cowboy boots kicking up dirt and twigs. "I think the girl just got spooked. She's powerful, but she's never been in such a dangerous situation before."

"None of your group has ever been in a situation such as this," Axiom pointed out.

Wayne's mouth curved in a lopsided grin. "Good point, my friend. Good point."

The bird hopped from branch to branch, observing the two men as they walked back through the trees toward the house. It flew after them, stopping every so often to survey its surroundings. Detecting movement below, it spotted a rodent scurrying through the bushes. It poised to dive for its next meal, but those controlling the bird held its small body still and turned its head to the south. The bird obeyed, knowing it could do nothing else, and soared to the place where They wished it to go.

Once there, it fluttered to the foliage nearest the girl with the long black hair. She crouched near the ground, conversing telepathically with a raven. Though she used no words, the bird could hear the conversation nonetheless.

They wished to view this one, the woman who talked to birds. The bird had been scouting for Them ever since it had come across the other woman in the woods far south of here. The woman who had been running. That's when They came and took over the bird and made it follow the woman here. The bird looked out at the world through its own eyes, yet They peered through them, too. And They determined when the bird could eat.

Soon, They said. *For now, just watch.* So the bird rested. And still as stagnant water, it observed, so They might learn.

CHAPTER TWENTY-ONE

Laurell sensed Axiom's presence before he appeared beside her. Even when warded, the yearning still seemed to know when he was near. A shiver of desire whispered over her skin, and she quickly stifled it, returning her attention to her lunch.

His arm brushed hers as he seated himself at the dining room table. "What are you reading?"

"A book on herbs Hillary gave me." She glanced up from the book. Axiom had forgone his usual formal attire for jeans and a cream-colored sweater. He looked different, more relaxed. *More human.*

Axiom nodded and took a bite of cheddar cheese. He motioned to his plate. "Would you like some?"

Laurell started to decline, but stopped herself. A variety of cheeses occupied his plate. She'd just finished a bowl of soup, but the cheese beckoned. "I'm from Wisconsin, so how can I refuse such an offer?" she joked, accepting a couple slices of herb-crusted white cheese. The flavors of tomato, basil, and sharp cheddar exploded in her mouth. *Ummmm. Delicious.*

Axiom smiled, seeming to enjoy her sighs of pleasure. "Please, have more if you wish." He lifted a grape to his lips and chewed slowly. He followed that up with a nibble of the cheese.

Laurell realized he was purposely trying to control his food intake for her benefit. She'd made fun of his eating habits before, and remembering this now, shame pierced her.

"So, what have you been up to?" she asked, hoping to make pleasant conversation.

"Wayne and I inspected the property to be certain all is secure." He lifted his water glass and took a sip.

"Oh? You had reason to believe it wasn't?"

"Only a feeling I had," he explained. "Nothing to worry about. This body experiences emotions at times that are not always my own. I must be careful to differentiate between the two."

Laurell stared. She had no idea what he'd just said, but nodded as though she understood. "Fiona tells me there's a ritual planned for tonight. For Samhain." October thirty-first, the witch's New Year—and according to Hillary, the time when the veil between the worlds was thinnest. She wondered what ghosts or spirits might attempt contact that night. *Hopefully, not Mother.*

"Yes. I believe she plans a Dumb Supper," Axiom responded. Hillary had explained that at a Dumb Supper, a place would be set at the table to represent the deceased ancestors of those present. Also, all would remain silent during the meal to honor the dead.

He'd said he wanted to be friends. Laurell struggled to find something to talk about. You'd think there would be lots to discuss, seeing as how they were to have a child together, but she found it tough to produce banal discourse. Axiom's presence made her want to touch, caress, kiss, not talk.

She cleared her throat. "Exactly how old are you?" She'd wondered about his background and statistics. As good a topic as any.

"It is difficult to say," he responded. "The Grays are

younger gods, by definition. Source started creating us approximately two hundred years ago in Earth time. The Light Gods and Goddesses have been in existence for as long as anyone can remember. None can recall a point of origin, just that they have always been."

"So, none of you were actually born? I mean, there is no beginning for you guys?"

He shrugged. "It is possible we have no particular starting point. Or perhaps it was so long ago, the memory of that time has disappeared from our consciousness."

"Do you recall your first moment of consciousness?" Laurell asked.

The fingers that had been about to press another slice of cheese between his full lips stilled. "Yes. It would be fifty years ago Earth time."

Laurell's eyebrows rose. "You look good for a fifty-year-old. You don't look older than, maybe, thirty," she teased. "Earth time, that is."

His piercing silver eyes roved over her face and settled on her mouth, which curved wryly. "When you smile, your face could light an entire room."

Laurell blinked. Where had that compliment come from? A rush of pleasure bubbled through her. *Wait a minute. Is he trying to distract me?*

"What was it like being born from Source?" she pressed.

He shifted, and his fingers drummed an agitated tune on the tabletop. "I do not remember. No one does. I recall only that it was very lonely." A private pain flitted across his fine features.

Laurell placed her hand atop his, quieting his restless tapping. "Why were you lonely?"

"Most of the Light Gods were kind to us, but they made it clear we did not belong. I was one of the fortunate. By the time I came, the Grays' ability to neutralize Umbrae had been discovered. Those that came before me were studied and observed, but not integrated with the rest of the gods. Some were sent to Earth and not allowed back into the Light Realm.".

Laurell's jaw went slack with shock. "Why in the world would they do such a thing?"

"Even gods fear what they do not understand," he murmured.

"I don't get it," she said. "I don't see what's so scary about you."

His slate eyes pierced her, penetrated to her soul. He didn't have to say it. She knew he remembered a time when she'd found him quite terrifying and had made sure to tell him so. Contrition lanced her. For the second time in the space of just fifteen minutes, she'd been made to regret her words.

She squirmed beneath the scrutiny of his stare. "I'm not afraid of you anymore," she managed to eke out on a shaky breath. Axiom's gaze softened. His arm snaked out and he trailed one finger down her cheek. Electricity slithered through her veins.

"I am glad to hear this," he said, leaning close, so close their lips almost touched. But he didn't kiss her. His mouth hovered over hers, teasing, tantalizing. Sandalwood and spice engulfed her, his scent intoxicating.

"You are?" she whispered, the words released on a heady sigh.

She had to remind herself to breathe. Air swooshed in and out of her lungs. Blood rushed in her ears. Her heart raced in a chest grown tight.

She wanted him to kiss her. Abruptly, he pulled back, and instead of his lips, his finger traced her mouth.

"Yes," he said. "Because tonight you begin your ovulation. Tonight, we will mate."

The throbbing in her sex began as Laurell dressed for dinner. She'd showered, slathered Hillary's homemade, organic, vanilla-and-lavender lotion all over her body, and had just slipped into the chocolate brown peasant-styled dress Lynn had given her that evening, when the first pulse of desire hit.

Someone had told the coven she was ovulating. She suspected that someone was Axiom. First Reese had knocked on her cabin door announcing he'd readied Shakti's Den for them. Then Lynn had appeared at her door, sapphire eyes sparkling, dress in hand. Despite her embarrassment at the fuss, she'd been grateful for the dress, having run out of wardrobe ideas.

She was able to ignore the pulsing between her legs while she blow-dried and styled her hair and applied mascara, blush, and lip gloss. But how was she going to keep it under control during the Dumb Supper, when Axiom would be in the same room with her?

In the dining room, the coven crowded around the table, enjoying their lasagna. Periodically, one of them glanced at the empty chair next to Fiona, where a dinner setting had been arranged to honor the deceased family members of the coven.

Despite the distraction of the yearning, Laurell noted the sorrow behind the poised exterior of their High Priestess, whose hands shook a bit when she lifted her fork. A picture of her dead sister, auburn hair wild about an open and friendly face, sat at the empty spot, along with a faded photo of Hillary's mother and one of Thumper's deceased golden retriever.

Fiona had asked her if she wished to include a picture

of anyone. Laurell had searched her wallet for a photo of her grandmother. No luck. While digging, though, a very old picture emerged from between the mess of credit-card receipts, business cards, and forgotten "notes to self." Laurell had stared at it, trying to remember what it had been like to be the little girl in the photo, held on her pretty mother's lap.

Fiona had asked her about the picture and, upon learning whose likeness it was, suggested she bring it to the Dumb Supper to honor Elaine. Ignoring a twinge of guilt, she had declined.

Laurell turned back to her plate and away from the empty chair next to her, which seemed to her both an accusation and a confirmation of her own lack of familial loyalty. She sipped a glass of merlot, and as the liquid pooled in her belly, heat crept into her limbs that had nothing to do with alcohol and everything to do with the yearning.

Her skin tingled and she sensed someone watching her. *Axiom.* Her gaze twined with his. His silver eyes sparked with a desire dark and deep. His obsidian hair shone in the dim light cast by the chandelier above the table, and his face looked tight and strained. *He's having trouble holding his ward*, she thought.

Though he occupied the seat directly across from her, he seemed much closer. The air around him pulsed, and tendrils of lust swirled through the air, caressing her bare arms like fingers. Her responding shiver didn't have anything to do with temperature.

How much longer could she hold her own ward? Axiom clearly struggled. *No offense to the ancestors, but when will this supper end?*

As though he'd heard her silent plea, Reese cleared his throat and stood. "This concludes our time of silence, but our love, respect, and admiration for those departed continues."

He then offered an explanation of the meaning of Samhain, the witch's New Year, and asked for everyone to state goals and aspirations for the coming year.

Laurell tried to focus on his words, but that proved impossible, given the maelstrom of desire pulsing in and around her.

The responses of the coven, their hopes and dreams and plans for the time ahead, buzzed in and out of her consciousness until their voices mingled, transforming into the white noise of static. She tapped the tabletop with one hand, willing the yearning to calm.

Axiom's hand engulfed hers, sparking a jolt of pleasure that momentarily kicked the air from her lungs. At her sharp inhalation, Axiom rose and was at her side quick as lightning. She didn't even startle at his inhuman speed, just sighed in gratitude when, with one hand under her elbow, he helped her from her seat.

"We must take our leave now," he said, perhaps a bit too loudly. His declaration caused Dawna to jump and interrupted her litany of New Year's resolutions. Almost as one, the coven turned to them with wide eyes and knowing smiles.

Fiona jumped to her feet. "Give me just a few minutes," she said, then hurried from the room. Laurell suspected the woman planned to perform some task at Shakti's Den.

Ten minutes later her suspicion was confirmed. Her limbs trembled with a need so powerful, Laurell found it difficult to walk to the cabin. She leaned on Axiom for support, but couldn't help noticing that his breath sounded labored and short—no doubt from his effort to keep the yearning under control until they'd secured some privacy.

Inside the cabin, candles flickered from every windowsill and available surface. Incense burned in one corner, nestled at the base of a four-foot-tall, golden-hued statue of

Shiva and Shakti locked in a passionate embrace. The sweet aroma filled the room. Paintings of gods and goddesses kissing, touching, holding one another—and one of them doing much more than that—hung on the walls. She might have blushed had the yearning not already squashed her embarrassment.

A king-size bed dominated the space, sheathed in silky sheets of crimson, violet, and amber. She stared, vaguely aware of what that bed represented.

Then Axiom's large frame filled her vision, blocking her view, and all thoughts of the bed, the room, and anything else she might have conjured up fled. He trailed his fingers over her cheek, traced her lips, and then lifted her chin until his smoldering gray eyes danced with hers. The way he looked at her made her heart race with excitement.

"Are you ready for this?" he whispered.

"As I'm going to be," she replied, her voice wavering.

"I have longed for this moment since the first time I saw you," he murmured. She felt her eyes widen at this admission, but hadn't the time to ponder what he meant before a torrent of desire assailed her.

Axiom had released his hold on the yearning.

CHAPTER TWENTY-TWO

Laurell's precarious ward proved no match for the onslaught of Axiom's unrestrained passion. Pleasure arched through her and she grabbed his shoulders with fingers turned claw-like. His mouth crashed into hers and tasted, devoured, and consumed. His tongue plundered, seeking hers, and she gave it willingly. Images of a deeper and more intimate joining invaded her mind as his tongue darted between her lips and then out again. In. Out.

Greedy hands tore at cumbersome clothing. A faint tearing noise met her ears as her dress gave way under Axiom's fingers. She struggled to undo the buttons of his shirt with shaking hands and sighed in satisfaction when he made quick work of it himself. White dress shirt and black slacks pooled between their feet, mating with brown dress and black bra.

Somewhere along the way, she'd kicked off her shoes, though she couldn't remember where. Apparently, Axiom had kicked his off too, as he now stood before her utterly, gloriously nude.

God, but he was a sight, all lean muscles and pale, almost luminous skin with just the right amount of dark hair sprinkled over his chest and trailing to his groin. Desire—sharp, almost painful—stabbed into her in response to the vision of him hard and ready. She reached out, intending to wrap her fingers around the tender tip of his sex, but Axiom stopped her.

"No, not yet," he said. He buried his hands in her hair and his lips pressed hers again. She fell against him, heated flesh molding to heated flesh. Her nipples tingled where they rubbed against his chest. Her sex pulsed with need, and she knew her panties were drenched.

His fingers left her hair and he lifted her easily, dropped her to the bed, and blanketed her with his body. The sheets, cool and soft against her hot skin, mocked the blaze that raged through her veins. She gasped in delight as lips and tongue tasted her neck, then suckled her ear.

She let her own hands explore him, trailed them along his spine, and tickled, teased at the crease of his buttocks, eliciting a harsh intake of breath from Axiom.

When did I get so bold?

The yearning, much as she'd previously hated it, destroyed her usual inhibitions. And right at that moment, as Axiom's seeking mouth closed over one rigid and anxious nipple and another current of sharp pleasure lanced her, Laurell thought the yearning was a wonderful thing.

His tongue licked and teased first one erect nipple, then the other. Cool air tickled her pubic mound and she dimly registered Axiom pulling at her panties.

She started to lift her hips, desperate for his touch there, in that place where she wept with desire, but before she could, he let out a frustrated groan, and a second later the thin scrap of cloth disappeared. Seeking fingers slid through her wetness, a thumb swept softly over her engorged, sensitive nub, and she thrashed beneath him, unable to control herself in response to the waves of exquisite pleasure his touch produced.

Her breathing came faster, laborious. Axiom positioned

himself between her legs then, and at the first nudge of his aroused organ against her entrance, she gasped and her gaze flew to meet his. His eyes glinted with sparks of silver and light, his face taut with his struggle for control. He hesitated, waiting.

For what? she wondered. *Ahhh. For me.* He waited for her acquiescence. For some reason, that small gesture meant everything to her. The slightest tilt of her head signaled her assent, and he plunged inside her, filling her completely.

More magical energy surged, and Laurell's body broke into tremors. Her muscles twitched and pulsed as though they'd turn her flesh inside out. Axiom slid his arms beneath her back and cradled her tightly. Her legs closed over his hips and pulled him into her, and she recognized that the same energy moved through him as his massive frame shook and convulsed. He placed one palm on each side of her face, forcing her gaze to his, as though to watch the ecstasy flicker across her features with each of his thrusts.

His movements inside of her were shallow, then deep. More pleasure. More currents surged until her nerves were raw from sensory overload. Then his jaw clenched and his body tensed. A moment later he roared his release. A heat so intense it bordered on pain shook her womb, and Laurell cried out her surprise.

An inferno flared in her pelvis and she saw stars. It passed as quickly as it had come, and she could see again. Axiom's body grew still atop hers. She blinked, and released her vise-like hold on his shoulders. He lifted his head from its resting place in the crook of her neck and stared at her.

In that moment, she knew without a doubt that she'd conceived. And by the look on his face, Axiom knew it too.

Hours later, Axiom cradled Laurell against his chest, where she feigned sleep. He knew she was awake, he could sense it in the tenseness of her body and the way her pulse sped when he brushed his finger over her neck. He observed through hooded eyes the way the flickering candlelight cast shadows over her creamy, voluptuous curves and highlighted the red streaks in her hair.

She seemed so small, so fragile there, curled into him, her legs tangled with his, long lashes spiked against high cheekbones. His chest constricted with some unnamed emotion, and he did not bother to try to reason that sensation away.

Instead, he let it simmer inside of him. If it was just this body, this human flesh, that ached with adoration and tenderness for the mortal woman, he did not care. The feeling was almost as pleasurable as their mating had been.

An erection stirred at the remembrance of Laurell's passionate response to his touch. His ability to experience her pleasure had intensified his own, making him lose control. He had intended to bring her to orgasm before seeking his own release, but had underestimated the power of the yearning coupled with Laurell's desire.

Now that the Earth Balancer lay safe inside her womb, additional matings were unnecessary. *There is no reason to couple with her again.* The yearning, no longed needed, had dissipated. They could spend the months until the Earth Balancer was born being merely civil and friendly if they should choose to do so.

Axiom chose not to do so. He could not imagine those long months without Laurell's flesh against his own, without seeing desire reflected in her exquisite hazel eyes. He especially enjoyed his part in creating that desire.

At this thought, he decided that he had let her rest—or at least, pretend to rest—long enough. His hand drifted slowly along her spine, then cupped her round, full bottom. He squeezed one cheek and let his finger tease the crevice there. Her eyes flew open, and she jumped, startled.

He grinned with satisfaction. "Ah," he murmured, "did I wake you?"

Her brow knit. "An unexpected hand on my ass will do that." Her tone was light and teasing.

He shifted her to her back and cupped her still-moist mound. "Is this a better placement for my hand?"

Her head jerked in response, and desire darkened her eyes, answering his question. He rubbed the outer lips and playfully tugged at the black, springy curls.

"What are you doing?" she gasped.

"It is time for your pleasure," he answered. His head dipped and he lapped at one nipple. Her back arched and she threaded her fingers through his hair.

"But we already made the baby," she said, each word huskier than the last.

Axiom scooted down the bed, careful to keep his hand on her sex, his fingers sliding up, down, and around the little pearl that peeked out from amidst the closely trimmed triangle of hair.

"True," he said, "but I have not yet brought you to orgasm this night." He had been unable to remove the vision of her flushed face, twisted in rapture, from his mind. He had given in to his body's need for release twice since the day she had burst into his cabin demanding answers and pushing him to the brink of losing control of his ward. Self-pleasuring only left him hollow and still aching for her.

I will witness her pleasure again. Here. Now. Without the yearning to fuel her desire. It will be only me who brings her to her peak.

His face hovered over her pubis and he blew on the area, teasing Laurell until she squirmed. Without the yearning to fuel his actions, Axiom had wondered how he might fare with mating. The intense energy of the yearning had erased all thought and caused him to act on instinct.

This was different. He still desired Laurell—gods, did he desire her!—but he wanted to please her, more than he wished for his own sexual gratification. He recalled the lovemaking rituals he had witnessed between mortals in the past. He had rarely observed human coupling for long, realizing that participants typically considered the act a private one and probably did not appreciate prying eyes.

However, once he had been assigned the role of fathering the Earth Balancer, learning about lovemaking had been one of his assignments.

Now, as his fingers parted Laurell's slippery folds and she lifted her hips in invitation, he was pleased he had paid such close attention to the couples he had viewed in the love act. He knew exactly what Laurell wanted and just how to go about giving it to her.

He slid his tongue along the soft skin, over the outer lips, then deeper. He suckled on the inner lips, tugging them oh, so gently with his mouth.

"Oh god," she moaned.

He released the succulent flesh. "Yes?"

"Don't stop," she pleaded.

Happy to oblige, Axiom dipped his tongue into her entrance and rolled it around inside. She grabbed his head and pressed him closer. She tasted salty and sweet at the same time, a flavor he found pleasing. Her hips began a rocking motion and she used his tongue as she earlier had used his manhood.

His erection grew almost unbearable, but he resigned himself to letting it pulse against the sheets beneath his belly. For now. He lifted his head and then closed his lips over the tiny bundle of nerves shaped into such a pretty kernel.

Axiom licked and sucked the engorged nub as Laurell bucked against his mouth. He pressed one finger, then two, inside of her and moved them in and out in quick succession and sucked harder. With his free hand, he took one nipple between thumb and forefinger and tugged.

"Oh," she breathed, then shuddered and tightened around his fingers, and he knew she had found her release. He wished he could see her expression, but dared not take his tongue from her until certain her orgasm was complete.

Without giving her desire a chance to wane, he lifted himself and positioned his hips between her thighs, erection pulsing.

"Yes," she groaned before her fingers circled him and guided him inside.

What came over him, he could not fathom, but his movements, which he had intended to be slow and leisurely, turned quick and frenzied. An inexplicable need to feel her, to see her, to be felt, to be seen, overcame him. Suddenly, the world slowed and narrowed to that moment in time, to her trusting eyes opened to his, to her slender hands holding his face.

He wanted to . . . to . . . He knew not what.

Axiom grimaced and tried to keep the raw need from his face, but must have failed. In the next moment, moisture welled in Laurell's eyes and in a husky voice she said, "I see you."

The orgasm that ensued shook him to his core.

Afterwards, Laurell feigned sleep again. Axiom held her tightly against his chest and she tucked her head beneath his chin. Despite the fact that he held her, she sensed that, at least right for this moment, she had assumed the role of protector. She didn't know why she'd said those words.

I see you. What had she meant by that? Where had the words come from? Something in Axiom's eyes, something about the way he'd looked at her in that moment before he reached his peak, had touched a place inside of her she reserved for just herself. An isolated, lonely place, where she hid her longing for acceptance, for someone to come along and love her. Just as she was.

Not try to change her. Not try to force her into the mold of a Hollywood legend's daughter or some warped idea of perfection.

Laurell lifted her head. Axiom's full lips and angular jaw were slack with sleep, his brow, normally furrowed with intent, wrinkle free. His breathing, even and strong, sounded in time with her heartbeat. Her chest constricted with an unfamiliar sensation. She tucked her head back under Axiom's chin and bit back the fear that accompanied her realization of what the sensation was. *Hope.*

CHAPTER TWENTY-THREE

A cool hand stroked her cheek, light as air. Sleep departed slowly, and with muddled mind, Fiona woke in the middle of the night and lifted her eyelids.

"Hey, Fi."

Fiona bolted upright, heart thumping so loudly she could hear it. Her sister sat perched on the edge of her bed. Or rather, a filmy, see-through version of her sister.

"I'm dreaming," Fiona said and rubbed her hands over her face. When she removed them, though, Anne was still there.

"No. It's really me." Anne smiled reassuringly.

Fiona's jaw went slack. She ran one hand through her hair and gave herself a minute to focus. Anne was here. In the flesh—well, in the spirit, actually.

"You're really real?"

"As can be. It's Samhain, silly. Did you think I'd miss the opportunity to say hello?"

Fiona felt like clapping herself over the head. Samhain. Veil between the worlds at its thinnest. Why hadn't she realized her sister might try to contact her? "I'm so glad to see you. What's it like on the other side?"

Anne tilted her head to one side. "It's good. I'm good. I'll probably reincarnate soon."

Fiona's eyebrows rose in surprise. "You always said you

wouldn't come back to this place again. You said you'd done all the learning you intended to do on this pit of a planet." Fiona paraphrased her sister's earlier words.

Anne laughed. "Yeah, I did say that, didn't I?"

"Numerous times," Fiona said.

"Well, things look different once you're on the other side. I've still some stuff to learn, things I want to do differently."

"Things that are worth another term on the worst planet in the universe?" Fiona teased, vaguely realizing she and Anne had settled into their usual sisterly repartee.

For a moment, she forgot Anne was dead and that this was a mere spectral version of her sitting on her bed in the middle of the night.

"Yup. Even worth another stint on Earth," Anne agreed. Her laughter faded, and her expression turned serious. "Listen, sis, we need to talk."

"Is it the mission? Do you have a message?"

Anne shook her head. "I'm not the Liaison. As far as I know, everything is going okay with that. I'm here to talk to you about Reese."

Fiona's cheeks heated. Did her sister know she had feelings for Reese? Had she known when she was alive? Guilt pierced her insides.

She forced herself to meet Anne's gaze. "What about him? Do you want me to give him a message for you?"

"No. I want you to give him a message for you." Anne's lips curved into a half smile.

"What? I'm confused."

"Tell him you're in love with him."

Fiona's face turned so hot she feared it might melt off. Shit. She hadn't stopped to think that once Anne was in spirit form, she might be able to pick up on Fiona's feelings for Reese. What else did her sister know? An image of herself thinking of Reese, moaning his name while her hand slid between her legs late at night flashed through her brain. Did her sister know about that too?

"I don't know what you're talking about," Fiona insisted.

Anne rolled her eyes. "Fi, don't deny it. Quite frankly, I knew you were in love with him long before I died. I just wasn't sure I was ready to let him go. Even if it was what he wanted. And I guess I was a bit envious of you."

Fiona frowned. "Envious of me? Why?" And what did Anne mean about letting Reese go?

"Because you still had a chance with him. I don't know if he has feelings for you or not, but I know he sure didn't for me." Anne sighed and shrugged.

"Wait a minute." Realization dawned. "Did you and Reese break up?"

Anne nodded. "Yeah. About a month before I died."

"Why didn't you tell me?" Fiona bit back a surge of anger. She hated the idea of Anne keeping a secret like that from her. They'd never kept secrets from each other. Except she'd neglected to tell Anne she loved her boyfriend. So maybe that was two secrets.

"I hoped he'd change his mind. As if Reese ever changes his mind once it's made up," Anne said with a rueful smile.

Fiona sighed. Reese could be stubborn, alright.

"Why did he break up with you?" Fiona asked.

"He said he just didn't feel the same way for me as he had. We'd been dating so long, you know, we'd become more friends than lovers. I guess if I was honest with myself then, I'd have realized we'd been drifting apart for a while. I just got used to him being my boyfriend. I wanted to hold on to that."

"You never did like change much," Fiona said.

"Well, I'm learning to deal."

They both laughed. Fiona thought it hard to imagine a bigger change than death.

Anne looked serious again. "So tell Reese how you feel. And stop torturing the mother of the Earth Balancer. She is not to blame for my death. And she doesn't have any feelings for Reese or he for her. He's a consummate flirt, as you know."

"Why do you want me to tell him how I feel? I don't want to end up embarrassed." Fiona thought of something else. "And are you sure you're okay with all of this?"

Anne chuckled. "Come on. I'm dead. I'm over my jealousy. Besides, I want to see you happy."

"How do you know about Laurell— Wait a minute, you've been spying!" Fiona's eyes widened.

Anne shook her head vehemently. "I haven't been spying, Fi. I've only checked in on you guys a couple times and I saw you giving Laurell grief. That's all. It's not like you think, you know? We can't just hang out for hours watching your every move. We can only hone in on snippets of your life here and there. It takes immense amounts of energy to hover around the Earth plane."

Anne's form shimmered and grew more transparent.

"You're leaving, aren't you?" Fiona said sadly.

"Yes, my energy is waning fast." Anne smiled a smile so full of love and light, goose bumps broke out over Fiona's flesh, and it became difficult to breathe.

"Anne, there's so much I want to say to you," Fiona said, her words choked on unshed tears.

Anne's hand touched Fiona's cheek again, the barest brush, the puff of air from a sigh. "I know, sweetie. I love you too."

Then she disappeared, fading until all that remained was

a bedroom barely lit by a moon-shaped night-light, and Fiona's heart, which swelled with love for her brave, dead sister. A sister who had just reached out from beyond the grave to give Fiona permission to love her man.

Damn, he was pretty. Laurell slipped back into the only clothes she had with her in Shakti's Den. She pulled the peasant dress over her shoulders with a slight rustle. The dress was a wrinkled mess from spending the night on the floor. Axiom stirred in his sleep, and she stood stock-still for a minute. She didn't want to wake him. He lay on his side, one arm flung over his head. The crimson silk sheet pooled around his narrow hips.

She slipped her shoes on and crept to the door. She didn't know why exactly, but the idea of his waking up, of having to exchange the awkward "night after" banalities, made her stomach say hello to her throat. She needed some time. Time to shower. To think. *To make sense of last night.* She pressed one hand to her belly and thought of the life already growing inside.

A thrill sparked through her. She was pregnant. A *baby.* There would be a baby. A child of her own. Mixed emotions battled for dominance: elation, fear, sadness. She didn't know how to feel, but she was suddenly unsteady, and the room tilted slightly. She needed to lie down, to think. Laurell exited the cabin and hurried through the ice-strewn grass and biting morning air to her own cabin, careful not to look back.

CHAPTER TWENTY-FOUR

"The Earth Balancer has been conceived," Axiom announced that night as the group reclined in folding chairs around a small campfire beneath an ink-black, diamond-studded sky.

He did not miss the way Laurell's head pivoted toward him or how her forehead knitted. Perhaps they should have talked and reached a mutual agreement as to how and when to inform the group, but when he had woken that morning, she was gone. And when he had attempted to speak with her that afternoon, she had not answered his knock, though he had been able to sense her presence on the other side of the cold, wooden door. He had the distinct feeling Laurell was avoiding him. A feeling he strongly disliked.

"Congratulations!" Reese was the first to speak. He hugged Laurell. The others followed, calling out their well-wishes. Hillary hugged first Laurell, then Axiom. All the attention made him a bit uncomfortable. He glanced at Laurell. She wore a strained smile that did not reach her eyes. Apparently, she did not relish the attention either.

"Here you go, Ax," Wayne said, plopping into a chair beside him and holding out a brown cylindrical object. Axiom eyed the thing, then took it, turning it in his fingers. He raised an eyebrow and tilted his head in question. "What am I to do with this?"

Wayne chuckled and tipped his cowboy hat low, then

leaned forward, his voice a conspiratorial whisper. "It's a cigar. Cuban. Shhh. That's between us."

For some reason, Wayne wished the nature of his gift to be a secret. Axiom started to tuck the cigar in his jeans pocket.

"Whoa!" Wayne protested. "Don't do that. You'll bend it. We gotta smoke it now, buddy. It's good luck." Wayne motioned toward Laurell. "You know, for the little guy."

Axiom nodded, though he did not know what his friend meant.

"Here," Wayne said, taking the cigar back and pulling out a cutting instrument. He clipped off one end of the cigar, lit it, and then took a deep inhalation from the other end before blowing smoke from between his lips.

Axiom observed Wayne's movements with interest. He had seen humans performing this ritual before, but had never understood the point of it.

Wayne's brown eyes sparkled with delight as he handed the cigar back to Axiom. "Your turn. Take a puff." Wayne then placed his own cigar in his mouth and smoke came out. "Smooth," Wayne said, his angular features lit with pleasure.

Axiom placed his cigar between his lips and inhaled deeply. Heat seared his throat, and he could not breathe. He broke into a fit of choking coughs. *Not smooth*, he thought. *Not smooth in the slightest.*

"Not so fast, my friend. A fine cigar is a thing to be savored." Wayne patted him on the back.

When he could speak again, Axiom handed the gift back to the other man. "I appreciate your gift, but I think someone else here may enjoy it more than I."

Just then Thumper appeared at Wayne's side, eyes wide behind his round glasses. "Is that a real Cuban cigar?"

Wayne shrugged. "I only had two, but Ax doesn't want his." Wayne tilted his head toward Axiom. "You mind?"

Axiom waved his hand. "By all means."

A moment later, Thumper was happily puffing on the thing, and he and Wayne were immersed in a conversation about the best and the worst cigars they had ever had.

"Can we talk?" He heard Laurell's soft voice at his side. She stood next to his chair, wrapped in the cloak he had given her, cheeks flushed with cold, eyes wrapped in firelight.

"Of course," he agreed. He rose and they left the warmth of the fire circle and found a quiet spot near Laurell's cabin.

Once out of earshot of the others, she spoke. "I think we should get some things straight. You know, lay some ground rules or something."

He had no idea of what she spoke, but he nodded. "Ground rules," he repeated. The sweet scent of vanilla drifted around them. He breathed it in with pleasure. Her scent.

"First off, you don't make announcements about me or the baby without talking to me first," she said. "We need to work together, you know?"

"Yes. Work together," he agreed. Her plump lips were stained deep red. They looked soft and supple. He remembered their taste, their smooth texture, and his pulse sped.

"I mean, if we're going to be parents to this kid, we have to present a united front, right? We need to start that now," she told him, her jaw set with determination.

"We will start now. Of course." Axiom wondered what she wore beneath the cloak. When she had joined the fire circle earlier and had taken her seat, he had noted jean-wrapped legs, but the black velvet cloak hid the rest of her body.

The memory of Laurell's naked curves amidst satin sheets flashed through his mind. His groin tightened, and he shifted his stance; the jeans he wore to please Laurell suddenly seemed a bad idea.

"Axiom, are you even listening to me?"

He forced himself to focus. *How easily this human body becomes distracted by desire once it has tasted it.* All day he had thought of nothing but Laurell and their night together.

"I am listening."

Her lips pursed as though she did not believe him.

He touched her arm through the cloak. "How are you feeling? You are well after last night?"

Her face flushed with more than the chill air. Even in the limited lighting of the tiki torches that lined the walkway, he could make out her blush. He did not mention he had attempted to visit her twice that day to determine her well-being. He sensed she already knew this.

"I'm fine," she told him.

"You are not sore?" He had worried afterwards, in the light of day, whether he might have hurt her in his excitement.

She turned away, hiding her face. "I'm okay. Really."

He frowned and took her chin in hand, tilting her face to his. "Are you certain? I know the moment of conception may have been uncomfortable."

She shrugged. "A little." She stepped back from his grasp. "I'm no worse for the wear." She shivered and movement under her cloak indicated she was rubbing her arms to ward off a chill.

He shifted from one foot to the other and stuck his hands in his pockets. He too was cold, something he did not experience in god form. It did not please him, this new sensation.

Not as copulating with Laurell pleased him. He cleared his throat. Not just copulating. What was it the humans called it? Making love? What had occurred between them was something more than just a physical act.

"So . . ." he hedged, struggling to make conversation. He wanted to remain in her presence, but he could sense her nervous energy. Her stance was stiff, half twisted away from him, as though she were poised to flee. "Did you enjoy our evening together last night?" It was the first thing to pop into his mind.

She jerked back toward him, brows lifted, startled. "Our evening?"

"The sex. You enjoyed it?"

Her cheeks darkened again. "It was great, thanks for asking."

He detected a note of bemusement in her voice. "I should not have asked this question?" They had been as intimate with each other as two humans could be, yet he sensed her discomfort in talking about that intimacy.

"Let's just say I've never met anyone as forward as you. There are certain rules you follow when dating. A guy asking, 'Was it good for you?' is just so cheesy." Her lips lifted in a half smile now.

Axiom sighed. "I do not understand all of these rules. I merely wished to make sure my performance was satisfactory. I studied humans copulating, but it is a different matter to be engaged in such an act oneself."

Laurell's eyes widened, and she cocked her head to one side. "You were a virgin before me?"

Axiom shrugged. "Of course."

"Gods don't have sex?" She stared at him, incredulous. Why did she find this so hard to fathom?

"There is an energy exchange that can occur between two gods. The pleasurable sensations are very similar to what I experienced with you last night, but the mechanics of the process are different."

"Wow. I just assumed you—" She stopped herself and shook her head.

"You assumed what?" He stepped closer, enjoying their discussion, inexplicable happiness filling him as her body relaxed and she made no move to leave.

"It doesn't matter what I thought," Laurell said. "You know what they say about assuming." She chuckled.

No. He did not. She was hopping from foot to foot now, her teeth chattering. He slipped one arm around her waist and pulled her to him, to his warmth. She did not struggle to free herself, and this pleased him. Her head tilted, eyes luminous in shadows cast by twisted tree branches above them. Being so close to her made his chest tight. Her lips, slightly parted, invited a kiss.

"I know you are not comfortable discussing our"—he hesitated—"lovemaking, but I am happy you were pleased with me. I was more than pleased with you."

Dark lashes flew upward. Did he detect a trembling in her limbs? Her mouth drew him forward, his head descended, but just before his lips touched hers, she stiffened and jerked her head back.

"Axiom," she gasped, her voice breathy, anxious.

He blinked, bewildered. "Have I done something to upset you?"

She disentangled herself from his arms and put some space between them. "No. I'm just tired," she said, then quickly retreated to her cabin.

Axiom watched until the door shut behind her and the curtains were pulled tight. He tried to ignore the way her speedy departure stung. *Sex*, he told himself. *This body just wants more of hers.* But as he entered his own cabin and prepared for sleep, he knew he had told himself a lie.

CHAPTER TWENTY-FIVE

The bird flapped its wings and sent dew flying. The night was cold. It wanted to seek shelter in the trees and sleep, but They would not allow this. The bird teetered on the edge of a windowsill of one of the smaller buildings where the people lived. It peered inside and saw the girl that They made it follow, the one with the black hair, reading, while next to her slept a blonde woman.

Keen eyes detected movement, and the bird's neck twisted to see the raven that spoke to the black-haired woman hobble to the cabin's front door. The raven tapped its bill on the door and let out a *rronk* noise. The woman set down her book and hurried to the door. She opened it and the raven hopped inside. The woman smiled and touched one finger to its head, stroking the feathers there.

Then she reached behind her, producing a piece of apple, and the raven took it in its bill before moving back out the front door and edging toward some trees, likely to rest for the night. *Follow*, They commanded. And knowing resistance would prove fruitless, it did.

Laurell tossed in her bed until the covers were a tangled mess. Her lids flipped open to stare at the ceiling. The cabin was pitch-black, save for a sliver of moonlight peeking between the curtain at the window. When she breathed in, she smelled Axiom. It was as though his scent, that combination of musk and sandalwood, was trapped in her nostrils, refusing to fade after their interaction hours before.

He'd made it clear he wanted to have sex with her again. *But he called it making love at least once.* She wondered if that had been a slip of the tongue, or if he really understood what the term meant. She'd been tempted. No doubt about it. She wasn't even really sure why she'd turned him down.

Part of her delighted in the knowledge that, with or without the yearning, he wanted her. The other part of her was scared to death by how she'd felt lying in his arms after their second round of lovemaking.

Laurell lifted her hand and trailed her finger over her bottom lip, remembering how Axiom's mouth felt pressed to hers. He'd said she pleased him sexually. A little smile curved her lips. Here she'd been so worried about her appearance and lack of sexual experience, and he'd been a virgin all along. Not that she'd have had any clue from the way he touched her, the way he kissed, or how his body, fitting perfectly with her own, moved against her.

Laurell rolled to her side and pressed her thighs together in an attempt to relieve the dull ache between them. Funny, now that the yearning was gone, she sort of missed it. It would have given her an excuse to climb out of bed and go to Axiom.

Why do I need an excuse? Why can't I just relax and enjoy myself with him? Because she wasn't a casual-sex kind of girl. And she didn't want to be with Axiom for sex alone. The yearning had made it impossible for her to refuse her body's desires. Without it, whatever happened would be her decision entirely.

Laurell let out a frustrated groan and forced her mind to clear. She had to get some sleep. She found a comfortable position, sank farther into the mattress, and drifted off.

Moments later, her feet stepped onto the now familiar

crystalline ground of the Astral Plane. The sky was a brilliant indigo this time, and the air was heavy with the scent of lilacs. Her mother's favorite flower. Flowers Laurell too enjoyed, and missed once she moved from Wisconsin to Florida; they didn't grow well in the hot climate.

"I'm glad you're here. We need to finish our last discussion."

Laurell whirled to see her mother standing behind her, clad in her usual white flowing garb. She shook her head vehemently. "I don't think so, Mother. I told you they needed to send a new Liaison. I meant it."

"Laurell, I get it. You're angry with me."

Laurell raised her brows. "You think?"

"We need to work through that. And I'm still hopeful we will, but regardless, the Council needs to confirm the progress of the Earth Balancer. You have conceived, have you not?"

Laurell's chest tightened. Well, of course the purpose of her mother's visit was to discuss the mission. She doubted the woman even meant what she'd said about trying to make things right between them.

"You can tell them I'm pregnant. Step One accomplished." Her voice wavered slightly. She grimaced. She would not show any emotion to her mother. And why was she getting upset anyway? Because in any other situation, a woman telling her mom she was pregnant would be cause for celebration?

Elaine nodded. "That's good news."

What did I expect? A hug? Even if it had been offered, the gesture would have felt forced and awkward to Laurell. "That's all I'm going to say. We're done here. Next time, I won't respond to you at all."

A pained expression took over Elaine's face, and her eyes narrowed in warning as if she knew what Laurell was about to do. "Laurell . . ."

Laurell tilted her head to one side, ignored the warning in her mother's voice, and promptly woke herself up.

She blinked her eyes open to confirm she was back in her cabin. The bedside clock indicated she'd been asleep for only twenty minutes.

Maybe she was behaving badly. Maybe it was childish to hold on to her anger at her mother. But the woman sure had given her a lot to be angry about. Was she supposed to forgive and forget just because Elaine was dead?

But Elaine wasn't guilty of everything Laurell had assumed: she hadn't killed herself. *At least she says she didn't.* Yes, she'd reneged on her pre-life agreement to be the Earth Balancer's mother and left Laurell holding the bag—but if she hadn't, Laurell would never have conceived a child of her own.

A pang of guilt sliced through her, but then she remembered the years of being ordered around by her mother and pushed the guilt away. She couldn't let her anger go. That anger had given her strength, kept her going during all the years when she had felt so alone.

She yanked the covers to her chin and reveled in her newfound ability to thwart the astral visits from her Liaison.

"She can't do that," Elaine cried, fists clenched in frustration. She paced the main hall of the Divine Council's meeting chamber, white gown flowing behind her like a flag.

Mobius touched her arm to calm her. "Your concern is understandable. You must give this some time."

"Time?" Elaine snorted. "I'm dead. I have to reincarnate soon. I don't have time."

He cocked his head to one side. She spoke the truth. Her descent to Earth was delayed only by her role in the mission. Once it was complete, she would be reincarnating to learn from the mistakes of her past life and continue her soul growth.

"You said the child has been conceived?"

"That's what Laurell told me."

"Then we have approximately three months' time before the Earth Balancer will be born."

"Three months, not nine?"

"The Earth Balancer will not be completely human, and therefore will not require the usual gestation period," Mobius explained. "Do not give up on Laurell. I believe she will reconsider."

"But she won't talk to me. How am I supposed to make amends if she won't even talk to me? For that matter, how am I supposed to be the Liaison if she keeps waking herself up when I try to contact her?"

"I may have a solution." Willow's soft voice announced her arrival in the chamber. Her golden hair curled over her shoulders, and the full skirt of her robe made a swishing sound as she crossed the room. As usual, her scent, fresh and clean as the air after a summer storm, followed her.

"Do share," Mobius encouraged.

"The grandmother, Helen? Does Laurell not feel affection for her?"

"Yes."

"Why do we not send her to converse with Laurell? Perhaps she can pave the way for Elaine."

Mobius pressed one finger to his chin. "Where is the grandmother, exactly?"

"She is in the Soular Realm." Anticipating Mobius's next question, she said, "And yes, we can break her away from her studies. I spoke with the Soular Council, and they have agreed to release her without penalty so she may assist us."

The Soular Realm was where humans went to study all

of their past lives, in order to determine what errors or progress they had made so they could decide whether or not to return to Earth to continue their learning.

"I believe that is an excellent solution, Willow. Let us brief the grandmother, shall we?" Mobius took Willow's arm then and pulled her out of earshot of Elaine, who had returned to her frantic pacing and appeared lost in thought. "Have you any news of the investigation?"

Willow would know he spoke of the undercover investigation he had initiated after learning that one of the gods had tainted Helen's visions. It was imperative they determine who had attempted to thwart the mission.

Willow shook her head. "Simply questioning the goddesses and gods is getting me nowhere. I have enlisted Avina's assistance."

"We are certain Avina is not suspect?" Avina was the beautiful, fiery-tempered goddess of justice. She was the only deity who could tap into the thoughts of other gods and goddesses, and so could prove instrumental in determining the culprit.

"I am positive, Mobius. Just as you trust me, I trust her," Willow said.

Mobius nodded his agreement. If Willow trusted Avina, he did as well. Willow's judgment was sound. And as the goddess of justice, it was nearly impossible for Avina to be deceitful.

Laurell wandered into the kitchen for the third time that afternoon in search of a snack. The child was making her ravenous. At least, she blamed the child. Maybe she was just stress-eating.

"There's some chocolate cake in the fridge. Hillary made it yesterday," Fiona offered as Laurell walked by.

The two had yet to really discuss the tainted glamour spell, but they'd called an unspoken truce.

"Thanks, that sounds good." Laurell rummaged through the fridge until she found the Tupperware container with the cake in it. Moments later, dessert in hand, she was about to leave when Fiona patted the chair next to her at the dining-room table.

"Sit," she said. Laurell hesitated. The other woman gave her a warm smile and a nod. "I'm serious, have a seat. I want to talk to you."

Wary, Laurell took the chair next to Fiona. The other woman wore a red sweater and blue jeans, and her cherry red hair was tied in a casual ponytail.

Her green eyes were wide with sincerity as she spoke. "I've been a real jerk to you, and I owe you an apology."

Laurell blinked. Was she serious?

"I know I don't deserve your forgiveness, but I hope you'll consider giving it anyway," the High Priestess continued.

Laurell chewed, and stared at Fiona, uncertain how to respond. Should she believe her? She'd seemed just as sincere when she was giving Laurell the fake glamour spell.

"Say something. Please," Fiona pleaded. She twisted her hands in her lap. Laurell had to admit she liked seeing Fiona nervous. She'd started to think the other woman never had a moment of uncertainty.

Laurell tilted her head to the side and took her time formulating a response. When she did speak, her voice was low and even. "Perhaps you can start by explaining why you've been such a bitch to me. I mean, I didn't even have any choice about coming here. What do you have against me?"

"Nothing. Not anymore, anyway." Fiona threw her hands

in the air. "There is no excuse for my behavior. Even saying 'forgive me' seems stupid and it doesn't make my actions excusable, but I think"—she paused and twisted her ponytail through her fingers—"I think I was jealous of you."

Laurell's jaw dropped. "Of me? Why?"

"Well, first off, you're a natural witch, and I've had to work long and hard to learn my craft."

"I assume you realize now that I've had to work hard, too," Laurell responded.

Fiona nodded vigorously. "Yes. I do. I also think I blamed you for my sister's death. I know that part doesn't make any sense."

Laurell sighed. What *does* make sense when you're talking about the death of a loved one? *I blamed my own mother for her death.* Even if she had killed herself, that would have meant Elaine was ill. Could she really be blamed for something done when she was unwell? Laurell shoved these thoughts away for another day.

"And then," Fiona continued, "I thought Reese liked you, and that was driving me crazy." Fiona's face flushed at this admission.

"I can assure you, he isn't interested in me. Nor am I interested in him for anything beyond friendship," Laurell said.

"I know that now. He's a flirt. He's always been a flirt. I've been acting crazy and not like myself." Fiona's voice wavered.

Laurell touched her hand and offered a reassuring smile. "It's okay. Men make us act crazy sometimes."

Laurell grimaced, thinking of how she'd been avoiding Axiom since their lovemaking several nights before. He'd arrived in the kitchen once at the same time she did, and she'd darted around the corner before he saw her. As silly as she knew the behavior was, she was afraid to spend time with him, terrified he'd look at her with those sultry, sexy eyes, and she'd jump him on the spot. She had to snap out of this. There was no use getting more involved with him than she already was. She had to control her raging hormones.

Fiona rose and hovered by Laurell's chair. "Are we okay, then?"

"Sure," Laurell agreed. Fiona bent and engulfed her in a lavender-infused hug. When she pulled away, Laurell halted her with a hand on one arm.

"When are you going to tell Reese?" she asked.

Fiona sighed and opened her mouth to speak, but before she could, a male voice broke in. "Tell Reese what?"

Both women spun around to see Reese's tall, slim frame filling the doorway, blond hair swinging around his shoulders, mouth curled in a sexy smile.

Fiona's quick recovery impressed Laurell. "That you'd better get some cake before it's gone," Fiona said before she hurried from the table to the kitchen. Reese followed, but not before flashing Laurell a quizzical look, to which she simply shrugged in response. She wasn't getting in the middle of this one.

CHAPTER TWENTY-SIX

Dawna dropped to the ground and settled onto her blanket. It was nearing dinnertime, and she could smell the lasagna Fiona had just pulled from the oven. It was Lynn's night to cook. The woman made one mean lasagna. The others were making their way to the main house. She'd join them soon, but at the moment, she just wanted to enjoy the night and some quiet. Chill air caressed her skin and threatened to find a way into her thick, wool jacket. Dawna pulled it tighter and lifted her eyes to the sky—inky black and dotted with diamonds.

A flash of movement at her side and a *rrronk* signaled the arrival of her familiar. Poe swooped down and settled on the ground beside her. He hopped close and tilted his head up, staring at her.

Dawna held her hand out and the bird rubbed his head in her palm. *Hello, my friend. What have you been up to?*

Food, he responded.

Ah, well, what else is new? Dawna scratched Poe's neck.

Must leave. Not safe here. She frowned at Poe's warning. She was quite certain she was not imagining it.

What do you mean? she pressed.

Circle not safe. Umbrae will find you here. Poe fluttered his blue-black wings and wobbled back and forth on his little legs. If a bird could look agitated, this one did.

Do they already know we're here? she asked, her chest constricting with worry and her heartbeat speeding up.

Not yet. Soon.

Dawna's mouth twisted. She'd often gone to her familiar for advice in the past. The bird had an ability to connect with the unseen world that she did not possess. So far, he had always been right. She didn't like this. Not one bit. She scratched him beneath his bill and noticed his little piece of string was missing again.

Let's get you a new tie. Looks like you lost yours yet again. Maybe a new color? How does green sound? It's very Yule. The holiday was just around the corner.

Poe hopped onto her arm, and she rose and headed to her cabin, intending to talk to Fiona about Poe's message the first chance she got.

She was avoiding him. Of this, Axiom had no doubt. For the past week Laurell had all but run away whenever they crossed paths. She was not behaving in an adversarial manner, no, but some excuse always surfaced for why she could not remain in his presence. Either she had training with Fiona, or the child was making her hungry, or she needed a nap.

Always, an excuse. He was fairly certain she had been in the kitchen the other day, but when he had turned the corner, she was gone. Her familiar vanilla scent, however, had still clung to the air and made him ache.

He did not like it, this strange sensation in his chest. A painful hollowness had sprung up inside of him. When he breathed in, he could not achieve a full breath. And the nights. The nights were unbearable. He could think of nothing but Laurell. Of her touch, her scent, her taste. The entire situation was unacceptable.

He could not sleep. And he worried that if his human body did not get some rest soon, he would be unable to fight off the pull of his shadow side. He could sense that part of him, buried deep and held carefully in check, pushing at its boundaries. It seemed to be getting stronger as his time on Earth continued.

Which was why he stood outside her cabin door late at night, a week after they had conceived the Earth Balancer. There was no yearning to spur him to go to her, yet he was driven to be near Laurell just the same. Humans called it love. If that was what he felt, he hoped it would dissipate soon. *Perhaps, once I leave this human body and return to the Light Realm, it will fade.*

In the meantime, he could not bear the distance she seemed intent on putting between them. He raised his hand, hesitated for just a moment, and wondered at his nervousness. He was a protector of the Light Realm, a god.

And yet, facing this one small human female made his bones turn to liquid and his stomach twist. He felt like the most unseasoned of warriors being sent into battle. His fist met the wood door with a resounding thud. Louder than he had intended.

He sensed movement inside the cabin, then a dim light switched on. The door swung open to reveal the object of his desire. Laurell leaned against the doorjamb wearing a pink sweatshirt and gray sweatpants. Her hair, which had grown to just below her ears, was tangled and mussed, her big eyes soft with sleep.

"I am sorry I woke you," Axiom said.

She tilted her head and crossed her arms. "What's wrong?"

"Nothing."

"Then why are you here? It's the middle of the night. And it's freezing out there." She shivered and rubbed her hands over her arms.

Axiom climbed the last step to the cabin door. He stood close to Laurell, so close he could smell her sweet scent.

"Nothing, except that you are avoiding me," he added.

Her eyes narrowed. "Axiom . . ." She did not attempt a denial.

"Nothing, except I cannot sleep. I cannot stop thinking of you." He grimaced. "And this body wants yours. There is no yearning, yet I am unable to push you from my thoughts."

Perhaps she saw the desire in his gaze, because her arms dropped to her sides and her breath caught.

"Do you understand?" he asked. She nodded. Axiom stepped into the cabin and, twisting his arm around her waist, tugged her in with him. He kicked the door shut and pulled her tight against him, burying his face in her neck. She did not move to be free of his embrace. Her body melted into him, and she raised her arms and circled his neck.

Ah, but she felt good. His flesh sung with need for her. He wished for the yearning in that moment, because then he would know what she was feeling. Without its benefit, he had nothing but her words to rely on, and that made him feel powerless.

He pressed a soft kiss to the tender flesh at the nape of her neck. She shuddered. He lifted his head to read her eyes. They were wide, glistening.

"What is it?" he whispered. How beautiful she looked in the half light, face scrubbed clean, lips parted, eyes seeking. . What did she seek? He touched one finger to her smooth cheek. "You are upset. Tell me what troubles you."

"I—" she started, then stopped, her voice husky with emotion held stubbornly in check. The irony of this did not escape his notice; it seemed he was not the only one who struggled to control the feelings growing between them.

"You are afraid?" he spoke for her, when she could not.

"Yes," she said, her spine stiffening a little.

"Of me?" he asked. She gave a half nod, and he saw it: her fear. It lanced him like a sword through flesh. "What do you fear? You know I will not harm you."

Her eyes fluttered downward and her teeth worried her lower lip. "It's silly. I'm being silly," she finally murmured. "I know you wouldn't hurt me."

Axiom rubbed circles over her back and neck until her face softened and her body relaxed again.

"Laurell, I need you." The words left his lips before he could ponder them. *I do need her.* What that meant, exactly, he did not know.

She blinked, and her gaze bored into his. Her hands pulled at his neck, directed his head closer to hers. She stoop on tiptoe and kissed him.

Heat flared, and he gratefully relinquished hold on his desire. He moaned into her mouth, kissed her back. Her tongue darted out and met his as the kiss deepened and he could no longer tell who was kissing whom. Not that it mattered. All that mattered was that this time she did not turn him away.

Laurell stretched languidly and, lifting her legs, pushed her bedcovers aside. She allowed her legs to plop down atop the comforter, careful not to disturb Axiom, who slept soundly beside her. He lay on his back, one arm flung over his face as though to keep out the sunlight streaming in through the window. The slightest of snores drifted through the cabin, and his naked chest rose and fell as he breathed the deep breath of slumber.

Funny, he didn't look much like a god right then. She stifled a giggle, thinking she'd worn him out last night. In the next moment, she sighed deeply and shook her head. *Don't get giddy, girl. Giddiness means there's more going on here besides really mind-blowing sex.*

She'd slept well last night. In fact, for the past week and

a half, she'd slept better than she ever remembered sleeping in her life. Ever since Axiom had taken to appearing at her cabin door each evening, eyes filled with need, looking like the dark god he was.

He is gorgeous. Her gaze washed over his face and form. His hair was matted, his thick, black eyebrows slanted over lids pressed tight, long lashes fanning his cheeks. His jaw was slack, his full lips parted in repose. She thought of waking him so they could make love again. Moisture marked her thighs at the thought. Would she never get enough of this man?

She decided to let him sleep a little longer and settled back down beside him, breathing in his scent, sandalwood and musk. She'd have to ask what cologne he wore. She assumed it was cologne, anyway. Did gods wear cologne or did they just naturally smell yummy? She'd ask him when he woke up.

Her stomach growled and she patted her belly, silently communing with the child as was becoming her habit. *Hang in there, little guy. I know you're hungry too.* She froze, and the hand rubbing circles on her midsection stilled. She glanced down at the small bump there. Bump? How could that be?

Laurell lifted the bedsheet. Yup. There was a bump alright. Wasn't it too early for the baby to be showing? She scooted from the bed and made her way quietly to the bathroom, scooping up a cotton shirt and a pair of jeans on the way. She slipped the shirt over her head and grabbed her toothbrush from the counter. She made a mental note to talk to Hillary about the baby. Surely the midwife could shed some light on the stages of pregnancy.

"Dawna, I know Poe is your familiar, and I know you trust him, but there's no reason to think we're anything but safe here." Fiona shifted in her seat on the paisley-printed wingback chair.

Dawna and Lynn reclined opposite her on the over-stuffed beige couch. The faint aroma of the apple sausage Wayne had brought back from a recent supply run still hung in the air of the main house.

Dawna groaned and tucked legs sheathed in ebony leggings beneath her. "Why won't you guys listen to me? Poe doesn't lie, and you know ravens walk between the worlds."

Lynn leaned forward and touched her partner's knee in reassurance. She brushed her honey-colored hair over one shoulder. "What did Wayne say?"

Magic the cat leaped into Fiona's lap, and she rubbed his fur absently. His grateful purr filled the room. "I told Wayne what you said and he did a sweep of the property again. He senses no Umbrae anywhere near."

Dawna's eyes, heavily circled with neon green eye shadow, widened. "Poe said it would happen soon, not that it's happened already. You guys don't want to listen to me because I'm the least skilled of the group. You think I'm not seasoned enough to be able to tell when my own familiar is giving me a message."

Lynn grabbed Dawna's hand and shot her girlfriend a warning look, then smoothed her free hand over her jeans and turned back to Fiona. "We know you're not saying that, Fi. Dawna's been a bit jumpy lately. Ever since she accidentally got me with the athame."

Dawna dropped Lynn's hand. She shook her head vehemently. "This has nothing to do with that, Lynn. That was an accident. It could have happened to anyone."

Fiona noted Dawna's cheeks flush, though, making her lingering embarrassment over the episode clear. "Look," she began, "no one doubts your prowess as a witch, Dawna. If we did, you wouldn't be here."

Dawna's pursed lips softened a little at the remark, and Fiona pressed onward. "We also realize the strength of your ability to communicate with animals—"

"Well, just birds, really, so far," Dawna interrupted sheepishly.

"Poe in particular," Fiona finished. Dawna nodded. "Is it possible, however, that Poe could be mistaken? Could he be picking up a potential danger, versus a definite one? I thought sometimes it could be difficult to tell the difference between the two?"

Dawna frowned. "Sometimes it's tough, yeah, but this feels to me like a definite."

Fiona nodded. "And I know you've been working on enhancing your psychic ability—"

"Come on, Fiona. Next to Anne, Dawna's intuition is the best in the group." This came from Lynn, whose jaw was tense now, her brow knitted.

Fiona groaned inwardly. Dawna was inexperienced. She was powerful, yes, but still learning, just as Thumper was still learning. As Laurell was still learning. There was no shame in that, yet she sensed saying this would hurt Dawna's feelings.

"Even if it were true, if the Umbrae were to find us here, they can't break through the protection circle."

"What about when we recast at full moon?" Lynn pointed out.

"There's not enough time between circle fall and circle cast for more than one or two of them to slip through. As long as one of us guards each quarter, the circle will be cast before they can do any real damage."

"And Axiom could deal with the one or two that might make it through," Lynn responded.

Fiona nodded. "Not to mention us witches. I'm sure we'd be of some help." She gave a half smile, but Dawna only scowled.

"Why don't we pose the question to the rest of the group?" Lynn suggested. "Do a majority rules sort of thing?"

"Good idea. Let's take it to the rest of the group," Fiona agreed.

Later that night a coven meeting was held. The pros and cons of leaving the covenstead were discussed. The group decided to stay put. This news sent Dawna stomping out of the main house, Lynn trailing behind her. Axiom suggested Laurell attempt contact with her Liaison that evening to see if there was any word from the Light Realm, any indication they should be concerned about their security on Fiona's property.

Fiona didn't miss Laurell's grimace at this request, nor the way Axiom touched a finger to her forehead, smoothing the wrinkle from it and making her smile. Laurell's eyes flashed with affection, and Axiom gazed at Laurell as if she were the most beautiful thing he'd ever seen. Just that morning, she'd seen Axiom exit Laurell's cabin, disheveled and sleepy-eyed. She hoped Laurell knew what she was doing.

CHAPTER TWENTY-SEVEN

"I'll be pregnant for how long?" The words burst from Laurell's mouth in astonishment.

"Three months," Hillary responded, eyes soft with empathy.

Laurell placed splayed fingers over her rapidly thickening middle. "I look like I'm three months along already, Hill, and it's only been a few weeks."

They stood in Hillary's cabin. Laurell had sought out the other woman after waking up that morning and realizing her belly had bloomed seemingly overnight. As usual, Hillary's cabin was peaceful, with music tinkling in the background and nag champa incense burning. Her smooth, lovely face was serene. Laurell wondered if anything ever fazed the woman; she had an air of solidity and strength Laurell admired.

Hillary crossed the floor, her long velvet skirt rustling. She lifted Laurell's red sweater and put her warm fingers on Laurell's stomach. "Hmmm. Yes. You do look about three months along. But Axiom said you'd only be pregnant for three months, so I assume that means, technically, the baby is as developed as a child would be at three months."

Laurell grimaced. "No wonder I'm so ravenous all the time. This kid needs tons of food to grow so fast."

Hillary nodded. "A healthy appetite is good. Make sure

you're getting fruits and vegetables and well-balanced meals. Not just those cookies I saw you munching on yesterday."

Laurell couldn't hide the guilt on her face. "Well, I only ate a few of those." She couldn't seem to help herself. She craved sugary foods.

Hillary wagged a finger at her. "You heard me, young lady. You've got a very important baby cooking in there. He's going to need lots of nutrients so he can be strong when it's time for him to face down those Umbrae."

Laurell sighed. "Yeah. I know." It wasn't as if she could argue. It didn't take a medical background to know the baby needed more than sweets to thrive.

Laurell turned in front of the full-length mirror resting against the far wall. The bump beneath her sweater was already fairly obvious. Although on the one hand giving birth and being able to move on with her life sooner seemed a good thing, it also meant the reality of being a mother was going to come quicker than she'd anticipated. Her stomach twisted, and panic surged and threatened to take hold, but she stamped it down. She'd be a good mother. A great one, in fact. She'd be nothing like her own mother.

Elaine hadn't attempted contact with her since the last time Laurell had refused to speak with her. Which was just fine with Laurell. Mostly. Some part of her still experienced a twinge of guilt over the way she'd left things with her mother. Realizing she was going to have a child of her own was making her rethink that situation.

Would she want her child to be so unforgiving? Would she want her child to live in the past so much he refused to embrace his future? She might never be able to forget the harshness of her own childhood and might never be able to forgive her mother for making life so difficult for her, but shouldn't she try? At least call a truce—not for her mother, but for herself?

And the child in her womb for whom she'd be setting an example.

Laurell's brow furrowed and she focused on Hillary again. "Are you sure my body can handle this accelerated pregnancy? I mean, is it dangerous?"

Hillary tsk-tsked. "My dear, you are worrying too much. Of course you can handle it. Nothing is the usual here, you know. The goddesses and gods would not put you or the child at risk."

Laurell didn't point out that the entire mission put them at risk. But she understood what Hillary meant. Hillary's warm, brown gaze washed over her, and Laurell was suddenly overcome with affection for her new friend. She pulled the other woman into a hug. Hillary hugged her back, and Laurell found her touch comforting.

Then Laurell drew away, her cheeks warming. She wasn't usually so demonstrative; she'd been more emotional than usual of late. *It must be the baby*, she thought. The baby. An idea dawned.

"Um, Hill, this kid isn't going to come out like an alien child or anything, right? I mean, he's going to look and be normal?" *As normal as a child born from a god and a witch can be.*

The other woman let out a loud guffaw. "Oh my Goddess, you do worry a lot, don't you?" Hillary wiped tears of amusement from her eyes, chuckling.

"Come on. It wasn't that funny."

Hillary shook her head. "It was pretty funny." Then, when Laurell pinned her in place with the sternest look she could muster, Hillary said, "As far as I'm aware, the child will look human and, other than accelerated growth, will have all the normal human characteristics. Except for the ability to dispel Umbrae with a touch."

Laurell's lips lifted in a half smile. "Yeah. I guess that's not quite normal, huh?"

Hillary was still chuckling. "Not quite."

To work with the element of water, you must embrace your emotions. You must dive deep into the pains of your past while touching fresh hurts and facing them head-on. The fragility of life, of being human, must be acknowledged. You need to accept your vulnerability and be one with it. A surface attempt to touch the water element will not work. You have to accept your pains, release them, and realize they serve a purpose in your life. You must be willing to cry, to be needful, and to admit defeat.

Laurell perused the *Book of Shadows* and read over a spell for working with the water element, which apparently had been written into the journal by a great-aunt she'd never known. She'd been practicing with Fiona more on her elemental magic, and was still unable to draw the water into more than a half-inch stream.

Her fire skills, though, were top-notch. Just that afternoon, she'd sparked fire at least ten feet in the air simply by focusing on the flames and willing it so. Fiona told her that once she became really adept at elemental magic, she wouldn't need a physical vehicle to focus on; she'd be able to conjure the element out of thin air.

She set the book aside, rose from her bed, and peered through one of the cabin windows. It was the end of November, midnight of a full moon. The coven had held their usual full-moon ritual and afterwards, Fiona had shooed Laurell off to her cabin for protection, then led the group away to recast the protection circle about the entire property.

She hated being shoved away like some helpless child. She was a witch, too, dammit. And she had power—perhaps not as refined as the rest of them, but she was getting there. Laurell bit her lip. She paced the floor, her movements jerky, her spine stiff. She needed to get out of her cabin. Her need for independence was rearing its head.

She shrugged into her wool jacket and rifled through her dresser for the pair of black gloves Wayne had brought back for her from his last supply trip to town. Winter was settling in, and the air, especially at night, was frigid. Way too cold, Laurell thought, for someone whose blood has thinned from years of living in Florida. When she stepped outside, a pang of homesickness filled her. She'd have been wearing sandals and a tank top if she were in Florida.

The air still smelled of the bonfire Thumper had created earlier for the ritual. She inhaled deeply. She loved that scent. Scooping up the flashlight she had hanging on a peg by the door, she clicked it on and followed its thin beam as it bounced between the trees.

She entered the ritual circle and found only Thumper there, tending the fire. Flames leaped and danced as she approached him.

"Hey," he murmured, barely glancing up. Then, as he realized she was disobeying Fiona's orders, his eyes narrowed and anxiety crossed his youthful features. "You're not supposed to be out here."

Laurell patted him on the arm. "I know, I know. They're almost done, though. And I was going stir-crazy in my cabin."

Thumper sighed and gave a small smile. "I can imagine. I sometimes feel the same way being confined to Fiona's property."

"Exactly." Laurell sat on the log behind him. After another couple of moments spent poking the fire, he perched next to her, leaning the poker next to him. "So, how come you don't help cast circle?" she asked.

"Well, it's not a good idea to leave the fire unattended. And I'm the least experienced with casting the protection circle. I think they want to keep me safe or something." He looked embarrassed at this admission.

"You're the youngest of the group, right?"

"Dawna's younger, but I think the rest of them look at me like a kid brother or something."

"Or maybe they realize how much power you have and they don't want it jeopardized."

Thumper shrugged. "It doesn't matter. Dawna has the same problem with the group, but, you know, she's just so powerful, I think they have more faith in her abilities then they do in mine." His admiration for Dawna was obvious, and the tenderness in his gaze when he spoke of the black-haired witch made her heart swell.

"It must be hard to be in love with someone who doesn't return the feelings," she murmured. The words were out before she could stop them. Thumper's spine straightened, and he cleared his throat, glancing toward the fire.

"Oh! I'm sorry. That's none of my business," she muttered hastily.

"It's okay. I figure it's obvious to everyone how I feel about Dawna."

"It is." She touched his arm in reassurance. "There's nothing to be ashamed of, though."

Thumper shrugged. "I know, and I know she doesn't feel the same, but loving someone is never a waste."

He retreated to the fire, his head ducked toward his chest as he turned inward. Laurell's chest tightened. She was an idiot. An absolute idiot.

"You are not in your cabin." Axiom's deep voice interrupted her thoughts. The hair on the back of her neck rose, and her body hummed with his nearness. He was behind her, so close his breath tickled her ear. She breathed his scent in, and a familiar ache began between her thighs and traveled to her chest until she found it tough to breathe.

She twirled to face him, and pressed her hands to his chest. "I'm naughty," she whispered, suddenly feeling just that.

He chuckled and wiggled his eyebrows. She tried to do the same back, but failed miserably. *Must be another of his god powers.*

"Everything went okay with the circle casting?" she asked.

"Yes. No sign of Umbrae." He threaded his fingers through hers as raucous laughter trickled to them from the woods, signaling the rest of the coven was approaching. "Let's go before Fiona sees you and insists you do penance for your disobedience." Amusement sparked in his gaze.

"Did you just make a joke?" She couldn't remember Axiom as anything but serious and focused on the mission. With the jeans and sweaters he'd started wearing instead of suits, the way his hair had grown and started to curl over his collar, and now, his joking manner, she hardly recognized him as the same man who had whisked her away from that graveyard not so very long ago.

"It was an attempt at one, though no doubt I need practice. Is that such a surprise to you?"

"Frankly, yes."

"Come to my cabin, and I will give you more surprises," he said, leaning closer, his voice a whisper.

CHAPTER TWENTY-EIGHT

"Some of the Council members have refused to submit to my questioning," Avina announced, breezing into Mobius's private chambers. He glanced up from the amethyst tablet he was studying and thought the doors humans had in their structures could be very useful. His dwelling, like all structures in the Light Realm, was created and maintained with his mind. Today, Mobius resided in a room made entirely of violet and silver quartz crystal. He had also discarded his usual white robe for one of deep purple.

Unfortunately, gods and goddesses could move into each other's mind dwellings without effort, though out of politeness, most refrained from doing so without announcing their arrival. Avina had to be quite agitated and distracted to have entered his chambers in such a hurried, informal manner.

The raven-haired goddess's amber eyes assessed him with one sweep of her lengthy lashes. "That color suits you, Director. It presents a pleasant contrast with your hair." Mobius thought the purple probably contrasted rather harshly with his red hair, but accepted the compliment nonetheless.

Mobius nodded. "Thank you. Now what is this you speak of? Who is refusing to speak with you?"

Avina's jaw hardened in frustration. "Helios, Rhakma, and Willow."

"Willow?" Mobius could not hide his surprise.

Avina nodded. "Yes."

"She would not cooperate? Why? She has nothing to hide." Helios and Rhakma he could well understand refusing interrogation by Avina. After all, they had both made their views on the mission quite public. Avina's ability to read their thoughts would ferret out even the tiniest inclination either one of them might have toward usurping Mobius or thwarting the mission. No doubt they had considered at least the former. Their involvement in the latter remained to be determined. Either way, it was unlikely they would want Mobius to know of their desire for him to give up his seat as Divine Director.

But why would Willow refuse?

"I do not know for certain, but she seemed very uncomfortable with the idea that you would be given a transcript of my session with her." Avina folded her arms across her chest.

"It is unavoidable. I must review all transcripts."

"Yes, I know."

"Arrange for the three to meet with me individually. I will assess their motivations and make them understand the implications if they continue to refuse questioning." He frowned. If Avina had to force her ministrations on them, it could be quite painful, even for a god or goddess. It would be infinitely better for all were they to acquiesce.

Axiom was woken in the middle of the night by a soft hand wrapped around his most sensitive part. His eyes flew open to a sight that made him appreciate his superhuman vision. Cast in shadows and moonlight, Laurell crouched between his legs, pert breasts swinging, nipples tickling the hair on his thighs. She was naked, her skin still flushed from their earlier lovemaking. Her hazel eyes were dark with devilish intent. His cock immediately hardened.

"What are you about down there?"

"Down here?" She teased him, brushing her chest over

his engorged flesh, her supple skin like a whisper of silk against him.

He groaned. "You could not sleep?"

"No. I want you again." Her tongue darted out and licked the tip of him. His jaw tightened, and he sucked in air.

"I haven't done this for a while," she murmured. "I didn't think you'd mind if I practiced."

Practiced what? A second later he knew just what when her plump lips closed over him and she suckled his engorged length. She took him deep into her mouth, impossibly deep, and the sucking motion sent rivers of pleasure flowing through him.

"You have not done this to me before," he gasped. With her free hand, she traced circles over his scrotum until the flesh there grew taut.

She lifted her head for just a moment. "You never give me a chance. You're so busy pleasuring me that by the time we're done, I can barely keep my head up." Her breath tickled his wet skin. "Not that I'm complaining," she added.

Before he could respond, she took him into his mouth again. Her hands and lips worked him until his heart raged so fast he thought it would burst from his chest. He fought to breathe.

The orgasm burst forth with such ferocity, he howled, a sound that was rife with joy and ecstasy. Afterwards, she curled next to him, wrapping her shapely curves around him like a cat. She tucked her head beneath his chin and trailed slender fingers in lazy patterns over his chest.

He cupped her shapely bottom in his palm and pulled her closer. She sighed and pressed tiny kisses to his neck. Goose bumps shivered over his skin.

Axiom lifted his free hand and trailed it through her shiny hair, letting the strands fall from his fingers before repeating the process.

"You're petting me," she murmured into his neck.

His hand stilled. "Is that acceptable?"

"Hmmmm."

He continued his stroking. He was completely satiated, one hundred percent satisfied. Laurell's warm body close to his, her contented sighs, the ache in his chest, all of these things made his heart dance with delight. In that moment he could think of no place he would rather be.

"Laurell," he murmured.

"What?" came the sleepy reply.

"Is this what love feels like?"

She stiffened and tried to pull away, but he held her fast and continued touching, smoothing her hair.

After what seemed like a very long time, she whispered, "Yes."

The bird watched the women from the trees, cloaked in night. It listened intently because They wished to hear. It hopped to the furthest branch when the dark-haired witch started to walk away from the light-haired one, careful not to make a sound.

"Dawna, you've got to stop this. The group made a decision, and we have to support that decision," the blonde said.

"I can't believe no one will listen to me. I'm so tired of being treated like I'm some kid who needs the coven's protection. I have just as much power as any of them."

"Why are you taking this so personally?"

"Because it *is* personal. It's not only me they won't listen to, it's Poe. He's never lied to us before. He has no reason to lie to us now."

The blonde touched the black-haired woman's arm and shook her head. "No one said Poe is lying. We said he may be mistaken. You may be mistaken."

The black-haired one pulled her arm from the other's grasp. "Doesn't my intuition count for anything?"

"We've gone over this a zillion times. It counts, but even the most accurate psychic is only about eighty percent accurate, Dawna. You know that as well as I do."

"Except Anne was more like ninety-nine percent accurate."

"No one is expecting you to take Anne's place."

"Of course not. How could I? I clearly don't have the same power she did." She stalked off, disappearing into the trees, her black garment making a swooshing noise.

"Come on, Dawna. You know I didn't mean it like that!" the blonde called after her.

Should I follow? the bird asked Them.

No. The rest of the evening is yours.

Several days later, Laurell stepped from Axiom's cabin on a windy Saturday morning that was dark and overcast. It was the most beautiful morning ever, to her, though. White powder dotted the frozen ground and clung to the tree branches. Tiny flurries cascaded all around and landed on her nose and lashes. She stuck her tongue out and tasted one as she used to do as a kid. The flake immediately melted.

"Axiom, hurry up!" she called, descending the outside stairs.

Axiom appeared behind her wrapped in his usual ankle-length black coat and tugged the door to the cabin shut behind him. Together, they made their way to the main house for breakfast. Axiom walked slowly, stopping to look at the sky and touch the falling snow with his fingertips.

"You've never seen snow?" she asked.

"I know of it, but have not seen it firsthand."

Laurell grinned. "It's been ages for me." She bent and scooped some snow into her palms, rolling it into a ball. She darted away from Axiom and tossed the snowball at him. It smacked his chest and left a wet trail down the front of his coat.

He frowned, confusion flashing over his face. "You pummeled me with ice."

She grabbed more snow, forming one, two, three little balls. "Pummeled you? Hardly! This is pummeling!" She threw the snow at him, each ball in quick succession. All three hit their mark. Of course, she was only ten feet away.

"What—" he started, but then his mouth curved and his eyes flashed with mischievousness as he realized it was a game. He followed her lead, grabbing snow and packing it into balls. Laurell figured she'd better put more distance between them and ran ahead, scooping another snowball as she went.

He lifted his arm and a moment later, a snowball made impact with her shoulder.

"Not bad for a beginner," she teased.

"Perhaps I can do better." Another chunk of snow hit her in the thigh.

"Better, but still needs work." She tossed one back at him, but missed.

"Ha!" he cried.

She took aim, and this time the snowball struck Axiom's forehead, eliciting a wide-eyed look of surprise from him. His eyes narrowed and suddenly his arms were a blur of motion and a stream of snowballs came flying her way. Laurell yelped and ducked behind a nearby oak just in time. The snowballs made a loud *whack, whack, whack* as they hit the tree.

"Not fair! You can't use your powers," she called from her hiding spot. She'd forgotten how quick he was.

"You did not explain that rule to me." Axiom's deep voice directly behind her and his breath tickling her nape made her jump and whirl. He wound one arm around her and pulled her close to his body. With his free hand he brushed stray hair from her eyes. The snow fell more densely around them, and little specks of white dotted Axiom's thick ebony hair.

His gaze was soft, adoring. "You are beautiful," he said.

Laurell's insides turned mushy. Her throat constricted. Right then, in his strong arms, she *felt* beautiful.

Later that day, Axiom left Laurell with Fiona, who was intent on teaching her various aspects of spell work, and took a walk in the woods. Wayne was finishing his lunch and said he would join him shortly to assist in their weekly sweeps for any indication of the Umbrae nearby. Laurell promised him she would attempt astral contact with her mother that night. He knew she did not wish to interact with her Liaison, but he pushed her to do so anyway. He would feel better about their safety if the Council were to confirm it. He could not seem to erase his feelings of unease.

It did not help matters that ever since her warning of doom was disregarded by the coven, Dawna had been sullen and withdrawn. She spent most of her time with the raven Poe, conversing silently with the bird. Her partner, Lynn, had expressed her worry to Axiom just that morning. He had reassured her all would be well, but was not so certain of this himself.

He trudged toward the north side of the property, keeping his senses open for any hint of Umbrae. He took in each tree branch, each leaf left on every plant or bush. All appeared normal.

His midsection suddenly burned, and it became difficult for him to breathe. He almost lost his footing but managed to stumble a few feet to a nearby tree, where he leaned and struggled for air. Pain sliced his stomach, sharp and hot. Every muscle in his body clenched, released, clenched again.

"Ahhhh," he groaned as a wave of dark energy made his body spasm. His teeth ground together hard enough that, had be been human, they would have cracked. He knew what it was, of course.

Earth's dark side. The evil force that was spreading corruption, depravity, and cruelty over the planet like a virus. That same malicious power seeped into his veins, pulsed through his heart, and called to the part of him buried deep. Axiom gasped and willed it away. *Not now. No. Not ever.*

Would it never admit defeat? How many times must he fight the dark force before he was left in peace? Images vulgar and horrifying flooded him: hatred, blood and pain, unspeakable and repulsive things that made bile rise in his throat and his stomach lurch with nausea.

He called to his own light, focused it, and made an effort to strengthen his aura. The black power still clung. It assaulted all that was bright and luminous in him, and he fought against the attempt to defile his spirit.

"Ax, what is it?"

With great effort, Axiom lifted his head. Wayne stood a few feet away, wearing an expression of concern. Axiom tried to speak, but could not. The evil sensed Wayne's luminosity, his inner radiance. And wanted to stamp it out. Wayne stepped closer to him, and the Gray God held his hands up to ward him off.

"Don't!" Axiom managed to grunt the word from between jaws tense with his inner struggle. He closed his eyes tight, clenched his hands into fists, and pushed, thrusting his light force through his entire being until he was flooded with the potent wash of its vibrant current. Air returned to his lungs and he gasped it in greedily. The god force pulsed and threaded its way through his aura, dug beneath his skin and through his organs, soothing, calming, battling the shadow force until it had dissipated completely.

Seeming to realize the threat was gone, Wayne stepped close and grabbed Axiom's arm. "Are you alright? What just happened?"

Axiom nodded and focused on the other man's open face, the warm concern in his eyes. He would have to explain this to Wayne. His shame would no longer be just his own private disgrace.

"I will tell you, but I must have your complete and total silence on the matter. No one else may know of this." His heart was finally slowing, his pulse returning to normal. He could actually hear more than the sound of his own blood rushing.

Wayne's eyebrows rose. "You have my word, Ax. Now tell me what the hell is going on."

CHAPTER TWENTY-NINE

Laurell stepped onto the Astral Plane and willed the place into a symphony of metallic colors. Gold, bronze, silver, and rose hues sparkled and shone over the ground and sky, brilliant, dazzling. She scented the air with lilacs and waited. She took a seat on a large crystal boulder and smoothed the plain white gown she wore.

"Mom," she called out. "I'm here." No answer. She turned her head this way and that, searching for any sign of life.

"Well, well, if it isn't my favorite granddaughter from my favorite past life." A familiar voice broke the silence, and she whirled to see her grandmother, Helen, striding across the silver turf, resplendent in a flowing pink gown. Pink was Helen's favorite color.

Laurell jumped from her seat, heart swelling with joy. "Grandma," she gasped. Helen pulled her into a hug, swift and earnest; then Laurell took a step back and took a good look at her grandmother. Helen's skin was smooth, save for small laugh lines at her eyes and forehead. Her dark hair was thick, with only very slight touches of gray. "You look so young!"

Helen chuckled. "We get to decide our appearance here. Most folks choose to look as as they did in their twenties. Not me, though. I chose somewhere in my mid-forties." Helen's eyes grew distant. "That was the happiest time in my last life. My body was still strong and your grandfather was alive and well."

Laurell shook her head in disbelief. "I can't believe it's you. I'm so happy to see you." Her stomach clenched with guilt. "I'm so sorry I didn't see you before you died. I didn't know you were sick." Of course, that had been her own fault, because she'd cut off all contact with her mother and refused to provide a forwarding address or phone number when she moved to her last apartment.

Helen put a finger to Laurell's lips. "No apologies now, my dear. They simply aren't necessary. We have bigger things to talk about."

"Are you my new Liaison?"

"A temporary replacement," Helen responded. "Which is something we need to talk about. But first, an update from the Council is in order."

"Yes, Axiom wants me to be sure you don't sense any Umbrae near the covenstead."

"No Umbrae that we know of," Helen confirmed. "But you must stay on guard. The Divine Director of the Gods, Mobius, indicated that as you get closer to delivering the baby, they'll become more desperate. There's no telling what they may do to find you and keep you from giving birth."

"I understand."

Helen touched Laurell's hand, and her expression turned serious. "Darling, it's time you made peace with your mother."

Laurell sighed and averted her eyes from Helen's knowing, penetrating gaze. "I'm sorry, Grandma. I can't seem to forget all the crap she put me through growing up. All the times she tried to make me be someone I wasn't, all the attempts to mold me into the perfect little Hollywood daughter."

Helen tilted her head. "Your mother was certainly no saint—goodness knows I had my own issues with her—but we've called a truce and come to terms with what we did and didn't do in life."

Laurell shrugged with a nonchalance she didn't feel. "I wish it were that easy."

"She was never the same after your father died, you know."

Laurell's ears perked up at the mention of the father she'd never known. "I imagine she was pretty distraught. They were high-school sweethearts, right?"

"More than that, darling. She was devastated. He was her first and only love."

"I'm sure it was hard for her," Laurell said, uncomfortable with the sympathy her grandmother's words inspired in her. She was not accustomed to feeling sorry for her mother.

"Beyond hard. Did she tell you they studied acting together? They intended to move to California and be big movie stars together, too. Like one of those famous Hollywood couples."

Laurell shook her head. "I didn't know my father was an actor."

Helen grinned. "He was a hell of a good one, too. Better than your mother. Though I never told her that, of course. When he died, fulfilling *her* dream became fulfilling *their* dream, to her. She told me once that if only she could make it big, it would be as if he'd made it, too. She was determined. I've never seen someone so focused as she was on doing everything she could to be the biggest, brightest, richest star in Hollywood."

Laurell frowned. "She succeeded."

Helen rubbed Laurell's arm thoughtfully, and her lips pursed. "She did, but at great cost."

Laurell trailed her hand over her face. "I'm not sure where you're going with this. Are you asking me to feel sorry for her and forgive her for the years of misery? Pretend it didn't happen?"

"I'm not asking you to do anything at all. I'm simply sharing information that might make it easier for you to understand how she became the person she was. It doesn't excuse her behavior. It certainly won't make you forget. As for forgive? Well, that's up to you, isn't it?" Helen took Laurell's hand in her own.

Laurell's insides shook. She blinked the moisture from her eyes. What was wrong with her? Maybe it was seeing her grandmother again, hearing her voice, feeling her gentle touch. She longed to fall into her arms and snuggle there and be comforted, as she had as a child. *But I'm not a child anymore. I'm going to be a mother soon myself.*

She cleared her throat. "I'm not sure about the forgiving part, but I'll make an effort to communicate with her as my Liaison. I guess that's why you were sent to talk to me, right?"

Helen gave a wry smile. "You always were a smart cookie."

Laurell felt her own lips curve in response. Then Helen pulled her into another hug. "I have to go, dearest. I'm so proud of you. You're going to be a wonderful mother and a witch to be reckoned with!"

The praise washed over Laurell and left a feeling of pride and reassurance in its wake. "Will I see you again?"

Helen shrugged. "I don't think so, but you never know. This reincarnation business is great fun. Maybe I'll come back as your cat."

Laurell's jaw dropped. "You will not!"

Helen blew her a kiss and in the next moment disappeared, her laughter tinkling behind her like tiny bells.

I love you, Grandma, Laurell thought, wishing she'd said it.

Then she heard Helen's voice call, "I love you too, dear one."

Moments later, she woke in bed, hearing Axiom's rhythmic breathing and feeling his body twined with hers. She pressed a kiss to his forehead and nestled closer, loving his comforting presence. The child in her belly moved, and she placed her hand on her abdomen, a small smile lighting her face.

Mobius stood outside of Willow's private chambers and mentally asked for admittance. *Yes, come in,* she responded. He entered an emerald room where varying shades of green vied for attention. Willow reclined on a stone slab the color of jade. She wore a form-fitting gown of forest green, and her golden hair was twisted atop her head.

She rose as he crossed the room. "Mobius."

"I believe you know why I am here," he said, getting straight to the point.

She raised her eyebrows. "Do I?"

"Avina's interrogation. Why do you refuse it?" He did not bother to hide his agitation. Willow was the one goddess he had trusted completely.

Willow averted her gaze and walked past him to a nearby stone table. "Come now, Mobius, you know I've nothing to do with tainting Helen's visions. I would never jeopardize the mission."

Mobius strode to her side. "I do know that, but refusing to cooperate with Avina makes you suspect."

Willow sighed. "I am sorry for that."

"Why be sorry? Why not simply acquiesce? I don't understand your reluctance."

Willow's eyes flashed with unreadable emotion. "Perhaps I do not wish to have my consciousness plundered."

"It is not a pleasant experience, I realize; however, it is necessary. Even I will undergo it." Mobius shook his head and pushed down his frustration. "If you refuse, I will have no option but to order you questioned by force."

Willow's eyes widened. "I am hopeful you will not do so."

"How can I avoid it? You know you leave me no choice."

Willow blinked. "As the Divine Director, you have the authority to grant me a reprieve."

Mobius grimaced. "You know the rest of the Council would take issue with that decision."

"They have taken issue with your decisions before, but in the end, they back down, do they not?"

Mobius sighed. This exchange was going nowhere. He needed to make her see reason. He touched her arm, and his voice softened. "Willow, as your friend, I must urge you to reconsider this course. What is it you are so concerned about sharing with Avina? What secret do you hide?"

"I did not think of it until after I enlisted Avina's help," she murmured.

"What did you not think of?"

"I had no intention of ever telling you. I would never presume to infringe upon our friendship." She twisted her hands, her agitation clear.

Her words made no sense. "I don't understand what you are saying."

She licked her lips and swallowed. "If Avina interrogates me, it will go in the official transcript."

"Well, yes, the results of her interrogations will be on record for the Council to read, if they so choose." Again, he had no idea what the weather goddess was getting at. "Speak plainly, Willow."

"I wish to experience a harmonization with you." The

words tumbled from her mouth so fast, he almost thought he'd misheard. She wanted to harmonize with him? It was akin to what humans called making love; their auras and energy bodies would merge in a highly pleasurable experience. Mobius had not connected with a goddess in this manner in a very long time.

"Willow . . ."

She jerked away from him, and he read the embarrassment in her movements. "I understand you probably have no such desire for me. I never intended to tell you, but if I am forced into interrogation, it will come out anyway."

For a moment, he considered what she was suggesting. Willow was a beautiful goddess, to be sure. He liked her well enough, and the power surge from a harmonization was intense and built enough energy for those involved to increase their god force exponentially. He quickly discarded the idea, however. Although it would be pleasurable, there would be no love between them. Gods and goddesses did not experience that particular emotion in the same manner humans did.

But he had felt it once, deeply, and afterwards, what Willow or any other goddess could offer him paled in comparison. Not to mention how the harmonization might affect their professional partnership. He did not wish the other Council members to lose faith in Willow. Or in him. "Willow, I am flattered by your interest, but—"

She spun back around to face him and cut off his words with her own. "Do not explain. It isn't necessary. Just do me the favor of keeping that part of my interrogation to yourself."

She was asking him to be less than completely truthful, and that was something he found difficult to do.

"Please, Mobius. It is difficult enough for me that you are aware of these thoughts of mine. I could not bear for the rest of the Council to have such knowledge." Her eyes pleaded.

It was a small omission. She had been his friend for a very long time. "I will do what I can," he agreed.

CHAPTER THIRTY

Laurell's second month of pregnancy passed in a blur of activity. Her training continued, lessening as Fiona seemed more and more confident in her abilities. And a good thing, too, because the child in her womb was growing with amazing speed.

Yule came and went without incident. The coven, unwilling to leave the covenstead to go shopping, agreed to celebrate without gifts.

But to her delight, the group did present Laurell with a pendant made of gold. It was shaped as a five-pointed star with a moon behind it and a circle of people etched into the back of it, hidden from view—the emblem of Hidden Circle Coven.

Axiom had gifted her with a warm bath and massage, and a night of loving. Both gifts had made her insides mushy.

According to Hillary, she would deliver sometime in the next few weeks.

Laurell stood in the kitchen of the main house, holding a plate of cheese and sausage. She glanced down at her swollen belly, shaking her head.

"Whatcha thinkin'?" Reese strolled into the kitchen and swiped some cheese from her plate.

She smacked his hand. "Hey, you're stealing food from a pregnant lady. There's got to be some bad karma there somewhere."

He chuckled. "I've done worse things in my time."

Fiona rounded the corner and came to a stop beside them. "Hey, guys," she said. "Don't ruin your appetite. Dawna's making spaghetti for dinner."

Laurell gave Fiona a pointed look. "How is Dawna, by the way?" The girl rarely came out of her cabin of late, and when she did, she had a distant, gloomy expression on her face. She and Lynn had gotten into a huge fight, though Lynn refused to talk about it. A few days before, Lynn had moved out of their shared cabin and into the main house, where she was bunking on the pullout couch in the living room. "Just until Dawna gets her head together," she'd said.

Fiona worried her bottom lip. "I don't know what to make of it. Hillary thinks Dawna has sunk into some kind of depression. She's been offering her herbal remedies, but Dawna won't take them. She spends all her time alone, scribbling in her journal or hanging out with Poe."

"It's not healthy," Reese said. "I'm surprised she's surfacing to make dinner tonight." He grabbed another piece of cheese from Laurell's plate, and she scowled at him.

"Well, Thumper went in and talked to her today and she seemed to snap out of her funk for a little while. At least long enough to come in here and eat a sandwich and announce she's cooking dinner. We'll see if she follows through. If not, Thumper said he'd make the spaghetti."

Laurell scrunched her face. "I hope we don't have to go with Plan B." Thumper's culinary skills left something to be desired.

Fiona laughed. "Come on, Laurell, your cooking isn't much better."

Laurell chuckled. Fiona was right about that.

"You know, I sure am glad to see you guys getting along. For a while there, I didn't think you'd ever be friends,"

Reese said. He eyed a piece of sausage and Laurell tucked her plate behind her back.

"We weren't that bad," Fiona said.

"Puh-leeze. I can remember coming into the kitchen and finding the air so thick with tension between you, I could have spread my toast with it."

Laurell's mind drifted to the day he was referring to. That was when she'd been sure Fiona had more than just friendly feelings for Reese. She'd been waiting to see if Fiona would 'fess up to Reese, but so far, it hadn't happened.

Reese ducked into the fridge and surfaced with half a block of cheese. "I'm off to do some reading." He patted the cheese in his hand. "I'll just take this bad boy with me."

"Thank you. I was beginning to think you were going to get more of my snack than the baby," Laurell said.

He laughed and waved one hand over his shoulder as he exited the room. Once she was sure he was gone, Laurell gave Fiona a pointed stare.

"What?" Fiona grabbed a sponge from the sink and wiped the countertop.

"Don't 'what' me. When are you going to tell him?"

Fiona groaned. "I don't know. Every time I work up the nerve, I chicken out at the last second. My reluctance is ridiculous, I know. I can't keep on like this. Last week I almost kissed him while we were shoveling snow. I slipped on some ice, and he caught me, and when I looked up, he was just so adorable. I started leaning into him and then I realized what I was doing!" She clapped her free hand to her forehead. "I haven't had it this bad since I was in love with this guy in college. He was such a computer geek, but I swear, his pocket protectors were a total turn-on."

"I'm serious, Fiona. You have to tell him. Really."

Fiona cocked her head to one side and in a very sassy tone of voice said, "I'll tell him when you tell Axiom."

Laurell felt her cheeks heat.

"A-ha! You think I don't notice what's going on with you two? Everyone can tell it's more than just sex, though judging by the sounds coming from your cabin at night, you're having one hell of a good time in that department."

"Oh! Are we that loud?"

Fiona giggled and waved her hand in the air. "Yeah, but don't worry about it. We're pagans. We like all that sexy energy being raised. It's powerful stuff."

Laurell sighed. "I haven't said the L-word for the same reason you haven't told Reese how you feel. I'm just so . . ." She struggled for the right words.

Fiona tossed the wet sponge into the sink and placed her hands on Laurell's shoulders, looking her square in the eye. "I know, honey. Maybe we can help each other find some courage, huh?"

"Yeah," Laurell agreed. "Maybe we can."

Dawna slumped on the edge of her bed, held out a piece of apple to Poe, who was perched next to her, and brushed tears from her eyes. She was tired, hungry, and she missed Lynn. She'd noticed how the others looked at her, as if she were sick or something. She was sick. Sick and tired of being treated like a second-class witch. And she was tired of being ignored. The Council said the Umbrae didn't know where Laurell was. The Council was wrong. Poe's warnings were growing stronger.

She'd tried talking to Lynn about it, but Lynn told her she was obsessed and then insinuated Dawna was imagining Poe's warnings. At that point Dawna had told her to get out of their cabin, and Lynn had said, *Gladly*.

But she regretted her harsh words now. And when she thought of her girlfriend, her chest ached. They were talking, but only barely. At dinner, Lynn had been stiff and re-fused to do more than shoot pitying glances her way.

I don't want their pity, Poe. I have to do something to prove to them I'm just as good a witch as they are. The problem was, she had no idea what she could do to change their minds.

You deserve better. They should listen to you. Poe responded as any friend might, reassuring her as best he could, but that didn't really make her feel any better.

But how? she asked. *How can I convince them? They won't let me help them.*

The bird raised and lowered his blue-black wings, tilted his head to the side, and assessed her with tiny, knowing eyes. "Kraw!" *We will make a plan.*

Fiona bundled herself in a thick red jacket and gloves and hurried across the snow-covered lawn. Knocking on Reese's cabin door, she shifted from foot to foot in an effort to keep the bitter cold from seeping into her bones. Nighttime was always worse than the day. At least during the day, the sun warmed them enough to make the temperature bearable. Once the sun went down, it wasn't unusual for the air to chill to below zero.

Reese pulled open the door to his cabin wearing a thick, navy blue bathrobe and a grin. His long hair spilled over his shoulders in yellow waves. "What's up, Fi? You look a little cold."

She rolled her eyes, teeth chattering. "Let me in."

Reese ushered her inside, and blessed warmth surrounded her. The air smelled like soap and the bathroom mirror was foggy, indicating he'd recently showered. He kicked the door shut behind them and sat on the bed, watching her expec-tantly. Fiona swallowed. Now that she was here, her courage was faltering.

She hadn't been able to sleep the last couple nights. Ever since her conversation with Laurell, she'd been trying to work up the nerve to talk to Reese. Then, last night, she'd dreamt of Anne. In the dream, Anne held outstretched hands to Fiona and between her hands a miniature Earth rolled in circles and sparked light. *You can have everything you want, Fi. You just have to take a chance.* Fiona knew the "everything" Anne referred to was love. Which for Fiona, meant Reese.

She approached the bed tentatively, halting a couple feet away. He adjusted his robe, which had fallen open a bit and bared his smooth chest to her gaze. She gazed at his naked flesh with interest, then realized what she was doing and quickly focused back on his face. His eyes twinkled with amusement. Had he noticed her staring?

"I need to talk to you," she said.

He scratched his chin. "Um, yeah. I figured as much when you showed up at my door at ten o'clock at night."

Where to begin? "I've been meaning to tell you something for a while now. I didn't feel like I could when Anne was alive, but then I found out you two had broken up before her death. . . ." Her words trailed off and she took a deep breath, hoping to steady her erratic pulse.

Reese looked confused. "Anne didn't want to say anything about our breakup. We were going to tell the group together, but then—" He paused and looked at her questioningly. "How did you find out?"

"She visited me on Samhain."

Reese glanced up in surprise, then nodded as if her explanation made sense. "What else did she tell you?" He patted the bed beside him. "Sit down. You're making me nervous with your pacing."

Fiona halted. She hadn't even realized she'd been wearing a pattern into the floor. Her nerves were raw by the time she cleared the few feet between them and lowered herself to the space beside him on the bed.

Heartbeat thundering in her ears, she began. "So here's the thing. I'm in love with you. I've been in love with you for a long time. And whether or not you have any interest in me besides friendship, and you probably don't, I had to get it off my chest." She couldn't look at him. She just kept her eyes focused straight ahead.

Long moments passed before he spoke. "Fiona."

She couldn't move. Her neck wouldn't turn so she could look at him. What if she saw disgust—or worse, pity—on his face?

"Fi, you have to look at me." His hand closed over hers and squeezed. His voice was soft, reassuring. Slowly, she faced him. His pale blue eyes sparkled with tenderness. "I've had feelings for you, too, for a long time. Anne and I grew apart. We realized we weren't in love. I think she might have even known how I felt about you, though we never talked about it."

Fiona's chest tightened and her heart swelled. "Did you say you love me?"

"Not exactly, but I do."

She leaped into his lap and pressed her mouth to his. Her arms wove around his neck and he chuckled at her audaciousness, but she ate the sound with her kisses. His lips roved hers with fervor, and her skin tingled and heated.

First things first. She tugged her mouth away. "Why didn't you tell me?"

Reese blinked, looking a bit shell-shocked at the abrupt change in pace. One minute, passionate embrace, the next, interrogation. "I wanted to, but it seemed like terrible timing after your sister died."

She paused and sighed. "I know. Is it terrible we're here, now, doing this? She's only been gone a few months." Her eyes quickly filled with tears, and one fat drop slid down her cheek.

Reese tenderly kissed the moisture away. His gaze was serious. "Birth. Death. Rebirth. You know that's how things work, Fi. Anne knew that too."

"She wouldn't want us to spend too much of our lives mourning her."

"No. She'd want us to live," he agreed.

Fiona nodded and sank into him, letting her head rest on his chest. "Let's just stay here like this for a while. I've wanted you to hold me for so long."

"And I've wanted to do the holding." Reese dropped a kiss on the top of her head and she closed her eyes. The thump-thump of his heart beneath her cheek was the only sound she heard. It beat in time with her own.

CHAPTER THIRTY-ONE

"He confessed without need for interrogation," Avina said. Mobius, Willow, and Avina stood inside the Divine Council's meeting room. The rest of the members of the Council would arrive shortly to cast their final votes on what punishment should be dealt to the deity who had attempted to thwart the mission.

"No doubt he realized continued denial would be fruitless," Willow said, directing this comment to Avina. Since confessing her feelings to Mobius, she had been cooler toward him than usual, though she'd remained professional. He hoped their friendship would resume. Perhaps time would relieve her discomfort.

"Avina, do we have any reason to believe he had accomplices?" Mobius asked.

Avina shook her head, long ebony mane flowing like water. "No. It would have shown up in one of the others' interrogations, and they were all clean. I believe it is safe to assume he operated alone."

A moment later, Mobius sensed movement outside the chamber door. Then the gods and goddesses filed in, one by one, and took their seats. Two of them escorted the prisoner. Rhakma was held between them inside a crystal cage that had been forged with Source energy, a power strong enough to keep even a god within the bars.

Once the Council members had settled into their seats,

Helios, the war god, spoke. "Mobius, before we vote, we would like to hear from you on this matter. Do you have any recommendations?"

Mobius peered at Rhakma, who narrowed ice blue eyes and lifted his chin in defiance. "I am surprised and saddened by Rhakma's actions. It is rare one of our own turns on the rest of us. In this case, Rhakma's actions could have caused all of us grave harm. Including the people of Earth."

The Council members nodded and general murmurings could be heard.

Mobius continued. "I recommend banishment to the Astral Plane for a period of one hundred Earth years. At the end of that period, we will revisit his status and determine whether he has repented and can be trusted in the Light Realm. His Council seat, however, should be revoked indefinitely."

Rhakma emitted a harsh laugh. "How convenient. You now have a place for your beloved half-breed to occupy."

"Watch your tongue, Rhakma." Willow edged closer to the caged god, eyes dark with warning.

"It is alright, Willow. Let him speak before his sentence is decided," Mobius said. Then, to Rhakma, "Have you anything you wish to tell the Council before the decision is made?"

Rhakma threw his head back with a smile. "I made it clear from the start that I disagreed with the decision to utilize a Gray for this mission. Grays do not belong on the Council, and they have no place on a mission of this magnitude. I placed knowledge of the yearning in Helen's visions, yes. I did so hoping only to make Council members see the error of their decision."

"Two humans died because of your actions," Willow pointed out. "What have you to say of their deaths?"

Rhakma's jaw hardened. "I have no apology."

"Very well. Let us vote." Mobius took his seat at the head of the table and the Council recorded their votes. Moments later, the decision crystal was handed to Willow.

She cleared her throat and pushed her sparkling gold hair behind one shoulder. "The majority votes for banishment to the Astral Plane."

"I will avenge this deed, Mobius. Of that you can be sure." Rhakma's words were heavy with menace, and his eyes glowed clear as ice as he surged his god force at Mobius. Not that it did any good for him to threaten. The cage bars would not allow his power to reach its target.

"Take him." Mobius nodded toward the doorway and two of the gods stood to escort Rhakma out of the room.

Once the rest of the Council had also departed, Willow lingered behind. She must have noticed Mobius's pensiveness, because she touched his shoulder. When he glanced up, her gaze was filled with concern.

"What troubles you, Mobius?"

"It is very rare for a Light God to turn to such evil. It is an indication of the progress the Umbrae are making turning humans to the darkness."

Willow sighed. "Keep faith. Once the Earth Balancer is born, we will gain the upper hand."

Mobius nodded. "Yes. But for how long?"

Laurell leaped from the dining table in the main house and rushed to the bathroom, where she was promptly sick. Once the quivering in her stomach ceased, she stood and went to the sink to rinse her mouth. She straightened and peered in the mirror at the pale face staring back at her.

Hillary appeared behind her, face etched with concern. "Was my homemade turkey chili that bad?" she teased.

Laurell managed a small smile. "It was great, Hill. I just should have known better than to eat chili right now. I've been queasy off and on for days."

Hillary tsk-tsked and led her out of the bathroom, holding Laurell's arm and leading her to the couch. Laurell sank gratefully into the cushions.

Hillary handed her a glass of water, which she gulped in a few swallows. "That child sure is giving you grief. No wonder you haven't put on much weight during this pregnancy."

Laurell looked down at her stomach, which certainly appeared to be plenty large from her vantage point. "I've gained weight. My belly looks like I'm eight-and-a-half months along."

"Developmentally, you *are* that far along. However, you really haven't gained much considering all the eating you've been doing." Hillary's tone was teasing.

Laurell groaned. "I'm ravenous all the time. The wonderkid must be taking all the food."

"It takes a lot to grow a baby strong enough to save the world from the Umbrae," Hillary said.

Laurell leaned back into the couch and rubbed her hands absently over her belly. The nausea had subsided. "I thought nausea only happened for the first trimester. I mean, I know this isn't a normal pregnancy by any means, but doesn't it follow at least some of the usual patterns?"

"Some women are nauseated through their entire pregnancy. Be glad you don't have to deal with nine months of being sick," Hillary advised.

Axiom's voice drifted from the kitchen, followed by Thumper's. The sound of the refrigerator door opening and closing ensued. Minutes later, Axiom appeared in the living room with a sandwich and a soda. He took one look at Laurell's face, set his food down on the nearest end table, and approached the couch.

"You are not well?" he asked.

"I've been a little sick to my stomach. I'm okay."

"Is it the child?" He pulled a chair up close to the couch and dropped onto it, placing one hand on her belly as though he could ascertain the baby's well-being through her skin.

"He's fine too. I think it's normal for me to get sick sometimes."

Hillary touched Axiom's shoulder and he jerked around as though just realizing she was in the room. "She's right. It's normal. They'll both be just fine, Axiom."

"Thank you," he said, and Hillary disappeared around the corner, back toward the kitchen.

Once they were alone, Laurell touched Axiom's cheek. He had a few days' beard stubble, dark circles under his eyes, and his skin was pale and wan. He hadn't been acting himself of late. He'd been spending more time than usual in his cabin alone. When she'd rapped on the door to talk to him earlier that day, he'd called out he wasn't feeling well and needed to rest.

"Are you okay?" she asked.

"I am fine," he responded, but then his gaze turned distant and guarded. His big hand was still splayed over her stomach, warm and heavy. She liked the feel of it there. He'd taken to spooning her while they slept, one of his arms tucked beneath her head and the other lightly holding her belly. Once, she had woken in the middle of the night to feel his fingers stroking her stomach ever so slightly. Deep warmth and a hesitant contentment had surged inside her.

"Why do I think there's something you're not telling me?" She placed her hand over his so both their hands rested on her belly. The movement got his attention, and he focused back on her face.

"Mind reading is not one of my powers, so I do not know

why you think this." It was his attempt at a joke, but his smile was strained and didn't reach his eyes.

Laurell wasn't fooled, but if he didn't feel like talking about whatever was bothering him, she wasn't going to push it. Not yet anyway. "You know, the Axiom I met a few months ago wouldn't even crack a smile, let alone a joke. You've come a long way."

"A long way how?" he asked.

She shrugged. "I don't know. I guess you're behaving like a human being instead of—" She halted midsentence. She'd meant to compliment him, but the words had come out all wrong.

"Go on. How did I behave previously?" His expression was taut.

"I'm not sure exactly. You're just softer around the edges. That's all."

"This is considered a good thing? To be soft around the edges?"

Laurell squeezed his hand. "In my book it is, yes."

Axiom pulled his hand from hers and sat back in his chair. "It is not considered so in the Light Realm. A warrior god should not be vulnerable or, as you said, soft."

Laurell pulled herself into an upright position. "Axiom, I just meant you've loosened up a bit. I really did mean it as a compliment." She leaned forward, pressed her lips to his in a small, gentle kiss. She tilted her head back and flashed what she hoped was a reassuring grin. "Why are you being sensitive? Are you still feeling sick?"

"I told you, I am fine." He shifted away from her and stood up. "Can I get you anything?"

She shook her head.

"I am going to my cabin, then. I will see you at dinner." He left the room before she could protest. Laurell's stomach knotted. Why had he been so distant these past few days? She aimed to find out.

Axiom lay on his bed and stared at the ceiling, trying to determine how best to explain to Laurell that they should sleep in separate cabins. Since the episode in the woods with Wayne, when his shadow side had again attempted to take hold of him, he was becoming more and more concerned about his ability to hold the dark energy at bay. He noticed that as the child grew in Laurell's womb, his struggle for control became more difficult.

He sensed this had something to do with the enormous light energy growing inside of the child. The Dark would be attracted to that power, would want to snuff out the Light like a breath against a candle flame. He had known his shadow side might attempt an upsurge once he had been on Earth for an extended period of time.

He had not anticipated the pull to be so strong. Just as he had not expected to feel so deeply for Laurell. Nor had he been at all prepared for the possessiveness that surged within him when he gazed at her blossoming belly and when his mind lingered on the baby inside. His child. He shook his head and rubbed his eyes with fisted hands.

No. The child belonged to Earth. The child was to be the Earth Balancer, the one being who could save the planet from destruction.

Perhaps it is still the effects of this human form. These thoughts about the child, the desire for Laurell, and the need for her touch and companionship could all be created by this body I inhabit.

The strange hold Laurell had on him would likely dissipate once he returned to the Light Realm and his god form. His chest tightened painfully. He shoved the sensation aside. The Earth Balancer would be born soon, and he would have fulfilled his mission. All he had longed for would be his. His place on the Divine Council would be assured.

He needed only to fight the lure of the Dark a bit longer. And since the child in Laurell's womb beckoned and taunted the Dark inside of him, he would limit the time he spent with her. He did not think Laurell would take the news well. *I will discuss the matter with her soon*, he thought. *Right after a short nap.*

The inner battle to keep the darkness at bay left him more tired than usual, and he could not afford to be at less than his fullest power when the time came for the Earth Balancer to be born. Although they had been successful at keeping the Umbrae out of their protected circle, it seemed too easy. The Umbrae would be desperate by now to gain access.

They were crafty creatures. He did not doubt for a second they were formulating their plan of attack. They would find a way to infiltrate. It was merely a matter of time.

Axiom woke to an incessant pounding on his cabin door. How long had he been asleep? He sat up slowly, still dazed from slumber. Long moments passed before he could focus his eyes on the bedside clock. He realized he had missed dinner. Hours. He had been out for hours. Axiom ran one hand through his hair and rose from the bed. The room tilted and righted itself again. He frowned at the wave of dizziness that washed over him and shrugged his shoulders to dispel the sensation. He started toward the door, but halted when the air around him became heavy and electricity trickled over his skin. The hair on his arms stood on end. A spasm of pain sliced into his midsection and momentarily stole his breath. The sensation passed. He sucked in air, grateful as oxygen filtered through his lungs. It was happening again. Already. His dark half was vying to upset the perfect balance inside him.

The pounding on his door continued. Another sharp jolt hit him, agonizing in its intensity.

"Axiom, are you in there?" It was Laurell's voice, muffled by the barrier of the wooden door.

The darkness inside of him curled up his spine, unfurling its murky fingers and spreading beneath his skin. He silently willed Laurell to leave. He would not allow her to see him this way.

"Axiom, I know you're in there. I just want to talk to you. I want to show you a spell in my grandmother's *Book of Shadows*. I think it could be useful." A pause. "And I brought you some dinner too."

He ignored her, hoping if he did so, she would retreat. She pounded some more. The door shook.

"Open the door right now, or I'm coming in." Her words were strained, worry evident in her tone.

He remembered he had locked the door and was thankful for his foresight.

The door handle jiggled. "Fiona gave me the master key. I'm coming in one way or the other."

The shadow energy filled his vision with the usual horrid pictures of cruelty and misery. He surged god force. Every muscle in his body tightened as he mentally clamped the dark energy down.

"Not now," he managed to croak out between clenched teeth. He tried to cross the space between the bed and the door, intending to bar her entrance with his body if he must, but all his power was being directed at the battle waging inside him. He could not move even one limb forward.

"You sound weird," came the voice on the other side of

the door. A moment of silence, then, "I'm coming in." A clicking in the lock. A squeak as the door creaked open. Laurell appeared in the doorway, backpack slung over one shoulder, keys dangling from her fingers. He struggled to focus on her through the vile images that flashed through his brain. His body shook with effort.

Her jaw went slack. "What the hell?" The keys slipped from her fingers and made a jangling sound as they hit the wood floor. The backpack followed, issuing a thud.

She rushed to his side and ran her hands over his arms, his chest, his face. "Oh my god. What's wrong? What's happening?"

At her touch, his shadow side arched and twisted harder, deeper. His blood rushed through his veins and pounded with such force he could no longer hear her words. His palms burned, his hands itched to touch her belly, to encompass the child inside, but not in tenderness.

The Dark wanted to claw the baby from her womb, stomp on that tiny but luminous light until it was no more. This time, he used every bit of strength he had to *keep* his body from moving, to force his hands to remain at his sides.

"Get away," he growled. "Before I kill you."

CHAPTER THIRTY-TWO

Laurell's spine stiffened. Her hands stilled. Confusion flitted across her lovely face. "What's wrong with you? What can I do?"

Axiom felt his hands move of their own accord, toward her stomach and the mound nestled beneath her jacket and sweater. Just as his fingertips brushed the fabric of her coat, he mustered enough power to lift his hands to her shoulders with one swift jerk and give Laurell a shove backwards. She stumbled, grabbing the bed for support, and was now a few feet away from him.

Her gaze narrowed and met his, searching. Whatever she saw in his eyes turned her brief spike of anger to fear, stark and vivid. He could read it in the lines of her pursed lips, her heaving chest, and the shaking hands she held up to him.

"Don't move," she murmured. "I'll . . . I'll get help." She took a few steps backward, edging toward the door. He tried—gods, how he tried—to stay rooted to the spot. But that dark energy was now focused on the child and resisted his attempts to cage it.

Axiom's hold broke. He was on her in an instant, grasping her shoulders and pushing her toward the wall. She let out a yelp as her back made impact. A hideous rage spiraled through him. Not his rage—the shadow side of him tapping into the negative forces of Earth, feeding on the evil permeating the planet. His fingers dug into her shoulders.

She struggled, twisted, her eyes glittering with panic. "Let me go."

"No," he snarled.

Her gaze darkened, and she shoved at his chest. He did not budge. One of his hands circled her neck, held her there, tightly. She gasped for air, her fingers clawing at his. His other hand trailed to her belly, splayed across it.

Comprehension flickered through her eyes. She knew what he intended. Her jaw clenched, her brow furrowed, and one of her hands left his and curled into his chest. Her body spasmed, and heat spread over his chest. Surprised, he loosened his hold on her neck. She grunted, and the hand on his chest clenched and unclenched as pain arced through him.

"Argh!" he cried, letting her go. The pain had been enough to upset the shadow side; he'd regained a small measure of control. He glanced down at his shirt. Tiny flames leaped at his sweater. Instinctively, he grabbed the cloth covering a table nearby and pounded his chest with it, putting out the flames. His skin throbbed. She had summoned the element of fire and burned him.

She scrambled toward the door. "Help!" she screamed. She tripped over her backpack and stumbled to the floor. The backpack tangled in her legs, and its contents spilled around her.

Axiom could barely breathe. He heaved huge gulps of air, and his eyes teared from the searing sensation in his chest. His dark side crouched, waiting to take over again. He pushed with his god force. One last potent thrust of Light energy and the Dark fell back, but not before cutting him once more with its razor-sharp claws, eliciting a pain-filled roar.

His limbs trembled with exhaustion. He turned to Laurell, who had risen to her feet and was scrambling toward the door. He took a step forward. Her wild eyes swept downward, and she seemed to notice the weapon that had fallen from her bag at the same moment he did. A kitchen knife, half wrapped in one of the hand towels he vaguely remembered from the safe house.

Laurell snatched the knife up and clutched it in shaking hands, waving it at him as she straightened and used her free hand to grab for the door handle. "Someone help me!" she screamed again.

The door burst open before she could turn the handle. Reese came barreling through, almost knocking her over. His gaze swept from the charred remains of Axiom's sweater to the knife in Laurell's hand.

"What the hell is going on here?"

"How are you holding up?"

Laurell glanced over her shoulder. Fiona stepped from the front door of the main house and descended the porch steps, pulling her jacket tightly around herself. She crossed the yard to where Laurell stood several feet from the porch. Her boots made a crunching sound on the snow.

Laurell shrugged and gazed into the blackness of the woods in front of her. The cold air bit at the exposed flesh of her face and ears, but she could barely feel it. She was numb.

"I'm okay."

Fiona stood next to her and wrapped one arm around her shoulders. The scent of the peanut butter cookies the High Priestess had been baking clung to her clothes and drifted to Laurell's nostrils, comforting in its reminder of life's simple pleasures.

"Why are you out here? It's freezing."

Laurell tore her gaze from the starlit heavens and faced Fiona. "I don't know. I thought the fresh air might do me good." It had been several hours since her run-in with

Axiom, but her legs still shook and her heart had yet to resume its normal pace.

"Wayne said that Axiom has control over his dark half again. He doesn't think you need to be concerned for your safety at this point."

Laurell sighed. "It's not my safety I'm worried about."

Fiona glanced at Laurell's abdomen. "I know, honey. The baby is okay, too, though." She brushed Laurell's gloved hand with her own. "Whatever you did with the fire element seemed to do the job. Axiom said he feels like his hold on his dark half is secure now."

Concern surged through Laurell. "Is Axiom okay? How badly is he burned?"

"Hillary doctored him up. It looks like first and second-degree burns, but he's already healing. I guess being part god comes in handy when he gets injured."

Laurell nodded. "Speedy healing, huh?" Another power to add to the list of Axiom's abilities.

"Yeah, honey. He'll be fine. Don't worry yourself over it. You did what you had to do."

"I know. And I know Axiom would never hurt me or the baby. Not intentionally."

Fiona tilted her head to one side and gave a reassuring smile. "Of course he wouldn't. Apparently, the longer he's on Earth and the closer the baby is to being born, the harder it is to keep the dark energy from infiltrating his own shadow side. It won't be long now, though. That baby will be born soon."

"Hillary said I'm due close to the full moon." Laurell peered at the cloud-laden night sky, where no moon was visible. She wished she could see it; for some reason, its absence made her uneasy.

Fiona squeezed Laurell's hand. "You know, maybe you should go talk to him, Laurell. Maybe it's time for you two to come clean with each other. It worked for me and Reese."

Laurell gave a half smile. Seeing the joy in Fiona's eyes when she spoke of Reese made her own heart swell with hope. Fiona and Reese had announced their new partnership at dinner. The coven members had been excited and happy for them.

Maybe Fiona was right. Clearly, Axiom hadn't felt he could tell her about his inner battle against his shadow side. Maybe if he had, she could have helped somehow. She hated that there were secrets between them. Especially now, when they were growing so close.

He had asked her once if the joy they felt wrapped in each other's arms was love. At the time, all she could manage was the one-word response, *yes*. As professions of love went, it left something to be desired. Maybe it was time she made her feelings crystal clear. Once Axiom understood the depth of her emotions, he would surely feel comfortable opening up to her more.

And then he'd understand there was nothing they couldn't face and conquer together.

"You're right, Fiona," she said. "I'll talk to Axiom first thing in the morning. He needs his rest right now."

Fiona grinned her approval, teeth flashing white in the dim light. "Good. Now let's go eat some cookies."

The next morning, Laurell knocked twice on Axiom's door. She balanced the breakfast tray full of food on her belly and waited.

"Come in," came the response from the other side of the door. She entered the cabin and kicked the door shut behind her. Axiom was fully dressed, sitting in a chair beside a small table near the window. He wore blue jeans and a black sweater. His hair was wet, and moisture still clung to the air from his shower. She set the tray of food on the table and plopped into the chair across from him.

"How are you?" she asked.

"I am well." He rubbed one hand over his stubbled chin. The short beard gave him a more earthy appearance. It was a sexy look for him. His eyes, which had turned to sinister obsidian pools the night before when he'd cornered her in his cabin, were back to their normal slate gray.

He gestured toward the tray of food. "This was not necessary. I planned to come to the main house for breakfast."

She shrugged. "I didn't know if you needed more rest or not. I thought you might like to eat in bed."

"Thank you for your thoughtfulness." He wore a pensive expression on his face and his back was stiff, his hands folded neatly in his lap.

"You're welcome. Whatever I can do to help."

"I appreciate that." He lifted the cup of steaming coffee from the tray and took a sip.

Why was he being so formal? Suddenly that table seemed to put miles between them, and she couldn't stand that feeling. She half rose and scooted her chair around the table, closer to his. "Listen, about what happened . . ." she began.

He placed the cup back on the tray. "I apologize for my behavior. I could not control myself and I—"

She leaned forward and put a finger to his lips, halting his words. "It's okay. It's not your fault."

He grimaced. "I should have had better control. I should have been able to fight the pull of the darkness."

"You did the best you could."

Black eyebrows arched. "My best was not good enough. I would have killed you and the child."

Laurell shivered at those words, remembering the hatred and fury etched across his face at the moment when one of his large hands had closed around her neck and the other hand had palmed her belly. She pushed that image away. "I know you would never hurt us, Axiom."

His lips thinned. "Do you? Do you truly know that?"

"Of course."

"Then what of the knife you have been carrying with you? Did you think I would not recognize it? That I would not realize where it came from?" His gaze pinned her in place, a mixture of accusation and hurt.

She grabbed his hands and held them firmly. "No, Axiom. I know how that looked. I took that knife my second day at the safe house. I totally forgot it was in my backpack."

Axiom withdrew his fingers from hers and pushed his chair back. "You were right to fear me."

"Axiom . . ."

He stood. "You will understand, of course, why we cannot spend any additional time alone together."

She jumped up and shook her head vehemently. "No. You're overreacting now. We belong together. We can help each other."

"It is true your powers have grown strong. In fact, your use of elemental magic likely saved your life last night"— he glanced at her belly—"and that of the Earth Balancer."

His words drew her attention to his chest and the wound she knew her magic had caused. Her stomach clenched. "I'm so sorry I hurt you. I didn't—"

"Have any other choice," he finished for her. He waved his hand as though to flick her worries away. "I heal quickly. You need not concern yourself with me."

His cavalier attitude was becoming annoying. She needn't concern herself with him? Right! How could she keep that from happening? She was his lover, the mother of his child. She was falling in love with him, dammit. *Falling in love or already in love?*

"Axiom, let's talk about this. We've come so far over the

past few weeks." She drifted close to him, wrapped her arms around his waist, and lifted her face to his. The fact that his arms hung limp at his side, that he did not return her embrace, stung.

She steeled herself and pressed onward anyway. "We've grown so close. Don't put a wedge between us now."

Emotions, unreadable, flickered over his face. He lifted his arms as though to hold her, and her heart raced with anticipatory joy. A moment later, his arms dropped to his sides again. "That is all the more reason for us to keep our distance now. This attachment we have developed serves no purpose. It will only cause you pain when I am gone."

Attachment? Like what, a growth? He was purposely pushing her buttons. *He wants to make me angry so I'll keep my distance. He's trying to protect me and the baby.*

"Look, I realize you'll have things to take care of in the Light Realm and you won't be on Earth all the time to be with me and the baby. I understand how important the Council seat is to you. A long-distance relationship isn't ideal, but we'll handle it. *Together.*"

He reached back and grabbed her hands, removing them from his waist. He took a step away. "You misunderstand. There is no relationship once the child is born."

"What do you mean?"

"Once the Earth Balancer is born, this body will die. And I will return to the Light Realm. Permanently."

His last word rang with a finality that made Laurell's ears hurt, and the cavern inside her chest that had almost closed reopened and gaped—raw, aching, bleeding out all of her fragile hopes and dreams.

CHAPTER THIRTY-THREE

The wind whirled around them, bitter and biting. A few stars dotted the sky; otherwise the full moon was the only illumination. The coven had finished dinner and now trooped out of the main house and headed toward the ritual circle, where Wayne had gone earlier to start a bonfire. Thumper hadn't finished his dinner yet, so Wayne had offered to help. They wanted to get the full-moon ritual underway as quickly as possible.

Midnight wasn't far off, and the protection spell around the covenstead needed to be rewoven for the final time. The baby was due any day. Once born, the Umbrae would be repelled by the child's very presence and the protection circle would no longer be necessary. The mission would be complete.

Tears pricked Laurell's eyes at this thought and all of its implications. She steeled her spine and lifted her chin. She couldn't remember the last time she'd given in to tears. She wouldn't waste them now on Axiom. Not on the man who had broken her heart. The man who had told her that her child was doomed to live in a single-parent household, just as she had experienced growing up. *I'll be a better parent, though, than my mother was.*

She had spent the last two weeks avoiding him, just as he wanted. He seemed to be avoiding her, too. That evening, though, he'd taken his dinner in the main house with the rest of the group.

Still, she'd managed to keep her distance, refusing to look at him, save for a few sideways glances. She'd noticed the circles under his eyes and his worn appearance. It seemed she wasn't the only one not sleeping well of late. *Good*, she thought. *Let him suffer.*

True, he'd never said he was staying on Earth after the child was born. She'd assumed that part. Wishful thinking. *Foolish thinking.* But the way he'd looked at her, held her, made love to her, told an entirely different story than that of a god eager to depart for the heavenly realms. *Damn him for making me believe it was safe to need him. To love him.*

Laurell clenched her teeth and forced herself to focus on the task at hand. She sucked in the crisp winter air, and it stung. She shivered, glad for her thick coat, earmuffs, and gloves. A movement to the right caught her eye. She twisted her neck and glanced toward the trees on the east side of the property. What she saw stopped her in her tracks. She slowly made a full circle, finding the same disturbing vision at each turn.

"Uh, guys?"

The coven members chatted merrily, their voices carrying loudly on the wind.

"Guys!" she cried, her voice higher pitched this time as panic set in.

A hush fell over the group as all heads turned to where Laurell pointed with outstretched arm. There, in the trees, amidst blackness so thick she could barely make out the tiny forms attached to them, hundreds of pairs of eyes watched them. The eyes glowed, luminescent against the inky backdrop.

"What the hell is that?" Reese was the first to find his voice.

A shiver crawled up Laurell's spine. "I think they're birds." Axiom walked from the back of the group to the front and stood next to Laurell, his brow furrowed as his keen eyes scanned the trees.

"Yes," he confirmed. "Birds."

Her pulse sped and without thinking, Laurell shifted closer to Axiom, so close their bodies touched. She felt him stiffen in surprise, but he didn't move away. His nearness gave her comfort. She felt a little better, but only a little.

Hillary moved forward a few steps, and Laurell could make out the whites of her enlarged eyes. "Why are they here?"

"And what do they want?" Fiona asked, stepping behind Hillary and resting one hand on the other woman's shoulder.

Someone cleared her throat. Slowly the group turned as though they were one body.

Dawna stood with hands on hips, tapping one foot nonchalantly. She smiled, and her eyes took on a strange gleam. The shadows beneath them stood out even in the dim light.

"It was Poe's idea," she said.

"This better be one hell of an explanation," Fiona said, hands on hips, eyes narrowed on Dawna, who sat on the couch sipping a glass of water. Dawna smiled as though nothing strange were going on, as if they weren't experiencing their very own live version of an Alfred Hitchcock film. The group had returned to the main house.

Laurell was glad to get inside; all those eyes watching her made her skin crawl. She was grateful for Axiom's solid presence behind her. His body framed hers, and he stood close enough that the scent of sandalwood enveloped her.

"You guys wouldn't listen to me and Poe, so we came up with a plan," Dawna said. Hillary, Thumper, and Lynn all sat around her, wearing various expressions of shock, disbelief, and anxiety.

"What sort of plan?" This from Reese, who paced the floor and ran one hand through his thick, honey-colored waves over and over again. He then seemed to realize what he was doing and forcibly shoved his hands into the pockets of his jeans.

"Well, I called all the birds so when you guys leave, they can be a diversion," Dawna said.

"A diversion for what?" Fiona asked.

"Who's leaving?" Laurell questioned at the same time.

Dawna glanced from one woman to the other and rolled her eyes as though they were missing a very obvious point. "You and Axiom are leaving. Or at least, you should be." This to Laurell. "And I'm talking about a diversion to distract the Umbrae." That to Fiona.

"Have you completely lost your mind, girl?" Hillary demanded. Lynn shot her a warning glance. Hillary clamped her mouth shut, but folded her arms over her ample bosom and glared at Dawna.

"You guys don't need to be afraid. I called the birds. They're on our side," Dawna insisted, taking another swallow of water.

Lynn leaned forward, shrugging out of her jacket. "If what she says is true, we're worrying for nothing, right? I mean, Dawna says the birds won't hurt us."

"Dawna's been acting like a nut for days, and she's got crazy eyes right now," Thumper burst out. Dawna glared at him, and he blushed. "Sorry, Dawna, but it's true. You're not yourself."

"I'm perfectly fine," she insisted. "You're the crazy ones. The Umbrae are practically breathing down our necks, and none of you want to do anything about it but sit here waiting for them to find a way in."

Fiona let out an exasperated groan. "How many times do we have to go over this? Even if you were right, and the Umbrae were somehow here and undetected by Wayne and the Council, they couldn't get in. They—" Her words broke off. "Oh shit. Someone needs to go get Wayne and let him know what's going on."

"He's probably still at the ritual circle working on the fire," Reese said.

"I was supposed to be there by now," Thumper said. "I'll go get him."

"No need," Wayne's voice called from the kitchen. A moment later, the man himself appeared in the doorway, shaking snow from his boots. He swiped at his cowboy hat, dusting the white powder from its brim. "Oh, sorry," he said to Fiona, who harrumphed her disapproval when the snow hit her carpet.

"Did you see the birds?" Laurell asked him.

He nodded. "Oh, I saw 'em alright. I think we've got a mighty big problem on our hands."

"Dawna says the birds are on our side," Lynn protested.

"It was Poe's idea," Dawna said for the second time that night, eyes bright with glee over her familiar's fabulous plan.

"Well, I think that's the problem," Wayne said.

"What do you mean?" Fiona asked.

Wayne bent and placed a rolled-up blanket on the floor. Fiona looked at it suspiciously. "I'm almost afraid to ask."

"You should be." And with that Wayne unrolled the blanket. Something dark lay amidst the folds covered in ice. Laurell blinked. It took several moments for her to realize a black bird lay there, dead and partially decomposed. No doubt the ice had delayed the process. That wasn't so upsetting. No. What was so upsetting was the purple string tied to its left foot.

Dawna sobbed into Lynn's shirt while the other woman rubbed reassuring circles over her back. In between sniffles, Dawna muttered, "I thought he'd lost his string. He's lost it before." She clearly realized she'd been duped. The raven that had been following her around and communing with her of late was not her familiar. Her familiar was dead.

Laurell's chest ached for the girl. Wayne had covered the bird back up and taken it from the room once Dawna identified it as Poe. Now Wayne perched on one of the wing-back chairs, his broad faced creased with concern.

"I don't understand it," Wayne said. "Somehow, the Umbrae must have tapped into the bird."

"Would you not have sensed their presence if that was true?" Axiom asked, stepping from his place behind Laurell and leaving her feeling suddenly alone, bereft.

Wayne shook his head. "I don't think they're *in* the bird. Not in the sense they enter Finders. I think they must be controlling it somehow from afar. That's something I wouldn't be able to detect and quite frankly, not something they've ever done before."

"How did they find us here?" Fiona asked. "I thought they could only trace Laurell through the yearning, and only if the yearning happened outside of protected space."

"That is true," Axiom said, scratching his chin in thought.

A memory drifted back to Laurell. "I think I know."

All eyes turned to her.

"The night I tried to escape, I was in the woods and I remember this black bird, a raven, sitting on a branch above me and sort of following me through the woods. I'll bet it's the same bird."

Fiona nodded. "And they used Dawna's connection with birds to initiate a bond with the imposter Poe."

"No doubt that bird's been hovering around here, listening to our conversations and giving all sorts of information to the Umbrae," Thumper remarked, pushing his glasses up his nose.

Laurell shuddered.

"But what do they hope to accomplish with all these birds?" Hillary asked.

"I think I know," Axiom stated. All eyes turned to him for an explanation. "If indeed the Umbrae control these birds, and I believe that they do, then during those brief moments between the death of one protection circle and the birth of the next, as many of them as possible will swarm the coven."

A horrible realization dawned. Laurell shook her head, trying to will the truth away, but it lingered like a rotten smell. "We can fight them, but they could distract one of us long enough to keep that person from casting his or her part of the circle. The birds aren't a problem once the circle is cast, but if the circle isn't complete, it will be an Umbrae free-for-all."

"What if we paired up at each quarter? We've got enough people to do it," Thumper offered.

Axiom shook his head. "If we send Laurell out, she and the child are easy targets. And Dawna is in no condition to cast circle. It is too risky."

Laurell groaned. He was right, of course, but it didn't make it any easier for her to accept that once again she would have to be tucked away and hidden for her own good. She placed her hands on her round belly and rubbed it absently. *You'll be born soon, little one, and this nightmare will be over. Couldn't you come a little faster, though?*

"This is getting worse by the minute," Reese murmured. "Does anyone else have any ideas?"

Fiona stepped forward, bright green eyes flashing, lips curved in a half smile. "I think I might. Dawna, I'll need your help. Are you up for it?"

Dawna jerked her head off Lynn's shoulder and wiped moisture from her cheeks. For the first time in weeks, she almost looked like herself. "I got us in this mess. I'll get us out of it."

CHAPTER THIRTY-FOUR

The bird peered inside the kitchen window. They'd told it to keep close watch, but it could not obtain a clear view of the people inside. It had already attempted a view from the living area windows, but the curtains there were drawn. Periodically, one of the humans walked past the kitchen doorway, face scrunched, mouth twisted, hands flailing animatedly.

They are arguing, the bird reported.

About what do they argue? They asked.

I do not know.

Several of the humans burst through the kitchen doorway, grabbed jackets from the backs of chairs, and emerged from the house. The raven swooped away from the window and dropped to the ground behind a bush. It remained close enough to hear their words. The black-haired witch stood in the snow along with the ones called Lynn, Thumper, and Reese.

"I think Fiona's plan is stupid," Dawna said. "She'll get us all killed."

Thumper nodded his agreement. "No kidding. I don't think we should stay here a minute longer."

"The birds will distract the Umbrae," Dawna said. "That should help us get away."

Lynn shrugged. "What does it matter? It's not us the Umbrae want. It's Laurell and the baby."

Reese stepped forward and sighed. "I don't think I can get Fiona to leave. She's insistent on staying here to help Laurell and Axiom."

"I can't believe they're going to attempt to recast circle," Thumper remarked, shaking his head in disbelief.

"Maybe they stand a chance. Who knows? Maybe the birds will be able to help. I'll talk to Poe and see what he can do," Dawna told them.

"I don't see how they can do it without our assistance," Reese muttered. His face was twisted with worry. "I just wish I could convince Fiona to come with us."

Dawna touched Reese's arm. "You know she won't go, Reese. Neither will Wayne or Hillary. We're divided on this one. We all just have to do what we think is best."

Reese groaned. "I feel like I'm leaving her here to die."

Dawna shook her head vehemently. "No, you're not. She's a powerful witch. So are Wayne, Hillary, and Laurell for that matter. And Axiom is hardly helpless." Dawna glanced at her watch. "Whatever we do, we'd better do it soon. We've less than an hour until midnight."

Reese raised his hands in a sign of defeat. "Fine. Everyone, pack your bags quickly. We can take my car."

The group scurried in all directions, heading toward their cabins. Only Dawna remained. She shivered and tucked her hands in her jacket pockets, glancing around her as though looking for someone or something. She stared at the birds she'd called to the camp and sighed. Then she hurried off in the direction of the cabins.

A moment later, the bird felt Dawna probe his mind from afar. *Poe, the group is divided. Some will leave with me. Others will not. I'm afraid Laurell and the baby are in the group who insists on staying.*

Not your fault, the raven replied.

I know you will want to follow me, but please stay here with

Laurell and Axiom. I need you to help direct the birds when the time comes. Maybe you can help them distract the Umbrae long enough to save my friends.

I will stay. I will do what I can, the bird assured her.

Thank you, my friend, came the reply; then the connection was severed.

It sensed Them lingering, listening to this inner conversation. When the dialogue had ended, the bird could sense gleefulness in his masters.

Must sleep, the bird declared.

You are free to go now. The heaviness oppressing it for the past few months lifted. The bird tilted its head, lifted its wings and flapped them. Free—free of Them. It had no night vision, and without the control of his masters, travel at night would be difficult, but the raven took flight anyway, twirling once, twice, through the air, before becoming one with the darkness.

By the time they reached Graves Manor, Laurell's nerves were frayed. During the entire drive there, she'd kept looking over her shoulder, expecting to see murky, twisted entities darting through the air after them. They had seen no signs of the Umbrae, however. Only those beady, glowing eyes of an army of birds, and the rustling of hundreds of wings as the creatures twisted and craned to watch four humans pile into the car and drive away from Fiona's retreat.

She sighed with pleasure as she walked through the front door, comforted by the familiar surroundings. Deep mahogany wood floors, covered by massive rugs of varying patterns. Light beige walls and high ceilings trimmed with stately crown molding. Directly in front of her was the sitting room and behind it, the library and the kitchen. To her right, a wide staircase spiraled to the second floor and six bedrooms and baths.

The place was immaculately clean and neat for a deserted mansion. Not a cobweb nor speck of dust in sight. Clearly, Abrams was doing a fine job of seeing the place was kept up.

"Now this is a house. It's gorgeous," Hillary spoke from behind her. Laurell turned to see Lynn's pale, delicate features fading into Hillary's cocoa-colored skin and broad lines.

"The glamour spell is wearing off," Laurell said.

Hillary grinned. "Thank Goddess. I made the mistake of looking in the rearview mirror on the way here. Talk about bizarre. I mean, Lynn is a lovely woman, but I've become attached to my own face."

Laurell pressed her hands to her own face. "What about me?"

"You don't look like Dawna anymore. All back to normal, sweetie."

Laurell sighed. "Well, the glamour spell sure worked." She frowned. "I'm worried about Fiona and the others though. I feel like we've abandoned them to the wolves."

Hillary patted Laurell's shoulder, her gaze warm with reassurance. "They will be fine. They're well trained. Besides, I doubt the Umbrae are particularly interested in them. Unless they're blocking the path to you and the baby, that is." She gave a pointed look at Laurell's round belly. Laurell placed her hands over the bulge instinctively. As though sensing the attention, the child twisted and moved inside. His movements had become strong and regular over the past month. A good sign, Hillary had said.

Wayne, whose face had earlier looked like Thumper's, appeared in the doorway behind Hillary, his gaze sweeping the room. "Nice place," he said.

"Yeah, well, the *Book of Shadows* said this is the location where I'd be strongest." She glanced around the room, her previous sense of safety suddenly overcome with a shadow of doubt. "I hope we made the right decision coming here."

"A witch is always stronger the closer she is to her ancestors. Hard to get much closer than this place." Wayne gestured toward the front door. "Where does that path lead to out there? To the right of the driveway?"

"Family cemetery."

"I rest my case."

Axiom was next through the door, carrying several bags and dropping them at his feet on the floor as he assessed the place. She was glad to see he no longer resembled Reese. Much as she liked Reese, it had been more than a little unnerving to see Reese's face every time she looked at the man she loved.

"We must erect the protection circle before the Umbrae realize our deception," Axiom announced.

"The others will maintain their glamour spells longer, to give us some time," Laurell said.

"Still, we don't want to take any chances. Let's get moving, kids," Wayne drawled, and the four hurried out into the frigid night.

Once the protection circle was cast and Wayne confirmed it was secure, they made a quick meal of some of the food supplies he had gathered for the trip. They dined on grilled-cheese sandwiches and sipped decaf coffee. Laurell was grateful for the hot liquid as it slid down her throat and warmed her bones.

She shivered off and on, but not from an outer chill. A deep, nagging fear had taken root inside and she couldn't tear it out. She wondered if her intuition, which she'd been working on with Dawna, was finally blossoming. If so, danger lurked outside Graves Manor, and their security there was only temporary.

Hillary and Wayne excused themselves to retire for the evening, heading up the stairs to the guest rooms. Laurell had decided to make her bed on the thick, comfy couch in the library. There was a bathroom attached to the room, and she didn't relish trying to climb the stairs to a bedroom on the second floor.

Her protruding belly made it more and more difficult to move around, and it had been all she could do to assist with casting the protection circle. Good thing she'd observed the coven as they cast circle at the last full moon.

She sat across from Axiom at the wooden table in the kitchen. No one had wanted to eat in the opulent dining room. It was too formal, too pretentious. Without the other two there to make conversation, an uncomfortable silence settled in.

Axiom lifted his coffee mug and sipped slowly, then set the cup down, his gaze meeting hers, guarded, pensive. "You look well, but tired."

"I'm okay." She tapped her fingers on the table, suddenly nervous about being alone with him. She'd missed him over the past weeks. She ached every time she rolled over in the middle of the night to find only cold, empty space next to her.

"Hillary tells me the child is due any time now," he said. "How are you faring?"

"Good. A little nausea now and then. And my lower back is sore, but otherwise, good." Her voice wavered on the last word and she cleared her throat, hoping to cover the tremulousness.

"I am sorry to hear that. How are you sleeping?"

"How the hell do you think?" she snapped, then immediately regretted her outburst. Tears sprang to her eyes and she wiped at them angrily. She'd told herself she wouldn't let him know how much she hurt inside. But dammit, how could he sit there making polite conversation as though they were nothing more than casual acquaintances? As though they hadn't spent the last month wrapped in each other's arms, sharing the most beautiful, amazing, ecstatic moments of her entire life? *Doesn't he know I love him?*

"I'm sorry. I—I have to go to bed now," she muttered as she rose and made to leave the room, embarrassed at her outburst.

His hand snaked out and grasped her wrist. "Laurell." His eyes were dark with unreadable emotion. The pulse in his neck beat erratically.

She glared at him, waiting for him to speak. Long moments passed while they simply stared at one another. She couldn't take it any longer. "If you've nothing to say to me, then let go of me."

"I am trying to do so, but it is harder than I anticipated," he replied. His silver eyes flashed with pain. She realized he spoke of more than just his hand circling her wrist.

She softened a bit. "What do you mean?"

He stood and dropped her hand, shifting closer to her until she had to tilt her head to meet his gaze. "I never wished to hurt you, Laurell. I tried to control the feelings of this body, but I failed. I tried to stay away from you, but could not."

Laurell bit her lip and shook her head. "Some things can't be controlled. Maybe that's the problem. You're trying to control everything, and sometimes it's better if you just let the universe move you where you're supposed to be."

Axiom tilted his head to one side. A wry smile pierced his lips. "This from the woman who would control everything in her life if she could?"

His words hit home. He was right. Here she was counseling him, and it wasn't so long ago her entire life had been regimented, planned. When had she learned to let go? When had she realized that allowing each day to create itself could be a good thing? *When the universe brought me a child of my own. And deep friendships. And a sense of power and inner strength like I've never known before.*

She blinked, taking in the beauty of Axiom's face, the way his thick hair curled over the black slashes of his eyebrows. Her fingers longed to twine through the strands of his hair. *And love.*

"Well," she said, "I guess I've learned a thing or two."

"It seems so," Axiom agreed. He lifted his hand and traced his index finger over her cheek. "I am sorry, Laurell. I did not intend to deceive you. I assumed you understood that I must depart once the child is born. I should have made it clearer. Perhaps it would have changed how you decided to spend your time with me over the past months."

She placed her hand over his, turned her head into his palm, and kissed it. She choked back a sob. No. She would not give in to the tears. Something shifted inside her. She wasn't angry with Axiom anymore. He had given her what he could. It would have to be enough. She remembered Thumper's words from so many nights ago: *Loving someone is never a waste of time.*

"It doesn't matter," she said, the words difficult to push out from a constricted throat. "I understand you'll go soon. But stay with me tonight?"

Axiom responded with a sharp intake of breath. "I want nothing more than to be with you, but I do not trust myself. I do not know when my shadow side will attempt to emerge again."

He tried to back away from her, but Laurell stepped forward and wrapped her fingers in his shirt, pressed her body against him. "I trust you."

He swallowed and hesitated, his gaze searching, seeking. She feared he would reject her, but finally, he nodded. "Let us go upstairs. The guest room Hillary prepared for me is comfortable and private."

She eyed the stairs. "I don't think I can make it."

"Of course you can." He bent, scooped her into his arms, and easily lifted her. With a speed that left her breathless, he ascended the stairs and entered one of the bedrooms at the far end of the hallway.

CHAPTER THIRTY-FIVE

Only a bedside lamp lit the room, casting shadows on the lavender wallpaper. Axiom set her on her feet, and her toes sank into the thick plush carpet.

She inhaled the scent of a single perfumed candle near the bed. Lilac. Her favorite flower. Her grandmother's too. Laurell had found a woman in Florida who made candles and scented them with essential oils. She'd mailed her grandmother several of the specially crafted candles for her last birthday. It was somehow fitting they should make love, likely for the last time, while basking in the glow of one of those candles, immersed in the scent of her childhood.

Axiom's hand twisted in her hair and tugged her mouth to his, erasing all thoughts from her mind except the sensation of his lips pressed to hers. He pulled her against his chest, trapping her hands there, kissing her with a fervor that made her dizzy with need. His tongue teased her lips and she sucked his tongue into her mouth, deepening the kiss.

Axiom moaned, the sound muffled by their mouths. He pulled back with a sigh of reluctance.

"I do not want to harm you or the child," he said.

Laurell shook her head. "You won't."

Needing no other prompting, his fingers made quick work of her clothing. Cool air hit her skin as her shirt fell to the floor, followed by her pants. Once naked, shyness overtook her. Her belly had grown so large over the past couple weeks, her hips had widened. Stretch marks marred her previously smooth flesh. Would he think her body ugly now?

Axiom discarded his own clothing and stood in all of his nude, taut glory. His body was so beautiful. She stared, committing every line, every hard and soft part, every inch of flesh to memory. She wanted this vision with her always, to remember in the days to come. His gaze swept over her and goose bumps broke out on her arms and legs. He ran his hands over her belly and hips.

"You are radiant, my goddess. Your body is exquisite." His fingers dipped from her stomach to the thatch of curls between her thighs. She gasped as one finger gently probed her folds.

"So soft," he murmured. Then he dropped to his knees and replaced his fingers with his lips.

"Oh!" She nearly lost her footing. He kissed her tender folds once, twice, three times, and desire heated her blood.

Axiom lifted his head, and his hands circled her buttocks. He guided her to the bed, pressed her backward until she lay sprawled across the mattress. He slid up her body, and his broad chest caressed and teased her taut, aching nipples. He kept his arms on either side of her, biceps and triceps tight as he held himself slightly aloft so as not to put any pressure on her belly. He rained kisses over her face and neck before his tongue tickled one nipple.

Her breath caught. She twined her fingers in his thick hair, urging him to deepen the caress, to suckle her. He obliged, and her back arched as raw need coursed through her.

She trailed her hands over his back, then circled around to his stomach, reached between their bodies to graze his cock. He released the nipple he had been tugging between his lips and raised his head to meet her eyes. His jaw was tense with the effort to control his desire. The length of him rested against her hip, searing her with its heat. She stroked him. He groaned, and his gaze went dark.

"I want you inside me." It seemed like forever since they'd connected body to body, reached deep inside of each other until they were one being.

"You must be ready for me first."

"I am," came Laurell's husky reply.

One of his hands dipped between her thighs, searching her core, stroking her, deliciously titillating. Dangerously arousing. She thought she might come just from those brief touches. He lifted his hand. His fingers glistened with her wetness. He touched those same moist fingers to his lips and a jolt of lust struck her. "Please," she whimpered, lifting her hips to urge him on.

Axiom nudged her legs open, and she let them fall apart, inviting his penetration. Then, his smooth length slid inside her entrance in one long stroke, piercing her to the core. He rested a moment, making certain she had accepted him without discomfort. And when she gripped his buttocks and pulled him deeper, he began slow, easy movements in and out. He held himself above her, careful not to put too much pressure on her belly, his arms and neck taut with his efforts to control his own passion so she could experience hers.

Each time he withdrew, only to merge more deeply with her, a dizzying, ecstatic need pulsed through her veins. She cried out in pleasure, over and over again. He tilted to his side just enough to remain connected to her, yet able to flick thumb and forefinger over the aroused nub at the apex of her thighs.

Their eyes met, and granite glittered into hazel as they both reached their peak, he with a shout of triumph, she with a moan of joy, and Laurell forgot for a brief, dizzying moment where she ended and Axiom began.

"Laurell, please, talk to me."

Laurell lifted her eyes. Elaine strode toward her across the sparkling landscape of the Astral Plane. Part of her wanted to run, leave her mother there, but she knew the time for running was over. She couldn't avoid her past any longer. She needed to make peace with it. That included making peace with her mother. After all, how could she teach her child to love, to forgive, to live his life to the fullest, if she herself couldn't do these things?

"Mother," Laurell said.

Elaine's silvery dress billowed in a lilac-scented breeze, and her dark hair fluttered around her face. The Astral Plane was silver and amethyst colored this time, dotted with lavender flowers.

Her mother paused a few feet from her, dark eyes probing. "You look different this time. You glow." Elaine closed the distance between them and raised one hand, grazed the back of it over Laurell's cheek. "Yet there is still sadness in you."

Laurell tilted her chin. "I am different. And I glow because of the baby I carry. As for why my life still has sorrow—" Her voice broke. She thought of Axiom. Of his departure, which was near at hand.

"Not because of me anymore, I hope? I had to die to realize how much I hurt you when I was alive. My re-visioning was awful." Elaine's eyes were full of tears. "Sweetheart, I'm so sorry for all I put you through."

"I was never good enough for you," Laurell accused, an old anger surging.

"I wasn't good enough for me either. No one was."

"All you cared about was work, your career."

Elaine sighed. "You're right." She focused on some spot over Laurell's head, and her voice became distant. "It was our dream to be actors, your father's and mine. We were in all the plays in our high school and we usually got the lead roles. He was a better actor than I was, but I was good too." Elaine's lips curved into a smile as an old memory consumed her.

"Grandmother said Dad was the better actor, too," Laurell replied, remembering her conversation with her grandmother.

Elaine chuckled and returned her attention to Laurell. "She was right about that. But once he died, it just became so much more important to me to make it, to be a real Hollywood actress, to be famous. I thought by doing so, I was honoring his dream as well. But I took it too far, I became obsessed."

"If this is supposed to be an apology, I'm not hearing it," Laurell said, unable to control her sarcasm or the hurt she knew was in her voice.

Elaine's brow furrowed, and she shook her head in self-derision. "Oh, Laurell. You have every right to hate me. But in my own selfish way I did—I do—love you. So much. I was horrible at showing it, but it's the truth."

Elaine's cheeks wore the tracks of her tears now, and she grabbed Laurell's hands and squeezed them tight. Laurell's own chest constricted with an ocean, a lifetime, of unshed tears.

Elaine continued, "I didn't believe your grandmother about the whole witchcraft, mothering-the-Earth-Balancer thing. And by the time I realized it was for real, when Anne showed up at my door and gave me a display of magic like I've never seen, I was so afraid, I turned her away. I've never been so terrified in my life. Then . . . well, you know the rest." Elaine cringed. "So I owe you an apology for that as well. Because of me, you are the one who has to make good on my promise, made a lifetime ago, to the Council."

Laurell swallowed, and sucked in a deep breath. "Mom, no. I'm not angry about that anymore. Really. If things hadn't happened as they did, I wouldn't be a mother soon. And I wouldn't know I was a witch or that I had all this power inside of me. Besides, I apparently agreed to be the backup plan in between lives, so it wasn't all your fault."

Elaine's eyes widened. "You forgive me?"

Laurell felt her lips curve ever so slightly. "Well, I can't say that just yet." Dismay washed over Elaine's face. Laurell squeezed the hands that still held her own. "But I'm working my way there."

Elaine smiled. She extracted her hands from Laurell's and pulled her into a hug. "I'm proud of you, Laurell. I really am. You're a hell of a witch, and you're going to be a fantastic mom."

At those words, Laurell couldn't stop the tears that sprang from her eyes and washed down her cheeks. She couldn't remember ever hearing her mother say *I'm proud of you, Laurell*. She returned the hug, squeezing her mother briefly, then, when she'd collected herself, she leaned back.

"Will I see you again?"

Elaine nodded. "Perhaps once or twice more. But I will have to reincarnate soon. A new Liaison will likely be assigned to you."

Laurell's heart swelled, and she bit her lip. "Mom—"

Elaine put her fingers to Laurell's lips. "I know, sweetie. I love you too."

Then, before Laurell could respond, Elaine arched her eyebrows and her eyes lit. "Do you realize you haven't called me Mom since you were a kid? I definitely prefer it to your usual *Mother*."

Laurell shook her head. She hadn't noticed.

Elaine disappeared then, fading until all that remained was the exquisite backdrop of the Astral Plane, brilliant and luminous.

Fiona stood, hands on hips, eyes narrowed, as she scoured the woods to her right. She made a full circle, wishing she had the ability to see in the darkness. Her very human eyes saw no sign of the birds.

Reese walked up and stood beside her. She glanced at him. He still looked like Axiom, but she longed to pull his face to hers for a kiss. He must have recognized the fire in her eyes.

"No time for that now, Fi." He grinned. "First we fight the bad guys. Then we get our reward."

She chuckled. "Sounds like a good plan."

"Oh, does someone actually have a plan for what to do now?" Dawna asked from behind them.

Fiona turned. "The plan was to fight, but where did the birds go? The protection circle has been open for hours. I thought we were going to be besieged by feathers and beaks and—"

"Umbrae," Thumper finished for her, shivering in the biting cold.

Dawna sighed. "I don't know. I mean, I still look like Laurell, don't I?"

Thumper nodded. "Yeah, and it's really starting to freak me out."

Dawna laughed. "You're just jealous because you have to wear Wayne's mug."

"Yeah, I definitely got the raw end of the deal—er, spell."

Fiona, the only one of the group who retained her original appearance, scanned the grounds of the retreat again. "You haven't seen your little feathery friend lately, have you?"

Dawna shook her head. "I don't feel his presence anymore. I think he's gone."

Snow crunched under footsteps and they all jumped nervously. Relief washed over Fiona. It was just Lynn.

Still disguised in Hillary's much larger form, she crossed the yard, holding a steaming mug. "I made coffee. Help yourselves."

The aroma of Lynn's infamous, not-for-the-faint-of-gut coffee drifted on the slight breeze. Fiona yawned. It was clear she could use some of the hot brew. She started toward the house, but a swishing sound emanated from behind, catching her attention. The noise increased in volume until it was a high-pitched buzz. The buzz grew louder, and a sliver of fear snaked up Fiona's spine.

"Tell me I'm imagining this," Reese said.

"I thought birds didn't fly at night," Thumper said.

"Umbrae-possessed birds apparently do," Fiona responded.

"Aw, shit," Thumper exclaimed.

Lynn's mug fell from her hands and hit the ground. "The birds."

The creatures swarmed like black bees in the moonlight, flying straight toward them. "Everyone get in the house!" Fiona cried. They ran toward the main house, the back porch light beckoning them.

Fiona glanced over her shoulder. The birds were fast. They weren't going to make it. At least not all of them.

Lynn reached the porch first. She flung the back door open. "Hurry! Get in!"

Reese and Fiona exchanged glances. An understanding passed between them. They both stopped dead in their tracks. Thumper landed on the porch and slid toward the door head first, Dawna close on his heels.

CHAPTER THIRTY-SIX

"What are you doing? Come on!" Thumper cried, waving them toward the door.

Fiona ignored Thumper and eyed the birds instead. "I really hate the idea of harming them."

"If we don't, they'll just attack the house and eventually peck their way in," Reese said.

"Killing themselves in the process," Fiona added.

"So what do you think? Fire?"

Fiona shook her head. "Air. Less damaging."

"Air it is."

The two raised their hands in unison, but it was Fiona who spoke the chant. "Element of the East, power of air, we summon, stir, and call you up. Where our focus goes, your current flows."

"So mote it be," Reese murmured.

The birds were less than twenty feet away when sparks of golden light arched from Fiona's and Reese's hands. The mild breeze of moments before turned swift and tumultuous. Energy surged inside Fiona, and she willed it toward the birds, who flapped their wings wildly, stalling in midair, unable to propel themselves forward. Their squealing and squawking pierced the night.

An inky funnel formed, twisting and heightening as Fiona and Reese continued to direct energy. Fiona's muscles clenched with the struggle to control the wind tunnel. She glanced at Reese, whose face still wore the mask of Axiom. The veins in his neck bulged with effort.

"Now!" she screamed, her voice barely audible to her own ears above the din of the birds and wind. Reese must have heard her, though, because he nodded and they pushed at the tunnel as one. The energy force wrapped itself around the birds and shot up and over the treetops, toward the east, carrying the possessed birds in its lethal embrace.

Once the birds were vanquished, Fiona bent over her knees, gasping for oxygen, unaware until that moment her breathing had been shallow. An eerie silence took hold of the forest.

Reese placed his hand on her back, rubbing circles. "You alright?"

She straightened. "Yeah. But why do I think that was just the beginning?"

The others hurried back out of the house. Thumper left the safety of the steps and crossed to where Reese and Fiona stood.

His eyes were huge. "Holy crap. Nice use of air."

Fiona shrugged. "You could have done the same."

Thumper shook his head. "Naw, my elemental magic is only so-so. But just in case it comes in handy later, I think I perfected my potion."

Thumper took his hand from his pocket and held out a tiny vial of bright green liquid that sparkled in his palm.

Fiona's eyes narrowed. Thumper had been forever working on his secret project. She'd thought he would never finish it. "What does it do?"

Before Thumper could respond, a loud pop reverberated through the night. It was soon followed by a hissing sound as something flew by her. Reese hurled his body at Fiona, taking both her and Thumper to the ground.

Dazed, Fiona struggled to sit up.

"Gunshot! Stay down!" Reese barked.

Fiona blinked, trying to see who was firing and from where. Her heart raced. "Who would be shooting at us?"

"Finders," Thumper said. As though he'd called them forth, two people emerged from the darkness, a man and a woman. Both wore head-to-toe black. Both carried guns and pointed them at Fiona and Reese.

"Guys, come on!" Dawna called from the doorway of the main house. Fiona craned her neck. Dawna waved her hands frantically, beckoning them to hurry.

Thumper heaved himself to his feet; Fiona and Reese scrambled right behind him. The three raced to the steps and sailed through the door, and Dawna slammed it shut behind them. Fiona searched for Lynn and sighted her, crouched low, back to the cupboards.

"Why wouldn't the Umbrae just attack?" Fiona directed this question to Reese.

He gestured toward Dawna. "She's still wearing Laurell's face. And I still look like Axiom. They're trying to distract us so they can get to Laurell."

More gunshots rang out. This time closer to the house. At the house. One bullet sailed through the back door, ricocheted off the countertop, and buried itself in the living-room wall.

"Holy shit!" Thumper carefully lifted the bottom edge of a curtain at the kitchen window. "They're climbing the porch steps. They walk like robots." His eyes widened. "Are there actual people in there?"

"Evil, rotten people," Lynn said.

"What do we do?" Dawna asked. "I wish my face was mine again. Maybe they'd go away."

Fiona shook her head. "Or just get more pissed once the Umbrae realize they've been fooled."

As if on cue, Dawna's features morphed from Laurell's to

her own. Fiona's gaze flew from one witch to the next. Everyone's faces had returned to normal. She glanced at Reese. His jaw clenched. He'd noticed too.

Footsteps sounded on the stairs outside the kitchen door. The wooden deck creaked and groaned beneath the weight of ice, snow, and the Finders. Fiona made eye contact with the rest of the group and jerked her head toward the living area. Reese reached out and carefully slipped the kitchen-door lock in place. The group scurried into the living area, with everyone crouching low.

Thumper cast a furtive glance Fiona's way. "Now what?"

Fiona pursed her lips. She groaned inwardly. She didn't have time to think. They needed to act. "What does your potion do?"

Thumper grinned. "Let's just say it's my version of working with the earth element."

"Can we use it against the Finders?"

Thumper's smile widened. "They'll be hating life."

Fiona held out her hand.

Thumper shook his head. "Uh-uh. You can't use it in here. Not if you like your house."

Fiona gritted her teeth. "This better be one hell of a potion, Thumper."

"It is."

"Fine. Out the front door. And everyone start making a racket so they follow us around the house." She looked over her shoulder toward the kitchen. It was a little too quiet out there. She'd expected banging on the door, more gunfire. Something.

"Oh, goody, we'll be live bait." Sarcasm dripped from Dawna's tongue. The girl was definitely herself again.

Coats were buttoned and gloves pulled on as Fiona hurried to the front door, the group following at her heels. Once outside, the bitter air nipped at Fiona's cheeks and nose. She barely registered the cold. Her body hummed with nervous energy and an adrenaline surge. She jogged away from the house, toward the woods, and the rest of the coven followed.

"Noise!" she reminded them. Everyone started hollering at once. Reese yelped, "Yee-haw." She rolled her eyes at him.

The Finders took the bait; the man and woman rounded the corner of the house and raced toward the group. The female raised her arm, and moonlight glinted off the surface of her weapon.

"Thumper, now!" Fiona cried.

"Everyone down on the ground," Thumper commanded. The group obeyed. Fiona's heart did a crazed jig, and she hoped she'd made the right decision putting him in charge for the moment.

Thumper's arm arched, and the vial sailed from his fingers, landing a few feet in front of the Finders. As soon as it hit the snow, a loud explosion filled the air. Snow burst in flurries, twenty feet into the air, and the ground shook. The Finders were knocked off their feet. The woman shrieked in surprise as her gun went flying and her body made impact with the ground.

The snow settled like white dust over the clearing. When the Finders didn't rise, Fiona stood. Her ears rang from the blast. She stuck her fingers in them.

"Huh," Thumper said, "the ground was supposed to break open. I'll keep working on the potion."

Fiona raised her eyebrows. "I think it worked just fine."

Reese slowly ventured over to the two people lying on the ground. He bent and touched his fingers to the neck of the man. He then checked the woman's pulse.

"They're alive," Reese said. "Just knocked out."

"What do we do with them? We can't have them waking up and trying to kill us again," Fiona said.

Reese frowned. "Good point."

"Why don't we tie them up good and just keep an eye on them? Once the baby is born, he can rid them of the Umbrae's taint, right? Turn them good again?" Thumper suggested.

Fiona shrugged. "I'm not sure exactly how that works, but it might be possible."

"Our other option is to kill them," Lynn offered.

The group exchanged glances. "Harm none," Fiona said. "It would be different if we were forced to kill them in order to save our own lives. In this case, though . . ."

"Killing them isn't necessary," Reese finished, strolling back to Fiona's side. "Better make it quick, though. One of them is waking up."

Thumper hurried to the house to fetch rope.

"Why aren't the Umbrae here? I thought for sure they'd show up," Dawna said, pushing her dark hair out of her eyes.

Fiona grimaced. "My guess is they've realized our true identities. Someone should call Laurell and let her know what's going on. They'll do everything in their power to figure out where she is now."

The female Finder groaned and tried to lift her head. Thumper rounded the bend, dropped to his knees and started wrapping rope around the woman's hands. Reese dashed over to assist.

"But how can they find her without the yearning to trace?" Lynn wondered.

Fiona brushed snow from her stomach and sighed. "They found her here, didn't they?"

CHAPTER THIRTY-SEVEN

At six-thirty the next morning, Laurell sat up in bed with a start. She glanced around the room and struggled to orient herself. The floral wallpaper was familiar. So was the antique wood furniture. Her hand brushed the lump in the bed next to her, and she shifted. He was definitely familiar.

Axiom lay on his stomach, arms flung above his head and twisted beneath his pillow. His head was turned toward her. Thick, ebony hair curled over a brow smooth and free of worry lines. Black lashes feathered his cheeks. She was overwhelmed with tenderness for this man. She pushed the lock of hair out of his eyes.

Images of the night before flashed through her mind. *The last time we'll make love.* Her throat constricted at the thought.

She knew it to be true. The baby was due any time now. And any time now, Axiom would return to the Light Realm.

Laurell slid from the bed, careful not to wake him, overcome with déjà vu. It wasn't so long ago that she'd left a bed she'd shared with Axiom in order to avoid him. How silly she'd been. She should have been cherishing every precious moment with him. *I'll just make us some breakfast. And once he wakes up, I'll ask Hillary to help me bring it to him in bed.*

Then I'll tell him how much he means to me.

She pulled on a long, black skirt and a bright red

sweater. She glanced furtively around the room for her purse. Downstairs. Along with her toiletries. She made her way down the staircase carefully, taking small steps.

The sound of the refrigerator door opening and closing echoed in the quiet house. "Who's there?" she called.

"Just me. That you, Laurell?" Wayne poked his head around the corner and smiled. He flashed her a grin. "You're up early."

"Couldn't sleep."

"Breakfast?"

"Yeah. In a minute." She found her bag in the library and took it to the half bath. She'd just finished brushing her teeth when she heard a rustling noise outside the front door. This was followed by a thud.

She dropped her toothbrush in the sink, wiped her mouth, and made it to the door at the same time as Wayne. He opened the door slowly. A man sat on the ground approximately ten feet from the porch. At about the spot where the protection spell barrier would be. The man rose and blinked, clearly dazed.

"Is anyone there?" he called. He peered at the invisible wall in front of him and held his hands out tentatively. He tapped at the air in front of him, shaking his head in confusion.

"Oh, right, he can't see us inside the circle," Laurell said.

"Nope," Wayne confirmed. Then, "You know this guy?"

"He's the family lawyer. He's okay," she said. She started out the door, but Wayne's arm barred her way.

"Lemme check him out first. We can't be too careful." He crossed the porch and descended the steps, then halted in front of Abrams. Wayne scrutinized the other man.

Abrams continued to stare at the air in front of him, pushing at the invisible wall. "What the devil is this?" he muttered.

Wayne shrugged and turned to Laurell. "He's no Finder. Should I cut him a door?"

She nodded. "Please."

Wayne lifted his hand. Ruby-colored light sparked from his fingertips as he slashed a rectangle in the air. A red line remained, hovering in the shape of a door.

Wayne stepped back. "Come on through."

Abrams's jaw hung to his chest. "Where did you come from?"

"Come on in, mister. Laurell says you're okay," Wayne said.

Abrams stepped through the door and turned, watching as Wayne closed the door again. The red lines faded. Laurell was impressed by how quickly Abrams regained his composure.

The lawyer made his way to the porch and climbed the few steps with a wary expression on his bland features. He paused in the doorway, eyes wide as he took in Laurell's protruding belly.

"Congratulations," he said.

"Thanks."

He tilted his head and tapped a finger to his chin. "I apologize for my confusion, but it has been only a few months since last I saw you. Yet your pregnancy appears to be rather advanced." He ran one hand over his nearly bald head. "Dear lady, are you carrying twins? Triplets?"

Laurell gave him a half smile and took his arm, pulling him into the house. "Come in and have some coffee. There's a lot to explain." She led him to the kitchen and sat him in a chair just as Hillary appeared, dressed for the day and wearing a grin too big to belong to the morning.

"Good morning, lovely witches," she sang.

"Witches?" Abrams said.

"I'll explain," Laurell said. She slid into the seat next to him just as a wave of pain clamped over her belly. She flinched.

"Hill?"

"Hmmmm?"

"Labor pains. Do they feel sort of like menstrual cramps times ten?"

Hillary nodded and paused in the process of pouring herself some apple juice. "At first. Once you get into the more advanced stages of labor, though, it's more like times a hundred, honey." Hillary glanced at Abrams then, finally noticing the thin man, who was sitting silently in his chair, taking the scene in with wide eyes. "Who's he?"

"I'll explain," Laurell said for what seemed like the tenth time that morning. "Once the pains start, it'll be like, what, hours and hours before I actually deliver, right?"

Hillary harrumphed. "Don't be so sure. I've seen women pop a baby out within a half hour of going into labor. I've also seen it take days. Either way, we don't know what we're dealing with as far as your baby goes. I mean, that kid is special, right?"

Hillary took a swig of her juice, then realization dawned in her chocolate brown eyes. "Do you think you're in labor?"

Axiom descended the stairs, still rubbing sleep from his eyes. His stomach rumbled as the smell of eggs and bacon drifted to his nose. He ran his fingers through his hair and smoothed his rumpled jeans and sweater, then started toward the kitchen. Before he reached it he heard a beeping sound emanating from the library. It came from Laurell's backpack. He reached in, pushed the *Book of Shadows* to the side, and found the culprit. A red light blinked repeatedly on a cell phone.

He went to the kitchen. Laurell sat in a chair at the dining table, lips compressed, hands pressed over her stomach.

"Are you alright?" He was at her side in an instant, the air sparking with silver.

She nodded. An older man with gaunt cheeks and thinning hair sat next to her. "How in the world did you just move so quickly?" the man asked.

Axiom glanced from Laurell to Hillary to Wayne. Wayne offered a lopsided grin. "We just finished explaining about the coven and the protection shield and how it is Laurell here came to be nine months pregnant in just three months' time. We didn't think to tell him about you yet."

Axiom frowned. "Just who is this man?"

The man offered him a trembling hand. "I'm Robert Abrams. I'm the Graves's family attorney."

Axiom ignored the outstretched hand. "Why are you here?"

"It's okay. He's clean," Laurell said.

Axiom focused on Laurell's face again. "You do not appear well."

"Women generally don't look their best when they're in labor, honey," Hillary said, hands on her broad hips, eyes sparkling with humor.

Excitement and sorrow mingled inside of him. His child would be born soon. His mission would be successful. He would have to return to the Light Realm. He placed a hand on Laurell's shoulder. "How may I make you more comfortable?"

"Hillary made me a bed in the library. I'm going to go lie down and just rest. I'll deliver the baby there when it's time."

"When will it be time?" He would not leave her side.

Hillary chuckled. "Oh my, now don't get the idea that child is going to pop out this instant. It could be hours yet before Laurell goes into active labor."

A temporary but sharp relief filled him. He would have to leave soon, but not yet.

"Why do you have my phone?" Laurell asked.

Axiom handed her the phone. He had forgotten he held it. "It is beeping."

Laurell took it from him and retrieved her message. Her brow furrowed in concern. "Everyone is okay at the coven-stead, but apparently there was a bird attack and then some Finders showed up. The Umbrae know they were tricked."

"It doesn't matter," Hillary said. "They don't know where we are."

"The Umbrae are resourceful creatures. They will proba-bly find a way to trace us here, but we are safe inside the protection circle," Axiom said.

"Is the rest of the coven coming here now?" Wayne asked.

Laurell shook her head. "No. They're afraid the Umbrae may be lurking around to follow them."

Her groin spasmed. Laurell grimaced. "That one really hurt," she said, rubbing her middle.

"Let's get you to the library. We'll work on some of those breathing techniques I showed you before." Hillary helped Laurell to her feet and led her from the kitchen.

After getting comfy on the mattresses Hillary and Wayne had dragged down from the upstairs bedroom and set up in the library, Laurell snuggled into the blankets and pillows and tried to rest. Hillary came in and out of the room a few times, bringing more pillows, sheets, and a long, cotton gown she'd found in one of the bedrooms. *Grandmother's*, Laurell thought. She obediently slipped into the gown. Hillary re-minded her of her breathing techniques, and determined that her contractions were only twelve minutes or so apart; she wasn't in active labor yet.

"I'm going to let you rest. You just keep breathing, and I'll be back to check on you soon," Hillary said. She placed a glass of water near Laurell's makeshift bed and left the library, closing the door behind her.

Laurell's eyes fluttered closed. She placed her hands on her belly, rubbed circles, and told the child within to go easy on her. So far, the contractions weren't bad at all. She'd almost managed to drift off when the swooshing sound of the library door opening brought her back to the here and now.

Axiom. He crossed to her bed and lowered himself to his knees beside her. His gaze was tender as he touched her cheek. "You are doing well?"

She nodded. "I'm surprised I can rest at all, but Hill said this stage of labor is mild and lots of women can even sleep through it."

"May I bring you anything?"

"I think I'm all set. Hillary's been buzzing in and out of here with so much anxious energy, I was actually kind of glad for the quiet."

He gave her a smile that didn't reach his eyes. His jaw was tense, and she realized something wasn't quite right with him.

"Can you stay here with me? Until the baby is born?" she asked.

He squeezed her hand and his eyes flashed with sorrow. "I wish I could, but as the child's birth draws near, I can perceive my shadow side trying to emerge. There is so much Light in the child."

Laurell pleaded with her eyes. "You can fight the darkness. You can keep it at bay."

He pressed a kiss to her brow. His voice was resigned. "Your faith in me warms my heart, my goddess. However, I cannot risk you or the child."

Axiom pulled her into an embrace, hugging her tightly. Her chest was tight with grief and she clutched him fiercely. "You know I love you." Having uttered the words, she no longer knew why she'd been so afraid of her feelings.

He settled her back into the bed and rained kisses on her fingertips, his lips hot, his gaze fierce. "You have come to mean a great deal to me." He glanced away, collecting his thoughts. When he faced her again, his expression was unreadable.

"You have done well, Laurell. The world owes you a great debt."

He hadn't returned her declaration of love. Tears pricked her eyes, but before she could speak further, another contraction took hold.

Noticing her discomfort, he stood and walked to the door. "I will find Hillary. You should not be alone."

Laurell rolled to her side and moaned into her pillow. *That's it? That's good-bye?* She thought of going after him, making him tell her he loved her, but quickly discarded the idea. It didn't matter whether he said the words or not. She knew he loved her. She felt it every time he touched her, looked at her, kissed her. Besides, she'd never see him again anyway. Why prolong the agony?

Minutes ticked by like hours. Where was Hillary? She couldn't just sit in the bed and cry. She pulled herself upright and stood on shaking legs. Hillary had told her once that walking could be a good way to speed up labor. She began slowly circling the room.

The library door opened again, and she spun around, expecting to see Hillary standing there. Instead, it was Abrams.

He walked over and handed her the glass of water he carried.

"Hillary said to bring you this."

She motioned toward the cup sitting next to the bed. "She already brought me some."

"Perhaps she thought you'd already drunk that."

Laurell took the glass from him and set it on the coffee table near the couch. "Where is Hillary?"

She craned her neck around Abrams. There was no one in the entryway or near the front door. The house was unusually quiet.

"I don't know, but the two gentlemen are outside. I was told to stay here with you for the moment. I sensed something was wrong, but no one would tell me just what." Abrams's eyes were glassy and bright. The small smile curving his thin lips seemed out of place. What was there to be happy about? He'd just said something was wrong.

Unease settled in Laurell's gut. She tried to push past him, but he stopped her with one hand on her arm.

"What are you doing? I need to see what's going on." She tried to push his hand off her arm, but he held on tight, surprisingly strong for such a skinny man.

"I was specifically told to keep you inside and out of danger."

"What danger?" Her voice sounded panicked to her own ears. Abrams's gaze had gone shifty, and his hands trembled. She got the distinct feeling she needed to get away from him. His explanation about where everyone was and why he needed to keep her in the library didn't ring true.

Her eyes narrowed. "Look, you'd better let me go or things could get very ugly, very fast."

Abrams's eyes widened in mock fear. A sharp laugh came from his throat. "Oh, yes, ugly indeed." He led her farther into the library, away from the door, and pushed her toward the wall, fumbling in his pocket as they moved. His hand emerged clutching a knife.

CHAPTER THIRTY-EIGHT

"Abrams—I mean, Robert, come on. You don't want to hurt me."

He waved the knife near her face. "Don't I?"

She struggled to pull away again, but that movement only caused him to push her more forcefully to the wall and to lift the knife to her throat. His hand hovered only an inch or two from her delicate flesh.

Fear knotted her stomach. "This is crazy," she said, unable to keep her voice from wavering.

"No. Crazy is serving your family for so many years without one little bit of gratitude. Your mother was a selfish, self-centered woman with enough money to live on for many lifetimes."

Laurell cleared her throat. "Well, we agree on that. I don't see what that has to do with me." Her attempt to establish common ground fell on deaf ears.

Abrams continued talking as though he hadn't heard. "Your grandmother was a good woman, though. She even had her will rewritten so if there were no more Graves descendants to inherit Graves Manor, it would go to me. Not that she anticipated such an outcome, mind you. It was more of a safety measure in case you met an untimely end. She seemed afraid that might happen."

Laurell groaned inwardly. No doubt Grandmother had worried the Umbrae might get to Laurell or something might go wrong with the mission. *She knew I would be in danger as a result of who I am. A witch. A woman fit to mother the Earth Balancer.*

"Yes, your grandmother was quite generous in rewriting her will."

"I don't remember that provision being in her will," Laurell said. She'd read the document carefully after her grandmother's death. There had been no mention of Abrams in it.

Abrams grinned. "You didn't see that version. You and your silly mother saw only the version I wanted you to see. The real document will come in handy, though, after you're dead."

"You don't mean it," Laurell whispered, her pulse beating frantically. She glanced toward the doorway. Just where the hell was everybody?

"Of course I mean it. I regret having lost my nerve the day we met here at Graves Manor when I delivered that book of your grandmother's." His eyes took on a distinct sheen. "I came back, you know, thinking you might still be here. I waited for you, but you never appeared. I half hoped you'd been kidnapped or murdered already and I wouldn't have to do the job."

"So you never reported me missing," she said.

Abrams shook his head. "I hid your vehicle and continued to check back here every so often, thinking you might return. For all I knew, you'd called a friend and taken a trip with someone. I assumed you'd come back for your car eventually. If you were still alive to claim it."

"And here I am," she said, catching her breath as another contraction arced through her.

"Yes, how convenient." His eyes darkened. "Only you're not alone. You showed up with three friends, two of whom are fairly large men. That made my task much more difficult."

"You mean you had to wait for me to be alone."

"Indeed."

"How are you going to cover this up? How are you going to hide your involvement?" She motioned to the knife. "Don't you think my turning up dead with knife wounds is going to be questioned? Once the police realize you had a million-dollar estate to gain from my death, you'll be a prime suspect."

She had to keep him talking until one of the others returned. Surely they couldn't have strayed far.

Abrams laughed again. His laugh was horrible. She scowled and felt some of her fear turn to anger. The man was clearly demented.

"I'm not going to kill you, dear. I'll wait for them to do it."

Laurell arched one eyebrow. "Them who?"

"Whoever it is you fear so much you constructed that amazing invisible force field about the property. When no one was watching, I went outside and cut a door in the same manner in which I noticed that Wayne fellow do it."

Anyone can cut a door from inside the circle. It's the casting that requires magic. Wayne's voice echoed in Laurell's mind from months before. Shit.

Abrams tilted his head to the side and continued. "So, it will be murder, but I will have had nothing to do with it. I will simply be the one who had the misfortune of coming to check on the property at the wrong time."

Her heart skipped a beat, and she pushed harder at Abram's chest. "Do you know what you've done? I have to warn the others."

"I can't allow it, my dear. I intend to make you easy to find for those who will do the deed. What was it your cowboy friend called them? Umbrae?"

Laurell bit her lips so hard she tasted blood. Something wet gushed from between her legs and puddled at her feet.

She looked down. The white nightgown was soaked. Her water had broken. Abrams glanced down as well.

"What is that?" he asked.

"My baby is coming," she bit out, rage now filling her and mingling with her fear. This was not how she wanted her child to be born. She gulped back a sob, thinking Axiom wasn't going to be there to witness the birth. And now she had to deal with this? With some crazy madman she used to think of as a family friend holding her at knifepoint until the Umbrae appeared? What then? Would Abrams keep her immobile while the Umbrae snuffed the life from her and left the child to die in her womb?

Sorrow, anger, fear, rage, helplessness, and despair rushed through her veins, and she was suddenly conscious of the moisture running over her thighs, legs, and feet. She remembered a line she'd read from the *Book of Shadows: A surface attempt to touch the water element will not work. You have to accept your pain, release it, and realize it serves a purpose in your life.* Tears streamed down her face as all of the reasons she had to feel sadness settled in her heart, pulsing and aching in time with the rapid cardiac beat.

She felt them then, the ghosts of her ancestors, all those who'd walked through these halls, who were buried in the family graveyard. They whispered over her, casting a chill. She couldn't see them, but she could hear the echoes of their lives, feel them surging through her blood—*their* blood. *I can do this. I'm a Graves. I'm a powerful witch.*

"You will not hurt me or this child," she ground out, her voice deep and ominous to her own ears.

She willed the pain into the water, into the amniotic fluid at her feet. The puddle grew; the liquid lifted and gained form, rising up over Abrams's ankles, legs, and hips.

He glanced down, and his eyes grew large with confusion. "What the—?"

Laurell moaned with effort and aimed all of her energy into the water. The liquid formed a swirling wall that soon encapsulated Abrams up to the waist. The water spouted into the shape of a claw, wound over Abrams's knife-wielding hand, and wrenched the weapon from his grasp. The knife flew across the room and made a clattering noise as it hit the wood floor.

"What are you doing?" he cried, struggling to move.

She ignored his question. Rage roared through her now. She imagined the stream of liquid covering Abrams to the chin, and the water obeyed. A moment later, the water pulled away from her and started to swirl like a tornado, with Abrams at the apex. It released him in an abrupt jerking motion and tossed him across the room with such force that he landed with a sickening thud. His eyes rolled back, eyelids fluttering shut. Free of its prisoner, the water immediately dissipated.

Shaking, Laurell ventured to the spot where Abrams lay. Kneeling, she touched a hand to his neck and found a pulse. He was unconscious, but alive.

Another spasm racked her body as she rode another contraction, sucking in a deep breath and letting it out as the pain cleared. They were definitely coming closer together now. She needed Hillary.

She rose and hurried to the front door. She was just about to yank it open, when it was flung inward by Hillary, who was in obvious distress. "Call Fiona and tell her to get the rest of the coven here. No need for them to stay away. The Umbrae have found us."

Axiom bounded through the front door of Graves Manor, heart racing, nerves on edge. Wayne swept in behind him and shut and locked the door. Not that a door would keep the Umbrae out. Wayne had sensed Umbrae activity near the property and the two had gone in search of the source. They had located an opening in the protection circle and closed it. However, they had been too late. Two Umbrae attacked. Axiom had fended one of them off.

Wayne had been struggling with the other when Hillary, apparently concerned about their delayed absence, had appeared to lend assistance. The two witches had impressed Axiom with their ability to utilize elemental magic to dispel the Umbra. Wayne had sensed more coming, though, and that they were already inside the protection circle, searching for Laurell.

The sight of Laurell, dripping wet and holding her belly, pale with obvious pain, made Axiom think for a brief, terrifying moment that he had been too late. That the Umbrae had already attacked her.

Hillary quickly told him what had happened. "The coven is on its way." She dropped the cell phone she held into her jacket pocket. "Abrams apparently cut the hole in the protection circle. He wants Laurell dead so he can take over this mansion. And I just timed Laurell's contractions. Her water has broken. She's in active labor."

"Go. Make her comfortable in the other room so the child can be delivered. I will do a re-visioning on this man to see if I can determine what he knows of the Umbrae."

Hillary rushed Laurell off to the library. Axiom squatted beside Abrams. He grabbed the man's shoulder, and closed his eyes. Visions flickered and raced. Abrams and the grandmother, Helen, discussing a will. Abrams leaving Graves Manor and returning on the day Axiom and Laurell first met. Abrams's preoccupation with killing Laurell. His repeated trips to Graves Manor hoping to find Laurell there. It was the man's memories of the day when Laurell and Axiom first met, though, that made Axiom pause and rewind.

He sensed a deep metaphysical connection that had been

formed on that day between Mr. Abrams and some negative force. After that day, Abrams was alone, but not alone. The Umbrae had left Abrams for months after that first day at Graves Manor, but the bond had remained, unbeknownst to the human.

Axiom released the man's shoulder and glanced up at Wayne, who watched the process keenly.

"What did ya get?" Wayne asked.

"The Umbrae must have traced the yearning that first day to Graves Manor, but upon reaching the place, Laurell and I had already departed. Mr. Abrams, however, was here. The Umbrae tapped into him much as they did the bird."

"And they've been hanging out with him since?"

"No. But they have kept track of him. And I assume once they realized Laurell was no longer at Fiona's camp, they revisited Mr. Abrams to see if he had knowledge of her whereabouts. He did not, of course, but as soon as he appeared at the mansion and saw Laurell here, the Umbrae were aware of her being here as well."

"Then he cut the door to let 'em in," Wayne said, shaking his head. "Could you tell if he knew about other Umbrae reinforcements coming?"

"If there are, he was not aware of it."

Wayne glanced back down at the man lying on the floor. "What do we do with him?"

"I will erase his memory of anything having to do with the mission. Then we will send him home."

"Like you did to those folks at the gas station way back when?" Wayne asked. Axiom nodded.

"He's okay then?"

Axiom nodded again and turned back to Abrams. Energy surged from his hands to the man's head. Moments later, he stood, satisfied that the process was successful.

Just then the unmistakable pop of gunshots rang through

the air. Axiom moved to one of the windows and lifted the curtain. Three men and a woman stood outside dressed all in black, wielding guns. One of the four inspected his weapon with a look of confusion while the others pressed their hands and bodies on the invisible force field, trying to push their way in, but not progressing very far.

"What is it?" Wayne asked, leaning over Axiom's shoulder.

"Finders. I believe one of them may have attempted to fire at the protection shield."

Wayne chuckled. "That wouldn't do 'em any good."

"No," Axiom agreed.

A sharp moan came from the library. Laurell. Fierce protectiveness raged through Axiom. He started toward the library, momentarily forgetting his earlier concerns about his shadow side. Laurell needed him.

A familiar, unwelcome odor permeated the air as he moved through the library doors to where Laurell lay on the mattresses, Hillary kneeling between her legs. Sulfur. The Umbrae. He spun on his heel just in time to witness the inky blackness emerge from thin air. Red eyes stared him down with wicked glee.

CHAPTER THIRTY-NINE

Laurell smelled the Umbra before she saw it. She yanked herself back from the edge of her pain to see Axiom hovering in the doorway of the library, arms in front of him as he struggled with the vile creature. Sparks of silver light emanated from Axiom as he pushed at the thing.

He groaned and grunted in effort, then more flashes of metallic energy jolted the creature, filling it until it shrieked and disappeared. Axiom gulped in air, broad chest heaving, and sank onto the couch. Just as he did so, another crack appeared in the air, and another Umbra, as black as a starless night, pulled itself into the room, snarling, its claws reaching for Axiom. This was followed by another, and then another, until Axiom was forced to ward off three Umbrae at once.

Wayne bounded into the room and started chanting. Something about fire. He lifted his hands and sparked crimson flame at one of the Umbrae. It squealed in pain and turned its focus from Axiom to Wayne.

Laurell groaned and bore down hard. She had to get the baby born. The baby could neutralize the Umbrae. Pain ripped through her, stealing her breath, as another contraction hit.

A fourth Umbra appeared and soon three of the nasty things were circling Axiom's body, rubbing themselves against him, pulsating, digging claws into his face. One of them ripped his claw down Axiom's cheek, leaving a bloody trail. Axiom continued to surge energy at the demons, and one of them became engulfed in a silver flame of god-force energy and dissipated.

Wayne continued throwing energetic flames at the Umbra whose attention he'd been successful in gaining. The creature hissed and undulated its transparent body, trying to grab on to Wayne and finally succeeding, although its body was alight with fire. It sunk claws into Wayne's back, and he shrugged out his jacket and tossed it to the floor along with the Umbra.

The Umbra attacked again, but this time, Axiom somehow managed to direct a spark of silver light at the thing and that, mingled with the fire energy from Wayne, seemed to be too much for the creature. It shuddered and disappeared.

Wayne stood on shaky legs and hurried to Axiom's side.

"No, go to Laurell," Axiom commanded, his voice strained.

Pain racked Laurell's body, directing her attention back to herself and the child on its way. Hillary's jaw tensed, and her gaze was serious as she peered between Laurell's legs.

"What is it? Is my baby okay?" Laurell gasped out, chest tightening with concern.

Hillary glanced over her shoulder to where Axiom had just destroyed one Umbra and still fought the other. Axiom fell to the floor, clearly drained from the fight. "The baby's fine. You're crowning already. He's almost here."

Come on, honey. Hurry. Be born.

"Push," Hillary commanded, for what seemed the hundredth time since they'd come into the library.

Laurell bore down and groaned as she rode another wave of agonizing pain.

"Good," Hillary cried. "Again. Push."

Dimly, Laurell heard Axiom grunt, and she glanced his

way to see he had successfully destroyed another Umbra. She took a deep breath in, preparing to push with all her might, when she sucked in sulfur. Terror arched through her as an Umbra appeared in the air above her, hovering, crimson eyes sparking hate and malicious intent.

Wayne lifted his hands toward the Umbra, but just as he did so, another demon appeared behind him and grabbed him by the throat. He turned and tumbled to the ground, writhing to get the creature off of him.

The Umbra above Laurell reached a hand toward her belly as it covered her nose and mouth with the rest of its body. She couldn't breathe. Her lungs burned. Her heart raced. *Oh god, no. We're so close.*

"I don't think so. Get off of her, you nasty thing!" Hillary cried before beginning a low chant. Laurell's eyes were covered by a weblike material. She couldn't see Hillary, but sensed a spell was in the works. Whatever Hillary was doing, the creature didn't like it.

Laurell could feel the Umbra twisting over her as it shrieked in pain. Still, it wouldn't release its hold on her. She was fading fast. She'd been deprived of oxygen for too long. Her hands, which had been clutching desperately at the air, at the being holding her hostage, fluttered to her side in surrender.

Her body continued to be racked with the contractions but she couldn't move, couldn't contribute to her child's birth. She was dying.

The demon squealed and finally let go. Then, suddenly, thankfully, air rushed into her lungs. She gasped and sucked in life's breath, her chest expanding with the effort. Her eyes fluttered open, and as her vision cleared she realized Axiom lay beside her, face wan and pale, body shaking from fatigue.

He grabbed her hand in his own and nodded. "Push, my goddess. Our child needs to be born."

Our child. Had he called the baby by that title before? She didn't think so. Her eyes pricked with tears. She gave one last, forceful push, bearing down until she couldn't hold the position for a second more.

"That's it," Hillary cried. Laurell felt the baby slide from her body. She fell back onto the mattresses, relief washing over her.

Hillary held the baby up, and it was tiny with red skin, fists flailing in agitation. Little legs kicked with force.

"You've got a girl," Hillary said, suctioning the child's mouth and nose to be sure she could breathe easily. She wiped the baby with a cloth and the child started to wail.

Hillary laid the baby on Laurell's chest, and Laurell stared at the most beautiful thing she'd ever seen. Tons of black hair. Wide eyes already sparking with silver light. A girl. Why had she thought the Earth Balancer would be male?

She turned her head to Axiom, whose breathing, previously labored, had gone suddenly quiet. What she saw made her breath catch and her heart lurch. His body was still; his silver eyes stared at her, but were blank, lifeless. And she knew he was gone. Her heart shattered like glass dropped onto stone.

"Oh, child," Hillary murmured, reaching over Laurell and pressing Axiom's eyelids closed. She touched Laurell's cheek. "I know this is so hard. But death is just what makes us appreciate living."

Laurell clasped the child in her arms and turned her head from Axiom. She couldn't bear to look at him any longer. And for the third time that day, she embraced her sorrow, her pain, and for all the tears she'd held back over the past years, she let them flow now.

She cried as Hillary cleaned her and the baby, changed the sheets beneath her, and bundled her in a clean gown and blankets. She cried as Reese appeared and helped Wayne remove Axiom's body. And the tears didn't stop when Fiona crept into the bed beside her, held her from behind, and smoothed her hair from her face, offering no words, just the comfort of her presence. In fact, it was days before the sobs stopped, and the only thing that made the absence of Axiom even slightly bearable was the little girl who looked so much like her father.

On the fourth day after the baby was born, Laurell looked up from the eggs she pushed absently around on her plate. "Aurora. I'm going to name her Aurora after the Greek goddess of the dawn."

Fiona turned from her place at the stove and nodded her approval. "What about a middle name?"

"Athtor, for the Egyptian goddess of night. To remind us of the importance of embracing both our light and our dark selves and finding balance between the two."

"For without night, there can be no day. Without evil, we would have no concept of good," Fiona said.

"And we need the darkness just as much as we need the light. It's part of us all. Without it, Aurora wouldn't be able to defeat the Umbrae," Laurell finished.

Fiona's smile was bittersweet. "I think you're getting it, sweetie."

The child she held in her lap giggled her approval.

CHAPTER FORTY

Mobius strode to Axiom's personal chambers with intent. He mentally rapped on the silver walls Axiom held in place around himself. He felt Axiom's power seep through the structure to see who came calling and then sensed the other god's permission to enter.

He found Axiom reclining in a clear quartz-crystal chair clad in a silver and white robe, face pensive and distant.

Mobius halted in front of his friend, head tilted to the side. "I have just returned from a meeting with the Council."

Axiom's eyebrows rose. "A decision has been made regarding who is to fill Rhakma's seat?"

Mobius nodded. "Yes, and it was unanimous."

"Do not delay, my friend. Please tell me what decision was made."

"They voted you to the Council, Axiom. Congratulations. I know you have desired this for some time."

Axiom rose from his seat and rubbed one hand over his face. His eyes were tired and lacked their usual silver of sparkling metallic light.

"This is good news indeed," Axiom said, though his words lacked conviction.

"You do not appear as pleased with the decision as I thought you would be. This is what you wanted, is it not?" Mobius asked.

Axiom nodded. "It was, yes."

Mobius's eyes narrowed. "Was?"

Axiom groaned. "I do not wish to be ungrateful. I know you have stood by me, pushed for me, and had faith in me when many others did not. For this I am forever in your debt." He began to pace the room with uneven, jerky movements.

Mobius sighed. "You owe me nothing. You and the mortal woman and her coven did us all a great service. It is we who owe you." Axiom's face was twisted with emotion, his expression heavy and troubled. "Speak frankly with me, Axiom. I can see something is amiss."

"It is the woman."

"The mortal woman, Laurell?" Mobius asked, though he already knew the answer.

"Yes. I am unable to stop thinking of her and yet, I wish to Source I could stop. Without her near, I feel hollow and ill inside." Axiom pressed one hand to his chest as though to illustrate where the emptiness resided.

Mobius knew that sensation all too well. "I understand."

"Do you?" Axiom's eyes were wide with emotion. "You speak little of your own mission or the Earth woman you were assigned to."

Mobius's chest tightened. He would not talk of her now. Speaking of the woman never produced pleasant sensations for him, only sadness and regret. He could not repair what had been broken so long ago, but he could make a difference now, for Axiom. He touched Axiom's arm, stilling him midstride.

"What if I said you have a choice?" he asked.

Confusion fluttered across Axiom's face. "How so?"

"The Council has agreed that, were you to give up your seat and return to Earth, you would have our full sanction to do so. You could assist in raising the Earth Balancer. It would be a noble mission."

Axiom stiffened. "Give up my seat?" The idea of such a

thing clearly put him out of sorts. Mobius knew of Axiom's ambition; to walk away now that he had finally achieved his goal would require terrific strength—and a powerful love.

"How long would I be able to last on Earth in human form? Is there some trick I do not know that allows a god to remain for more extended periods of time?" he asked.

"No trick. You would have to become fully human."

Axiom scratched his chin, and Mobius could almost see his mind racing over the implications. "If this is true, then you were given this choice once as well?"

Mobius nodded. "Yes. But I made the wrong decision."

Axiom's gaze penetrated his as though trying to read his very soul. After long moments, he spoke. "I see. And what of my powers?"

Mobius smiled.

"So, you're sure you don't mind us staying here for a while, right?" Lynn asked, pouring orange juice and champagne into a glass.

Laurell sliced a strawberry and set it on the rim of her champagne flute. "Stay as long as you'd like. This place is huge and there's no reason you and Dawna should squeeze into some little apartment while you finish school."

Lynn sighed. "I'm still wondering if going back to graduate school was a good idea."

Laurell smiled. "I think becoming a therapist is a great idea. I hear that the program at the University of Wisconsin is a good one. And Kenosha isn't that far from here."

"Thirty miles. I like the drive, actually."

"I intend to finish school, too," Laurell said.

"Oh? Did you talk to your college advisor?"

"Yes. Of course, I couldn't tell her the real reason I disappeared. I told her I went into a major depression once Mom died and dropped off the radar for a few months because of that. The department granted me an extension on my thesis work."

"That's excellent news. I'm glad you're finishing," Lynn said.

"Me too." Fortunately, Abrams hadn't listened to Laurell when she'd told him to give all her mother's money to charities. Apparently, he'd had plans in place to commandeer that money, in addition to obtaining Graves Manor, once Laurell was dead. Only his plan had failed, Laurell was very much alive, and she no longer felt the need to refuse her inheritance.

"I talked to Fiona today," Lynn said.

"What's the scoop?" Laurell asked.

"Well, she and Reese have their hands full with planning a Samhain festival for October. Thumper's off finishing his last semester of school. Hillary's visiting her son who is on temporary leave from the army. Oh, and Wayne is doing his usual thing, hanging out at the covenstead, enjoying his retirement."

"Does he ever take that cowboy hat of his off?" Laurell asked.

Lynn shook her head. "Dawna and I have an ongoing bet he's bald under there, but we've never been able to find out for sure." Both women laughed.

"So everyone's still coming here for full-moon ritual, right?"

Lynn grinned. "Of course. Fiona said they wouldn't miss it for anything."

"Mama, Mama," came Aurora's excited cry as she wobbled into the kitchen of Graves Manor, where Laurell and Lynn stood sipping mimosas and frosting Dawna's birthday cake. The child halted in front of the women, hand held aloft. Laurell set her spoon on the counter and ruffled the black mop of curls atop her daughter's head.

It never ceased to amaze her, Aurora's rapid growth. During her last astral visit with her mother, Elaine had informed her Aurora would continue the rapid growth spurts until she reached age eighteen. Then she would revert to the normal human aging cycle. Still, a child who was only eight months old was already walking around in the body of a two-year-old. *And Aurora's mind. Sheesh.* The kid was sharp as a new knife. Her mental functioning was on fast-forward as well.

"What have you got there, sweetie?" Laurell asked.

Aurora giggled and showed her mother the multicolored butterfly poised in her hand. "Pretty!"

"Gorgeous. But you have to take her back outside and let her go. Butterflies belong outdoors."

The child nodded. "I won't hurt her." She disappeared back out the door.

Lynn shook her head. "Probably Dawna's doing. I think insects are the latest addition to the animal species she can communicate with."

"She's outside still, right? With Aurie?" Laurell asked.

"Mm-hmmmm," Lynn confirmed, pushing a chunk of honey-blonde hair from her eyes. "She said she'd stay out there with her until we tell her it's safe to come inside. She knows we're doing something for her birthday in here. I don't know why we're attempting to surprise her."

Laurell sipped her mimosa, the liquid sliding smoothly down her throat, tangy and sweet. She set the glass on the counter and lifted her spoon to spread more fudge frosting on the cake. "Well, we have to at least try. She doesn't know what we're doing, so it will still be a surprise. Who doesn't love a surprise?"

"Indeed, who does not?" A deep male voice echoed off the polished wood floors and over the marble countertops. Both women spun around to see whom the voice belonged to.

Laurell, however, recognized that husky timbre immediately. Her breath caught, and the spoon slipped from her fingers and made a pinging noise as it clattered to the floor.

"Holy shit," Lynn gasped.

Axiom chuckled in response. He looked beautiful. Ebony hair, longer than Laurell remembered, curled over the collar of his three-piece, smoky gray suit. His mouth was lifted in a smile, even white teeth bared. His tall, broad frame seemed to fill the room. He crossed the kitchen until he stood close to her, so close she felt the hairs on her arm stand up and she had to tilt her neck to make eye contact. Musk and sandalwood drifted over her.

Tears sprang to her eyes. How many nights had she held that damn shirt of his to her face and breathed in the remnants of his scent, wishing like hell it was him she held?

"I've dreamed of this moment so many times," she said on a broken whisper, vaguely aware Lynn scurried out of the room, no doubt to give them some privacy.

"As have I, my love," he responded, his hands cupping her face, his gaze washing over her features as though he'd never seen her before and wanted to memorize every line, every angle. Her heart sped at his choice of words.

"How is it possible?"

"I was given a choice, Council seat, or Earth." His thumb traced her bottom lip, lightly, teasing, and she had to blink and shake her head to focus on the matter at hand.

"You refused a seat on the Council?" Her chest constricted. "But that's what you've wanted more than anything."

Axiom shook his head and pressed a kiss to her forehead, then his eyes met hers again and sparked silver light. "No. What I want most is you. And our child. And a life together. No political office I could hold would content me as being with you does. You accepted me, loved me when I was not acceptable to those in the Light Realm. I belong with you."

Moisture streamed down Laurell's face. Now that she'd opened up to her emotions, tears did not shame her; she no longer needed to keep strict control. Fear, sorrow, joy: these things were meant to be shared. A life lived behind a wall, no matter how safe and controlled, was no life at all. She understood this now. Axiom had helped show her the way.

"How long will you stay?" The question broke from trembling lips. Not that it mattered. She'd love him for as long as she could. She couldn't stop herself if she wanted to. And she didn't want to. She longed to kiss him, hold him as deeply, as much, as long as she could. She'd take what she could get. The last months without him had been the bleakest of her life.

Axiom pressed a kiss to her nose, then each cheek, raining them over her face.

"How long will I stay? Is forever long enough?" he whispered. "If I am with you always, Laurell, I do not think I will have had my fill of you."

Her heart swelled with elation. "But how is this possible?"

"I am human now."

Her breath caught. "You became human for me? I—I don't know what to say." She sighed. "Maybe instead, I'll show you." She stood on tiptoe, and parted her lips in invitation, begging for his kiss, not bothering to hide her need.

His lips crashed against hers, hard and hungry, his arms circling her and pulling her so tight against him it seemed they were no longer separate beings, but one body, one mind, one heart. Heat seared her insides, turned her legs to Jell-O, and she thrilled at the feel of him, the taut muscles bunching under her hands as she kneaded his back.

He lifted his mouth from hers just long enough to whisper the words she longed to hear him say. No matter that she already knew how he felt; she'd needed them to pass from his lips.

"I love you."

"I love you, too," she murmured.

A metallic sheen layered his gaze, and her own eyes widened. "You have powers still?"

He grinned. "An old friend made sure of it. How else might I be able to fight evil alongside my magical child and my powerful witch mate?"

Laurell laughed at this, and his head turned, his eyes searching the room. "Where is she? Where is our child?"

Laurell's throat grew tight. She swallowed, suddenly able to envision how their lives together would be—hers, Axiom's, Aurora's. How was it possible that in the space of mere months, she'd found everything she'd ever wanted and more?

She stepped from Axiom's embrace and tugged his hand, leading him toward the back patio. Through the sliding glass doors she could see Dawna tossing a Frisbee, her black ponytail bobbing, face flushed with delight. Little peals of laughter indicated Aurora was on the receiving end of Dawna's soft throws.

"She's outside. Come meet your daughter."

She heard his sharp intake of breath. Did his hand tremble just a little bit in hers? *My, how the mighty have fallen*, she thought with a small smile. Wait until he saw the little angel. Wait until he saw what they'd created together, *whom* they'd created.

She paused and glanced at him before they reached the door, eyes washing over his suit. "What's with the suit? I thought you gave those up."

Axiom chuckled and shrugged. "I wanted to look my best for you. And for Aurora."

Laurell laughed, thinking him the most gorgeous man she'd ever seen and anticipating Aurora's excitement when she met her father.

Then, hand in hand, they walked outside into the crisp, sun-kissed morning. Laurell blithely ignored the thunder that rumbled somewhere in the distance.

Autumn Dawn
NO WORDS ALONE

As The Only Woman In A Team Of Marooned
Explorers, Whom Do You Trust—
Your Friends...Or Your Enemy?

Crash-landing on a hostile planet with a variety of flora
and fauna intent upon making her their lunch was Xera's
most immediate concern, but not her only one. The Scorpio, sworn enemies of her people, were similarly stranded
nearby, and Xera didn't trust the captain of her team of
Galactic Explorers. He was belligerent and small-minded,
and he'd already caused one unnecessary death—Genson's.
Xera was the translator, and she should have been the
first sent to deal with the Scorpio. Even if she was a lone
woman and they were some of the galaxy's most merciless
soldiers.

For, on this inhospitable world, the warlike Scorpio were
their only chance. And in the eyes of the aliens' handsome
leader, Xera saw a nobility and potency she'd never before
encountered—a reaction she knew her male human com-
panions would despise. A future with Commander Ryven
was...something to consider. But first she had to survive.

ISBN 13: 978-0-505-52801-8

☐ **YES!**

Sign me up for the Love Spell Book Club and send my
FREE BOOKS! If I choose to stay in the club, I will pay only
$8.50* each month, a savings of $6.48!

NAME: _____

ADDRESS: _____

TELEPHONE: _____

EMAIL: _____

☐ I want to pay by credit card.

☐ **VISA**   ☐ **MasterCard**   ☐ **DISCOVER**

ACCOUNT #: _____

EXPIRATION DATE: _____

SIGNATURE: _____

Mail this page along with $2.00 shipping and handling to:
Love Spell Book Club
PO Box 6640
Wayne, PA 19087
Or fax (must include credit card information) to:
610-995-9274
You can also sign up online at **www.dorchesterpub.com**.
*Plus $2.00 for shipping. Offer open to residents of the U.S. and Canada only. Canadian
residents please call 1-800-481-9191 for pricing information.
If under 18, a parent or guardian must sign. Terms, prices and conditions subject to
change. Subscription subject to acceptance. Dorchester Publishing reserves the right to
reject any order or cancel any subscription.